NEW YORK REVIEW BOOKS
CLASSICS

NOTES OF A CROCODILE

QIU MIAOJIN (1969–1995)—one of Taiwan's most
innovative literary modernists, and the country's most
renowned lesbian writer—was born in Chuanghua County in
western Taiwan. She graduated with a degree in psychology
from National Taiwan University and pursued graduate
studies in clinical psychology at the University of Paris VIII.
Her first published story, "Prisoner," received the *Central Daily
News* Short Story Prize, and her novella *Lonely Crowds* won
the United Literature Association Award. While in Paris, she
directed a thirty-minute film called *Ghost Carnival*, and not
long after this, at the age of twenty-six, she committed suicide.
The posthumous publications of her novels *Last Words from
Montmartre* and *Notes of a Crocodile* made her into one of the
most revered countercultural icons in Chinese letters. After
her death in 1995, she was given the *China Times* Honorary
Prize for Literature. In 2007, a two-volume edition of her
Diaries was published, and in 2017 she became the subject of a
feature-length documentary by Evans Chan titled *Death in
Montmartre*.

BONNIE HUIE is the recipient of a PEN/Heim Translation
Fund Grant. Her rendition of Motojirō Kajii's story "Under
the Cherry Blossoms" was nominated for a Pushcart Prize,
and she has also translated the work of Tatsuhiro Ōshiro. Her
writings and translations appear in *The Brooklyn Rail*, *Kyoto
Journal*, and *Afterimage*. Huie lives in New York.

NOTES OF A CROCODILE

QIU MIAOJIN

Translated from the Chinese by
BONNIE HUIE

NEW YORK REVIEW BOOKS

New York

THIS IS A NEW YORK REVIEW BOOK
PUBLISHED BY THE NEW YORK REVIEW OF BOOKS
207 East 32nd Street, New York, NY 10016
www.nyrb.com

Originally published as *Eyu shouji* by China Times Publishing Co.
This publication was made possible in part by a grant from the PEN/Heim
Translation Fund.

Library of Congress Cataloging-in-Publication Data
Names: Qiu, Miaojin, 1969–1995, author. | Huie, Bonnie, translator.
Title: Notes of a crocodile / by Qiu Miaojin ; translated by Bonnie Huie.
Other titles: Eyu shouji. English
Description: New York : New York Review Books, 2017. | Series: New York
  Review Books Classics
Identifiers: LCCN 2017000237 (print) | LCCN 2017006563 (ebook) | ISBN
  9781681370767 (paperback) | ISBN 9781681370774 (epub)
Subjects: LCSH: Lesbians—Fiction. | Women—Taiwan—Fiction. |
  Gays—Taiwan—Fiction. | Taipei (Taiwan)—History—20th century—Fiction.
  | BISAC: FICTION / Lesbian. | FICTION / Coming of Age. | GSAFD:
  Bildungsromans.
Classification: LCC PL2892.5.U65 E913 2017 (print) | LCC PL2892.5.U65 (ebook)
  | DDC 895.13/52—dc23
LC record available at https://lccn.loc.gov/2017000237

ISBN 978-1-68137-076-7
Available as an electronic book; ISBN 978-1-68137-077-4

Printed in the United States of America on acid-free paper.
10 9 8 7

CONTENTS

NOTES OF A CROCODILE

NOTEBOOK #1

I

JULY 20, 1991. Picked up my college diploma at the service window of the registrar's office. It was so big I had to carry it with both hands. I dropped it twice while walking across campus. The first time it fell in the mud by the sidewalk, and I wiped the mud off with my shirt. The second time the wind blew it away. I chased after it ruefully. The corners were bent. In my heart, I held back a pitiful laugh.

When you visit, will you bring me some presents? the Crocodile wanted to know.

Very well, I'll bring you new hand-sewn lingerie, said Osamu Dazai.

I'll give you the most beautiful picture frame on earth, would you like that? asked Yukio Mishima.

I'll plaster your bathroom walls with copies of my Waseda degree, said Haruki Murakami.

And that's how it all began. Enter cartoon music (insert *Two Tigers* closing theme).

Forgot to return my student ID and library card but didn't realize it. At first I'd actually lost them. Nineteen days later, they were returned to me anonymously in an envelope, instantly transforming their loss into a lie. But I couldn't stop using them anyway, out of sheer convenience. Also didn't take my driver's exam seriously enough. Took it four times and failed, although two of those instances were due to factors entirely beyond my control. What's even better is that I publicly claim (and perhaps society buys it) to have failed only twice. Whatever, I don't care....

Locked the door. Shut the windows. Took the phone off the

hook and sat down. And that's how I wrote. I wrote until I was exhausted, smoked two cigarettes, and went into the bathroom and took a cold shower. Outside were the torrential winds and rain of the typhoon season. Halfway undressed, I realized there was no soap left. Got dressed again. Returned to the bathroom with a bar of soap, undressed again, then climbed back into the shower. That's how it is, writing a best seller.

Soap in hand, and the sounds of late-night TV in the background. Then a sudden clatter, as if the power station had been rocked by an explosion. I was enveloped in pitch-dark silence. The power had gone out. Nobody else was around, so I ran out of the bathroom completely naked, searching for a candle though I had no matches. Carried three tea lights with me into the kitchen, bumping into an electric fan on the floor along the way. Tried to light them on the gas burner, but the wax melted away. There was nothing else I could do. I threw open the balcony door and stepped outside to cool off. I hoped to catch a glimpse of other kindred souls standing naked out on their own balconies. That's how it is, writing a serious literary work.

Even if this book is neither popular nor serious, at least it's sensational. Five cents a word.

It's about getting a diploma and writing.

2

IN THE past I believed that every man had his own innate prototype of a woman, and that he would fall in love with the woman who most resembled his type. Although I'm a woman, I have a female prototype too.

My type would appear in hallucinations just as you were freezing to death atop an icy mountain, a legendary beauty from the furthest reaches of fantasy. For four years, that's what I believed. And I wasted all my college days—when I had the most courage and honesty I would ever have towards life—because of it.

I don't believe it anymore. It's like the impromptu sketch of a street artist, a little drawing taped to my wall. When I finally stopped believing in it and learned to leave it behind, I wound up selling a collection of priceless treasures for next to nothing. It was then that I realized I should leave behind some sort of record before my memories evaporated. I feared that otherwise it would be like waking from a dream, when the inventory of what had been bought and sold—and at what price—would be forever lost.

It's like a series of roadside warning signs. The one behind me says: DON'T BELIEVE THE FANTASY. The one ahead of me says: WIELD THE AX OF CRUELTY. One day it dawned on me as if I were writing my own name for the first time: Cruelty and mercy are one and the same. Existence in this world relegates good and evil to the exact same status. Cruelty and evil are only natural, and together they are endowed with half the power and half the utility in this world. It seems I'm going to have to learn to be crueler if I'm to become the master of my own fate.

Wielding the ax of cruelty against life, against myself, against others. It's the rule of animal instinct, ethics, aesthetics, metaphysics—and the axis of all four. And the comma that punctuated being twenty-two.

3

SHUI LING. Wenzhou Street. The white bench in front of the French bakery. The number 74 bus.

We sit at the back of the bus. Shui Ling and I occupy opposite window seats, the aisle between us. The December fog is sealed off behind glass. Dusk starts to set in around six, enshrouding Taipei. The traffic is creeping along Heping East Road. At the outer edge of the Taipei Basin, where the sky meets the horizon, is the last visible wedge of a bright orange sun whose radiance floods through the windows and spills onto the vehicles behind us, like the blessing of some mysterious force.

Silent, exhausted passengers pack the aisle, heads hung, bodies propped against the seats, oblivious. Through a gap in the curtain of their winter coats, I catch Shui Ling's eye, trying to contain the enthusiasm in my voice.

"Did you look outside?" I ask, ingratiatingly.

"Mmm," comes her barely audible reply.

Then silence. For a still moment, Shui Ling and I are sitting together in the hermetically sealed bus. Out the windows, dim silhouettes of human figures wind through the streets. It's a magnificent night scene, gorgeous and restrained. The two of us are content. We look happy. But underneath, there is already a strain of something dark, malignant. Just how bitter it would become, we didn't know.

4

In 1987, I broke free from the draconian university entrance-exam system and enrolled in college. People in this city are manufactured and canned, raised for the sole purpose of taking tests and making money. The eighteen-year-old me went through the high-grade production line and was processed in three years, despite the fact that I was pure carrion inside.

That fall, in October, I moved into a second-floor apartment on Wenzhou Street. The leaseholders were a married couple who had graduated a few years earlier. They gave me a room with a huge window overlooking an alley. The two rooms across from mine were rented by two sisters. The young married couple was always in the living room watching TV. They spent a fair amount of time on the coffee-colored sofa. "We got married our senior year," they told me, smiling. But most of the time, they didn't say a word. The sisters would spend all night in one of their rooms watching a different channel. Passing the door, you'd hear bits of lively conversation. I never saw my housemates unless I had to. Just came and went on my own. Everyone kept to themselves.

So despite the five of us living together under one roof, it might as well have been a home for the deaf.

I lived in solitude. Lived at night. I'd wake up at midnight and ride my bike—a red Giant—to a nearby store where I'd buy dried noodles, thick pork soup, and spring rolls. Then I'd come home and read while I ate. Take a shower, do laundry. In my room, there was neither the sound of another human being nor light. I'd write in my journal all night, or just read. I became obsessed with Kierkegaard and Schopenhauer. I devoured all kinds of books for tortured souls. Started collecting issues of the independence movement's weekly. Studied up on political game theory, an antidote to my spiritual reading. It made me feel like an outsider, which became my way of recharging. At the break of dawn, around six or seven, like a nocturnal creature afraid of the light, I'd finally lay my head—which by then was spilling over with thoughts—down onto the comforter.

That's how it went when things were good. Most of the time, however, I didn't eat a single thing all night. Didn't shower. Couldn't get out of bed. Didn't write in my journal or talk. Didn't read a single page or register the sound of another human being. All day long, I'd cry myself sick into my pillow. Sleep was just another luxury.

Didn't want anyone around. People were useless to me. Didn't need anyone. I started hurting myself and getting into all sorts of trouble.

Home was a credit-card bill footed by Nationalist Party voters. I didn't need to go back. Being in college gave me a sense of vocation. It exempted me from an oppressive system of social and personal responsibility—from going through the motions like a cog, from being whipped and beaten by everyone for not having worked hard enough and then having to put on a repentant face afterward. That system had already molded me into a flimsy, worthless shell. It drove my body to retreat into a self-loathing soul, and what's even scarier is that nobody knew or seemed to recognize it. My social identity was comprised of these two distinct, co-existing constructs. Each writhed toward me with its incessant demands—though when it came down to it, I spent more time getting to know my way around the supermarket next door than I did getting comfortable in my own skin.

Didn't read the paper. Didn't watch TV. Didn't go to class—except for gym, because the teacher took attendance. Didn't go out and didn't talk to my roommates. The only time I ever spoke at all was in the evenings or afternoons at the Debate Society, where I would go to preen my feathers and practice social intercourse. All too soon I realized that I was an innately beautiful peacock and decided that I shouldn't let myself go. However lazy, a peacock still ought to give its feathers a regular preening, and having been bestowed with such a magnificent set, I couldn't help but seek the mainstream of society as a mirror. With that peacock swagger, I found it hard to resist indulging in a little strutting, but that's how it went, and it was a fundamentally bad habit.

The fact is, most people go through life without ever living. They say you have to learn how to construct a self who remains free in spite of the system. And you have to get used to the idea that it's every man for himself in this world. It requires a strange self-awareness, whereby everything down to the finest detail must be performed before the eyes of the world.

Since there's time to kill, you have to use boredom to get you to the other side. In English, you'd say: *Break on through*. That's more like it.

5

SO SHE did me wrong. If my old motto was *I'm sentencing her to the guillotine*, my new motto contained a revelation: *The power to construct oneself is destiny.* If only it weren't for you, Shui Ling. In spite of everything, the truth is I still can't take it. I can't take it. Really, I can't. No matter how far I've come, it's never far enough. The pattern was already in place.

It must have been around October 1987. I was biking down Royal Palm Boulevard and passed somebody. I remembered it was their birthday. It was at that precise moment that all of my pent-up grief and fear hit me at once. I knew more or less that I'd been rejected and that was the bottom line. But somehow, I was convinced I had to get even.

She'd just turned twenty. I'd turned eighteen five months earlier. She and some friends from high school walked past me, and I managed to glance at her. But as for what significance that glance held, it was as if my whole life had flashed before my eyes. Though they were off in the distance, I could still feel the glow of her smile. It left me with the acute sense that she never failed to elicit the adoration and affection of others, that she was someone who radiated a pure, child-like contentment.

Even now I'm still in awe of her innate power to command such devotion—not only her charms but how it felt to be deprived of them. She maintained only a handful of friendships. In the past, the people around her had clung dearly to her, giving her their entire attention. She didn't need any more of that, but she didn't have much of a choice. She was trapped and suffocating. Whenever I was around her, I'd become clingy, too. If I wasn't by her side, I felt distant from other people, when in fact she was the one who was distant. That's how it worked. It was her natural gift.

I didn't see her my entire senior year of high school. I was careful to avoid her. Didn't dare take the initiative, though I longed for her to notice me in the crowd. An upperclassman and my senior, she was an ominous character, a black spade. To shuffle and draw the same card again would be even more ominous.

6

THE LECTURE hall for Introduction to Chinese Literature was packed. I got there late and had to sheepishly lift my chair up higher than the rostrum and carry it all the way to the front row. The professor stopped lecturing, and all the other sheep turned and gawked at me and my antics.

Toward the end of class, someone passed a note from behind:

Hey, can I talk to you after class?

—SHUI LING

She had sought me out. I knew it would happen. Even if I had switched to a different section, she would have sought me out all the same. She who hid in the crowd, who didn't want anyone to see her with her aloofness and averted eyes. When I stepped forward, she stepped out, too. And she had pointed with a child's wanton smile and said, "I want that one." There was no way I could refuse. And like a potted sunflower that had just been sold to a customer, I was taken away.

This, from a beautiful girl whom I was already deeply, viscerally attracted to. Things were getting good. There she was, standing right in front of me. She brushed the waves of hair away from her face with a seductiveness that painfully seared my heart like a tattoo. Her feminine radiance was overpowering. I was about to get knocked out of the ring. It was clear from that moment on, we'd never be equals. How could we, with me under the table, scrambling to summon a different me, the one she would worship and put on a pedestal? No way was I coming out.

"What are you doing here?" I was so anxious that I had to blurt something out. She didn't say a word or seem the least bit embarrassed.

"Did you switch to this section to make up a class?" She didn't look up at me. She just stood there, dragging one foot behind her in the hallway, and didn't say a thing, as if this one-sided conversation had nothing to do with her.

"How'd you know I switched?" Abruptly, she broke her silence. Her eyes were shimmering with amazement, and I could finally meet them. She was now looking right at me, wide-eyed.

"Well, of course I'd know!" I didn't want her to think I'd been noticing her. "You finally said something!" I said, heaving an exaggerated sigh of relief. She smiled at me shyly, even teasingly, and I let out a huge laugh, relieved that I'd made her smile. The glow on her face was like rays of sunshine along a golden beach.

She told me that she'd started to feel nervous as soon as I walked into the room. She wanted to talk to me, but didn't know what to say. I pointed to her shoelaces. She gingerly leaned forward to tie them. She said when she saw me, she couldn't bring herself to speak, and then she didn't want to say anything, so then she just stood there. She threw her purple canvas backpack over her shoulder and crouched on the floor. As she started talking, I felt the sudden urge to reach over and touch her long hair, which looked so soft and supple. You don't know a thing, but I figured it all out in an instant, I told her silently in my heart. I reached over and held her backpack instead, and feeling mildly contented by the closeness of its weight, wished that she would go on tying her shoes.

It was already six when class ended. Shadows had lengthened across the campus, and the evening breeze lilted in the air. We grabbed our bikes and headed off together. We took the main thoroughfare on campus, keeping with the leisurely pace of the traffic on the wide open road. I didn't know if I was following her, or if she was following me. Within a year, the two of us would come to cherish our ambiguous rapport, at once intimate and unfamiliar, and tempered by moments of silent confrontation.

"Why'd you come over and talk to me?" In my heart I already knew too much but pretended to know nothing.

"Why wouldn't I talk to you?" She sounded slightly irritated. The dusk obscured her face, so I couldn't read her expression. But as soon as she spoke, I could tell she'd had a tough freshman year. There was a curious note of dejection in her answer. I already knew her all too well.

"I'm just an underclassman you've seen, like, three times!" I nearly exploded.

"Not even," she said coolly to herself.

My eyes were fixed on her long skirt as it wafted in the breeze. "Weren't you worried that I wouldn't remember you, or wouldn't want to talk to you?"

"I knew you weren't like that." Her reaction was perfectly composed, as if everything to do with me was already set in stone.

We reached the school gates, not quite sure what to do next. She seemed to want to see where I lived. The way she suggested it conveyed a touch of familial kindness, like a tough but pliable cloth whose inner softness made my heart ache. Besides, as they say, if the floodwaters are rushing straight toward you, what are you going to do to stop them? This was how she treated me, for no apparent reason. I took her toward Xinsheng South Road, back to Wenzhou Street.

"How's this year going?" I tried to break through her gloom.

"I don't want to talk about it." She squeezed her eyes shut and grimaced slightly, lifting her chin in a hopeless look.

"You don't want to tell me?" I was practically edging her onto the road. I was sure she was going to get hit by a car.

She shook her head. "I don't want to tell anyone."

"How did you get this way?" It pained my heart to hear her speak such nonsense.

"Yeah, well, I've changed." Her eyes flickered with haughtiness, underscoring the boldness of her statement.

Her answer was so immature that I felt tempted to tease her. "Into what?"

"I've just changed, that's all. I'm not the same person I was in high school." I could detect a note of self-hatred in the viciousness of her tone.

Hearing those words, "I've changed," made me truly sad. The traffic had illuminated Xinsheng South Road in an opulent yellow. We followed the red brick wall that enclosed the school grounds, pausing to lean against a railing. To our left were the city streets, whose bright lights seemed to be calling. To our right was the dimly lit campus, teeming with the splendors of solitude. There's nothing that won't change, do you understand? I said in my heart. "Can you count the number of lights that are on in that building over there?" I pointed to a brand-new high-rise at the intersection.

"Uh, I see lights in five windows, so maybe, like, five?" she said brightly.

Just wait and see how many there are later on. Will you still remember? I asked myself, answering with a nod.

7

THE FIRST semester she was my lifeline. It was a clandestine form of dating—the kind where the person you're going out with doesn't know it's a date. I denied myself, and I denied the fact that she was part of my life, so much so that I denied the dotted line that connected the two of us and our entire relationship to a crime. But the eye of suspicion had been cast upon me from the very beginning, and this extraordinary eye reached all the way back to my adolescence. My hair started to go gray early. Life ahead was soon supplanted by a miserable prison sentence. It was as if I never really had a youth. Nonetheless, I was determined at all costs to become a person who would love without boundaries. And so I locked myself and that eye together in a dark closet.

Every Sunday night, however, I was forced to think about her. It was like a chore I dreaded. I'd resolve not to go to Intro to Chinese Lit, and every Monday I would sleep in until almost three, waking up just in time to rush to class on my bike. Every Monday after class, Shui Ling would follow me matter-of-factly back to Wenzhou Street, as if she were merely passing by on her way home. Afterward, I'd wait with her for the number 74 bus. There was a bench in front of the French bakery. Our secret little rendezvous were tidy and simple. They were executed with the casual deftness of a high-class burglary: bribing the guards with one hand, feeding a criminal appetite with the other.

The rest of the week, we barely spoke. She was an apparition seen only on Mondays. On Mondays, she would appear like the answer to a dying man's prayers—roses in hand, draped in white muslin, barefoot and floating, come to grant me a reprieve. In a primal mating dance, eyes closed in rapture, she scattered rose petals into the wilderness. Roses every week and she didn't even know it, and it was amid roses that it seemed I might live after all. I reached for those roses, and for a new life, only to discover a glass wall. When I extended my hand, so did my reflection. When Monday ended, the glass that stood between me and my reflection thickened.

The room on Wenzhou Street. Elegant maroon wallpaper and yellow curtains. What did I even talk to her about in there? She sat on the floor, in the gap between the foot of the wooden bed frame and the wardrobe, with her back to me, almost silent. I talked nonstop. Most of the time it was just me talking. Talking about whatever. Talking about my horrible, painful life experiences. Talking about every person I'd ever gotten entangled with and couldn't let go of. Talking about my own complexities, my own eccentricities. She was always playing with something in her hands. She would look up at me in disbelief and ask what was so hard to understand about this or what was so strange about that. She accepted me, which amounted to negating my negation of myself. Those sincere eyes, like a mirror, hurt me. But she accepted me. In my anguish, about every third sentence out of my mouth was: *You don't understand.* Her eyes were suffused with a profound and translucent light, like the ocean gazing at me in silence, as if it were not necessary to speak at all. *You don't understand.* She thought she understood. And she accepted me. Years later, I realized that had been the whole point.

Those wrenching eyes, which could lift up the entire skeleton of my being. How I longed for myself to be subsumed into the ocean of her eyes. How the desire, once awakened, would come to scald me at every turn. The strength in those eyes offered a bridge to the outside world. The scarlet mark of sin and my deep-seated fear of abandonment had given way to the ocean's yearning.

8

I AM A woman who loves women. The tears I cry, they spring from a river and drain across my face like yolk.

My time was gradually consumed by tears. The whole world loves me, but what does it matter since I hate myself? Humanity stabs a bayonet into a baby's chest, fathers produce daughters that they pull into the bathroom to rape, handicapped midgets drag themselves onto highway overpasses to announce that they're about to end it all just to collect a little spare change, and mental patients have irrepressible hallucinations and suicidal urges. How can the world be this cruel? A human being has only so much in them, and yet you must learn through experience, until you finally reach the maddening conclusion that the world wrote you off a long time ago, or accept the prison sentence that your crime is your existence. And the world keeps turning as if nothing had happened. The forced smiles on the faces of the lucky ones say it all: It's either this, or getting stabbed in the chest with a bayonet, getting raped, dragging yourself onto the highway overpass, or checking into a mental institution. No one will ever know about your tragedy, and the world eluded its responsibility ages ago. All that you know is that you've been crucified for something, and you're going to spend the rest of your life feeling like no one and nothing will help you, that you're in it alone. Your individual circumstances, which separate you from everyone else, will keep you behind bars for life. On top of it all, humanity tells me I'm lucky. Privilege after privilege has been conferred upon me, and if I don't seem content with my lot, they'll be devastated.

Shui Ling, please don't knock on my door anymore. You don't

know how dark it is here in my heart. I don't know who I am at all. What's ahead of me is unclear, yet I must move forward. I don't want to become myself. I know the answer to the riddle, but I can't stand to have it revealed. The first time I saw you, I knew I would fall in love with you. That my love would be wild, raging, and passionate, but also illicit. That it could never develop into anything, and instead, it would split apart like pieces of a landslide. As flesh and blood, I was not distinct. You turned me into my own key, and when you did, my fears seized me in a flood of tears that soon abated. I stopped hating myself and discovered the corporeal me.

She didn't understand. Didn't understand she could love me, maybe that she already did love me. Didn't understand that beneath the hide of a lamb was a demonic beast that had to suppress the urge to rip her to shreds. Didn't understand that love, every little bit of it, was about exchange. Didn't understand that she caused me suffering. Didn't understand that love was like that.

She gave me a puzzle in a box. She put the pieces together patiently, one by one, and completed the picture of me.

9

"I'm NOT coming to Intro to Chinese Lit next week, but I'll be there the week after," I said.

Shui Ling and I took the number 74 bus together at seven in the evening. She was headed home and I was going to private tutoring on Changchun Road. We sat together in a double seat; she had the window and I the aisle. She was wearing a white scarf. With the window halfway open, she rested her head on the ledge, her body tense, her eyes fixed on some far-off point in the dusk. Her isolation was apparent. I felt the distance between us.

"Okay," she answered in a tone that showed her waning enthusiasm. I wanted to leave, and she knew it.

"You're not going to ask me why?" I felt a twinge of regret. I was hesitant to be on my own.

"Fine. Why?" she asked me indignantly, with her head turned to conceal her wounded pride.

"I don't want to have a steady relationship with anyone. I've gotten used to seeing you every week, and I can't handle being tied down like this. It's a bad pattern that I have to break," I told her guiltily.

"Okay. Whatever suits you." She turned away again.

"Still mad at me?" I felt sorry for her.

"Yes. You're selfish." She had turned her back to me, but her reflection in the glass revealed her loneliness and dejection.

"How am I selfish?" I tried to make her say what was bothering her. It was so hard to get her to talk.

Finally, after thinking for a long time, she aired her resentment.

"You don't want to have this...bad pattern...but what I am supposed to do, now that I'm used to it?" Emerging from her silence, she could be rash with words, though she normally spared me.

"What are you used to?" I pretended not to know.

"You know what I'm talking about." Her fragile voice was especially attractive whenever she was angry.

"No, I don't know." Whenever she divulged her overwhelming feelings for me, it was always bittersweet.

"That's a lie. I'm the same as you...I've gotten used to seeing you every week, too." She spoke timidly, not because she wasn't supposed to have such feelings but because she was telling me about them. Because femininity meant having to hide one's true feelings.

"That makes it even worse. You shouldn't get used to it. After Chinese Lit ends, we're not going to see each other anymore."

"Why can't we see each other?" she asked instantly, as if asking for the solution to a math problem.

"Because there's no reason for us to see each other. Besides, I'll run off one day, and that's when you'll really feel bad." For the first time, I had spoken aloud my true feelings toward her, and my words were a slap in the face.

"I still don't understand. Whatever suits you." She gave up all resistance.

10

MAUVAIS SANG is a film. Not another Godard movie. A more youthful French film. Its male protagonist is built like a lizard and clearly has traces of crocodile in his blood. All the other men are short and stout and bald. They're all ugly old men in this film, aside from this sight-for-sore-eyes of a young Adonis in the lead role. The director is a contemporary master of aesthetics.

"I must ascend, not descend," the protagonist declares. As he nears his final moments, the female lead embraces him from behind, and he resists. It's moving beyond words. He closes his eyes with a dramatic flutter and utters his last words: "It's hard being an honest child." After he dies, a hideous old man squeezes a single blue tear out of his closed eyes. There's essentially no way the lizard can be honest. Even as it rolls over and turns its white belly up, it must take its hidden tears for its lover to the grave. The lizard has a good name: Loose-Tongued Boy.

Betty Blue is another film. It's relatively institutional fare. A French film made for a young mainstream audience. Just how is it made for them? There are only two colors, blue and yellow, which makes things easy to remember, and aside from the two protagonists—a man and a woman—there's no one else on earth. Time glides by in the film without so much as half a struggle or a long conversation. Anyone with eyes, even if they're color-blind, can sit with popcorn in one hand and soda in the other, and leisurely watch the whole thing. Fair enough.

The best thing about the entire film is when the main couple's friend, upon hearing news of his mother's death, lies in bed paralyzed, and other people have to dress him for the funeral and tie his necktie, which is adorned with naked ladies. The tears streaming down his face make you want to explode laughing. The female protagonist, Betty, says, "Life always had it in for me." She gouges out her own eyes and is sent to a mental institution, where they strap her to a bed. The male protagonist says, "No one can keep the two of us apart." He disguises himself as a woman in order to sneak into the institution, and with a pillow, smothers Betty to death. At that moment, his face, exquisitely white, radiates a ghastly feminine beauty. The director uses a crazy love to curse the hand of fate. Fair enough, though the last bit will make you gag on your popcorn and soda.

The first film is nauseating. So is the second film.

The difference is, the first film is sincere in its approach. From the beginning, you know that it's nauseating. The second film is deceptive in its approach. It tricks you into thinking that you're not on the road to nausea, until the very end, when the truth becomes clear.

"Nauseating is nauseating. Try to be the most honest child you possibly can," says *Mauvais Sang*.

"Who says you can't get away with a naked-lady necktie?" says *Betty Blue*.

11

MENG SHENG. Did I ever truly love this man? I don't know the answer to that question. I attended an arts camp in December 1987, in the town of Danshui. After I'd introduced myself in a fiction workshop, he stood up in the front row, walked back to where I was seated, and knelt down in the aisle next to me. The frivolous grin on his face hinted at an unusual astuteness beneath the surface.

"I'm a year older than you. I go to the affiliated high school. Next year I'll be at your school. Just hearing the few words you said, I felt as though you were the only one worth listening to. All that other garbage makes me sick. Coming here was a real waste of my time."

This pompous fool spoke as if no one else were around us. My heart was filled with utter disdain. I felt like scoffing but managed to indulge him with a smile nevertheless. After crouching for a while, he impulsively launched into a set of squats, as if it were some form of self-amusement. Though he was an archetypally beautiful boy back then, he was also not exactly what you would call a boy. I sensed he had the power to lead others astray, and this power was in part what kept him young. Apart from that supremely cheeky grin, there wasn't a whiff of boyishness about him.

"What are you doing? Scurrying away like I'm a skunk. . . . What's so important?" As I walked out, he followed right behind me. Even as other people were trying to talk to me, he stood there impudently, blocking the way. I was losing my patience.

"What's wrong with skunks?" he quipped. "At least they can make annoying people disappear!"

"So why don't you make yourself disappear, then? What are you doing here?" I said, letting my irritation show.

"What am I doing here?" he repeated. "Good question." He slapped me on the shoulder. "It's just that—I don't even know what I'm doing out here." He pouted innocently.

"How about if we have a talk, old pal?" I said, softening. I gestured for him to sit beside me.

"We're not old pals," he protested politely, putting his arm around my shoulder. I pushed it off.

"All right . . . big brother. Stop following me around. You're ruining my chance at happiness."

"You're the one with seniority here. What a joke—people like you have no clue what happiness is. That word has been erased from your mind," he said contemptuously. Then he did a gleeful somersault, right there on the ground.

Instantly, I recognized that he and I were of the same ilk, each embracing our own singular way of seeing things. Yet he seemed pure and whole compared to me, and in that respect, he was more precocious and more exceptional. Were it possible to love him, it would also mean loving his brand of exceptionalism. By winter of that year, he'd actually grown quite attractive. He was a tall, handsome youth.

12

JUST ANOTHER day, right? The last day of Intro to Chinese Lit. Exactly as planned, I went to class. In order to get there early, I sped down the road, pedaling at full speed. My heart was pounding. A million different thoughts had been swirling in my mind and now they were lodged there, unexpressed. She'd chosen a seat in the very back. Her purple backpack was on top of her desk. She'd put her head down, and her long locks hung over the edge of the desk. By that point, she wasn't talking to anyone at school. I knew she was lonely. Separated from her friends who'd looked after her, she had to try to be her own person. She just sat there, not moving. I paused at her side, contemplating her isolation. She looked miserable. I knew she didn't want to live this way. I was upset, and so I'd treated her badly.

"I'm here." It was almost time for class to start. I called to her lightly.

"Mmm," she answered indifferently, without lifting her head.

"You don't want to talk to me?" My guilt, and tenderness, were starting to spill over.

"Oh, I'm really tired. I want to go to sleep," she said softly. She still hadn't given me so much as a glance. She was pushing me away.

"Fine. You should rest for a while." Unwanted by her, I felt like my heart was being dragged around on a chain. I plodded over to the desk in front of her and sat down.

After class, I stood up front to observe her from a distance, but she wouldn't look at me. Moving slowly, she quietly packed up her things. I glanced over while chatting with an acquaintance. She was already gone. *Wait. There are so many things I want to tell you.* I barreled out of the building toward the bikes, searching frantically for a familiar one. Nothing. I sprinted toward the place where we'd always met before leaving together. No sight of purple anywhere. I made a mad dash in the opposite direction. I knew it was too late. I'd already gone down the wrong road too many times. I'd never catch up to her. After checking the bus stop by the rear entrance, I turned around and started walking home. *Please, no. I just wanted to tell you: It doesn't have to be this way.*

A dark night's rain. The storm was intensifying. With my clothes clinging to my skin, I was racing as fast as I could. But the faster I ran, the harder the rain and wind seemed to fight me. My socks were encrusted with a layer of mud. I could feel it. After wading through pools of standing water, my legs soon felt like wet logs. I checked every bus stop before turning onto the next street. I'd already run a long way. I sat down weakly inside a bus shelter. I'd never find her. I waited wearily for the next half hour....

Basically, what I wanted to tell you today was that we shouldn't stop seeing each other. I couldn't find you, and so we still can't see each other. I also brought you that book you wanted to borrow.

The rain turned to drizzle. My eyes stung as I finished writing the note and tucked it into the rear rack of her bike, which I'd found parked across from the Literature Department building. *Whatever. Really. It'll fall out by itself, which will save a lot of trouble.* With the slackening of a rope, I'd been sent tumbling to the ground, and now that I was on my own again I was at a loss. I missed her. I had gotten what I deserved.

The next day, around noon, I walked into class late, not even conscious of where I was. Someone passed me a note.

Your book is missing. I had to go to gym class in the morning. As I was walking over I noticed a whole bunch of bikes were missing. In my heart, I prayed that my beloved bike wasn't one of them and got really worried. But sure enough, it was lying there, on top of one bike and under another, covered in mud. I hurried to stand it back up, wondering if I should wipe off its frame with my handkerchief. I was crying inside. How could anyone have knocked it over so carelessly? Then I saw that the rear rack had a pink flyer stuck in it. I just hate those tacky flyers, and when I tossed it aside, I saw your note. There was no book. Someone must have stolen it. So I had to tell you: Your book is missing.

I don't understand your complicated reasoning, and I don't want to. You said it was for my own good that you stopped having anything to do with me, and that we should stop seeing each other so there'll be less grieving. I don't understand it at all, and I refuse to ever understand. Maybe you have it in your head that things are better this way, but it doesn't address my situation. Did you even consider me at all? Because my answer is: It's not good for me. I used to think that I could seek refuge in you. Those two words—*seek refuge*—were what I really wanted to do. You're the only person at this school I'm close to. It's happened three times now that I've gotten depressed and needed to escape. Each time I ran from campus, clutching my backpack and hoping I wouldn't bump into anyone I knew, and I found my way to your apartment. As I rang the buzzer, all I knew was that I needed to see you. But you were never there. The first time I was tired, so I sat down on the steps and stayed there. I was already a little closer to you. I could feel you there. Then I found the energy to go home. After that, I stopped ringing your buzzer. I just had to hang out on the steps for a while, and that was enough.

Did you know these things? If you don't want me to seek refuge in you, sorry my skin's not thick enough to handle it. What's wrong with that?

—Shui Ling

I still recall it. When I received that messily scrawled letter—messily scrawled and yet elegant—my hands wouldn't stop shaking. I read it several times and still couldn't comprehend it, but I couldn't read it again. My eyes were fixed on her name. I jumped to my feet and got on my bike and pedaled to the lecture hall where she had her afternoon class. With the wind in my hair, words flooded my mind. My heart swooned. That day I was wearing green jeans, and the color sparkled in the light of the afternoon sun. I stood out on the lawn, waiting for her to pass by. As any fool would tell you, there was never any book left on the rear rack. She walked past me and asked what I was doing there. I said, Can we start over? She turned around. The ocean wept. I knew it was mutual love.

13

THE SINGER Zhao Chuan has a new song out that goes: "A boy sees a rose in a field. . . ." Working on this notebook, I stayed up from the wee hours of midnight until nine a.m. listening to this song on repeat. Didn't listen to any other song on the whole tape. And now for this section's tangent:

I cannot resist your wildness swaying in the wind. I cannot imagine you would so much as shed a tear in the rain. In the early-morning wind, you are a rose beyond compare—ever dangerous, ever alluring. You are the rose of autumn's final reverie, so distant and absolute. A boy sees a rose in a field, this rose that grows in a wasteland. How full it is in bloom, this rose that grows in a wasteland.

This notebook constitutes part one. It recounts the period from October 1987 to January 1988. Each eighty-page notebook is quickly fading, having been filled out in pencil. Based on ten massive journals' worth of material, I wrote eight manuals that can be read as admonitions for young people. A clean transcription was made using a ballpoint pen before each notebook was stuffed into the bottom of a drawer. Whenever my memory failed me, I would take out a notebook and look at it, and go over the events that made me who I am. They illustrate a process.

The first two notebooks, though, are meager compared to the rest. They didn't have journals to serve as a reference, so I had to rely on dwindling impressions, which meant tinkering around until it sounded right. During my four years of college, I left a lot of things behind. Sometimes writing was like finding a parking spot: Just as I was about to give up, I managed to achieve a perfect fit, thanks to a bit of skillful maneuvering. Other times it was like examining food that had been left sitting out for so long that ants and cockroaches had gotten to it. On other occasions it was like a major year-end cleaning where I was forced to throw something away because I couldn't find anywhere to put it. And still other times, it was like trading in a used car for a new one: I didn't give it a second thought.

Freshman year was a total blackout. I burned all her letters. I gave her an exquisite beige journal as a gift. These were all things that happened later on. She was subjected to my every which way of purging things, and in the end, I was purged of her. Consequently, I discovered that I had no shortage of purging methods. By then, I was a purgeaholic. Because she was mine and illness had set in. And because purging her was the cure. What was gone was gone. There was no looking back. I wouldn't purge anything else important, or so I vowed.

By the time I'd invented a glue powerful enough to stop my purge-happy hand dead in its tracks, it was too late. No one was left in my inner circle. Since Meng Sheng left behind scarcely an eyelash, these days I have no choice but to become an archaeologist.

"A girl sees a rose in a field" is how it should have gone. That's the kind of song Meng Sheng wrote for me.

NOTEBOOK #2

I

IMAGINE an overstuffed bag of tricks. Those who belong to the class known as college students are given a free pass. You're handed an empty bag at the start of your education, and you're allowed to put anything you want inside of it. Then adults give you a break for the next four years. (There are unfortunate exceptions to this rule in certain departments. Adults have been chosen to uphold societal values, after all.) They'll turn a blind eye for the most part and let you put anything you want into that bag, as long as you hang on tight to that student ID of yours.

College—now there's a system. Though it's not quite death, it's a pretty close second. It's the nexus of three major institutions (compulsory education, compulsory labor, and compulsory marriage), and these three institutions happen to be the greatest achievements of human civilization. Contrary to expectation, when experienced in combination, they allow for an escape into a transient, self-absorbed greatness. Like death, college serves as a kind of escape hatch. But while death takes you straight to the morgue, college is a single rope dangling loose from the inescapable net of society. While in death everyone receives equal treatment, college is a place where certain people arrive covered in a layer of muck, a nastiness that they, in turn, smear onto others.

To sum it up, the usual bag of tricks consists of: going to class + taking tests + chasing the opposite sex + recreation + earning spending money + pretending to be interested in joining clubs + observing society + hanging out. The first seven constitute eighty percent of your waking hours. I don't even know how to explain what goes on that eighty percent of the time. I could go on and on, and still never get to the last one: hanging out. You just have to gather all the tools you can—as if in preparation to outsmart life itself—and keep them in that overstuffed bag of tricks.

2

FEBRUARY 1988. I spent my first winter vacation alone at the place on Wenzhou Street.

All week I holed up in my room. Ate instant noodles. Went for walks. Went to the bathroom. In between those three activities, I worked on a story a lot more disturbing than this one. Got a letter in the mail. On the white envelope was a hand-drawn sketch in red marker. It was of a naked woman with her legs spread-eagle.

> I want to see you. Reply, or else I'll chop off a finger and send it to you.
> —MENG SHENG, The Bridegroom from Hell

Meng Sheng. That annoying dude I met at arts camp. He was like a sinister shadow that made me want to run away. The next day, I'd said I was sick and left Danshui. As I was leaving, I could see him standing off in the distance with a strange, innocent smile on his face. It was as if that smile could encroach upon my mind, even if I was rid of him for the next few months and tried to console myself with the thought that we had no contact. That smile suggested the powers that he'd flaunted around me, to show that he was capable of dominating me. So when I got the letter, I was terrified. I'd never before feared being dominated in a relationship. I could practically feel his eyes probing me, using me as he pleased.

I decided not to reply. I refused to enter the dynamic in that premonition, and I also wanted to test his strength. Three days after the first letter, a second letter arrived. On the envelope was a drawing of a knife, and in red ink like the first. But this time, there was no mailing address. Evidently, it had been placed directly in the mailbox. I opened it. Inside was a letter, along with a plastic bag riddled with staples that, sure enough, contained a crimson, blood-soaked withered pinky finger. My entire body started to tremble. I got on my bike and pedaled as fast as I could to a distant canal. When the coast was clear, I tossed the plastic bag in the water and told myself I'd lost. The letter said:

> I'm not in love with you. I just want to see you. If you don't reply, I'll come over in the middle of the night on Sunday and beat the crap out of you.
> —MENG SHENG, Bridegroom among Bridegrooms

Ten p.m. on Sunday. I'd been scrambling to finish the story. I was completely exhausted, but I had to wait for Meng Sheng. It was strange, to say the least, to be waiting around for some guy I'd met only once to come over and beat me up, but in fact, I felt like we were old friends. And so I started to look forward to it. I didn't want him in my room, though. Shui Ling was the only one I'd let in. I dragged me and my throbbing, overactive mind down to the front steps of the building. The sound of passing scooters, big and small, grazed my ears. Seemingly able to distinguish their individual sounds, I felt extraordinarily sensitive. Focusing on my senses had forced my mind to stop thinking. Suddenly, out of this tranquil state came an internal directive: I was free to look him right in the eye and say whatever I wanted.

"So you've surrendered, eh? How long have you been sitting here waiting?" At exactly midnight, this dude Meng Sheng pulled up on a heavyweight motorcycle with no muffler. The rumbling noise it made was downright maddening. His bike had a white fairing and was fitted with a rear seat cowl that, like the glint of a razor's edge, signaled danger. Coupled with sensitivity, that ferociousness was echoed in his tone, which exhibited a manner that seemed all his own.

"What do you *really* want?" I shot back at him. But it was obvious that I was no match for him. In spite of the tenderness flowing between us, I had to toughen up and push back.

"What do I want?" he asked himself, as if my question were so good he had to mull it over. He took off his wraparound sunglasses, and a genuine smile flashed across his face: "I want to die."

I hung out with him for a while. When we were together, my masculine and feminine sides reached their highest state of dialectical tension. It was the same for him, and he knew that it was his optimal state. His words had sparked something in both of us.

"Take me somewhere," I said. Though his words were hard, I softened. His expression instantly changed, and he didn't say another word. Once he ditched that tough exterior, his face was like a blank sheet of paper. For the first time since we'd met, I felt as if I could let my guard down. His motorcycle shot down the overpass of Keelung Road. The streetlamps along the highway formed arcs of yellow light. I was singing but the sound was broken up by the wind.

"Do you know why I decided to talk to you, out of everyone?" He parked the bike underneath Fuhe Bridge and led me up a weed-covered path to an open area on a hill. There were no houses nearby. I looked up at the wild grass, which grew so tall that it towered over our heads.

"I read the story that you submitted to the writing workshop. You're the kind of person who'd die with me. You practically have horns growing out of your head. I recognized it in an instant." A sly grin escaped from the corners of his mouth.

"You're wrong. I don't want to die, or anything like that." My high hopes were crushed. "Why would you need another person to die with you? That's horrible." I started to feel I'd overestimated him.

"It's not my choice. I've never gotten an ounce of sympathy from anyone. I've always hated being alone, and I refuse to die alone. I don't want my life to end this way."

"Sounds juvenile to me. You still have to die alone, and it's the most alone you'll ever be. I never think about these things, but even I know that much. Where do you get these ideas from?"

"I talk about my fantasies too openly." His face betrayed his arrogance. "It's like being in the clutches of death and refusing the last breath of air with my eyes wide open and a sneer on my face. To have paid such a high price to live, only to die! Don't tell me I don't have the right to say no thanks?"

"I don't want to talk about this anymore. I don't agree with you. It doesn't matter what you say." I had all kinds of deep reservations that inhibited me from continuing this conversation.

"You and I are birds of a feather." He shot me the same strange smile as he did when we first met at Tamkang University. "The thing is, you're more strongly inclined toward realism than I am, so it's easier for you to escape yourself. I completely envy you. That's a commendable strength." He seemed on the verge of kissing my feet, which struck me as funny.

"Thanks a lot," I said, unable to restrain the loud guffaw that slipped out. My laugh set him off, and his laugh was even more outrageous. We were both cracking up so hard our stomachs hurt. I began slapping him on the cheek, harder and harder, and he started stroking my hair, faster and faster. In a burst of silliness, we released the tension that had built up from all the heaviness and arrived at an understanding.

"Tell me about yourself." I was curious about him.

"Perfect, flawless human being. My family has loads of money. I'm also so smart that it's easy for me to be the best at everything I do. I'm so bored that I wish I were dead. Whatever I want to do, I can do, and no one's going to stop me. When I was twelve and still in grade school, I pulled the pants off the girl next door and practiced putting my pee-pee inside of her body. Later on, I started feeling like there was a special kind of boredom awaiting me. When I was fourteen, I joined a gang. I left home for two whole years. I hunted to kill and was hunted myself. Those were exciting times. But I realized I'd meet a gruesome, senseless death before I'd even figured out what the hell was going on.

"I went home because I experienced a huge shock. One day I was in a hotel room getting liquored up with this underage prostitute, and I spotted a big black birthmark on the inside of her thigh. It was the same girl from when I was twelve. I cried out her name just as I was about to enter her, and suddenly I broke down sobbing. Pain was shooting through my heart and lungs. She started to cry too and ran out of the room naked. I'd done a bad thing, and I was being punished. I felt like I had it coming. And that's when I went home. I forced myself to live a normal life. I'd lost whatever right I had to object, so the best punishment for me was to have my hands bound and tied, to let myself be arrested by boredom.

"Later on, my story became one of a man in search of his destiny with a certain goddess. By the time I was a junior, I'd already skipped two grades to make up for the two years I spent on the streets. My life story is way too long. I'm tired. We'll talk more next time, okay?"

His final words sounded weak, though I sensed an inkling of goodwill within that weakness. I gave him my most gracious and sincere nod, and thanked him for everything he'd shared with me. It was a moving experience, one that I certainly wanted to repay in kind. The stream of headlights on Fuhe Bridge illuminated its arches to form what from a distance looked like a golden pavilion.

"Where did the finger come from?" I asked, my eyes widening.

"I told one of my old gang brothers to get it for me." He seemed slightly remorseful.

3

THE MOMENT I said to Shui Ling *Can we start over?*, the flood-gates of desire were thrown open.

We didn't see each other the entire winter break. It was a buffer between us, and the suspense built up—as if for an even bigger clash. "If I come out of hiding and treat you however I want, you'll wish you could hide from me, but you won't be able to—I'll be cast deep down into the inferno," I wrote to her. "Even if you were in the inferno, I'd follow you down just to see you. I'm capable of things you can't imagine." That was her response. Nice. She wasn't one to down-play her abilities. That last bit about being "capable of things" hinted at a strong feminine will.

"The other day... Saturday, I think ... yeah ... I was in Hsinchu visiting Zi Ming. I took the Zhongxing Line there by myself...." The way she spoke, it was as if she were teasing out a delicate thread. I didn't dare interrupt her. It was the first time we'd run into each other that semester. The two of us stood under the portico of the Literature Department building. It felt like our past had been a life-time ago. Zi Ming was her best friend from high school.

"I went to watch her basketball game ... yeah, it was fun. I hadn't had that much fun in ages." She turned and looked at me. I was lis-tening, mesmerized. "She took me out for some good food. That night, when we went to bed, we stayed up talking with the lights out." She leaned back against a pillar, staring excitedly off into the distance. "The next day, she even helped me wash my hair... and dry it...." As she recounted the details, the enraptured look on her face revealed how much she cherished every second. "Yeah, part of me really didn't want to come back." I asked her why, and she sighed. "I told myself to have as much fun as I could... because as soon as I came back and school started, things would stop being so laid-back." With a change of topic, a dimpled smile spread across her face.

We wheeled our bikes to Drunken Moon Lake. I said, "I used to imagine what you'd look like when you get older." She asked what I had imagined. I said, more melancholy, and later on, tall and slender. Someday, you'll grow into a tall and slender woman. Sitting there on that bench by the lake, she started to ramble, telling me her entire life story.

"All of a sudden, everyone's gone. I go to school alone, walk alone, ride the bus alone, eat alone, go home alone.... It's not like before, when there was always someone who'd let me copy their homework, or in Home Ec when someone would help me knit a sweater, and I'd just stand to the side during cooking lessons. Or in gym class, when someone would walk with me after doing sprints. Not to mention Zi Ming taking me to the bus stop every day and covering for me in everything. Even helping me tie my shoes, things like that. During freshman year, sometimes I'd feel this tightness in my chest, and I'd go to the pay phone by the Literature Department and call Zi Ming in Hsinchu, but I could never get through on the dorm phone because no one would answer.... Then I felt even worse, and I'd start crying...." Her eyes, now red, began to well over. She lay her head down on her purple backpack.

Afternoon. The sun came out, but then rain began to pitter-patter. Little by little, it started raining with ever greater intensity and soon the sky was covered by dark clouds. I tried to shield her with my umbrella, but she pushed it away, saying she wanted to get drenched. I closed it, and the two of us sat on the white enamel bench, getting drenched. The droplets were like a flurry of arrows, foiled by the lake's surface. The cold wind hit us, wave upon wave. I looked at her long hair, flattened by the rain. Beads of water were trickling down her neck and off the tips of the locks that were so perfectly framing her exquisite face.

We wandered through the pouring rain, our vision blurred and our eyes aching. The two of us walked down the center of a deserted road. With all human commotion at a standstill, we heard the scattered sounds of nature, the passing cry of a bird overhead. Soaked from head to toe, we found our way to the lush greenery of Wenzhou Street. The trees that lined the street appeared to have been reborn in shades of emerald. No need to be silent. Are you sinking into some corner of your melancholy? In my heart, I called out to you.

Didn't eat dinner, either. Said it was a waste of time. It was her idea to hang out at my place. When I got a towel and tried to help her dry her hair, she said she wanted to do it herself. She curled up in a corner of the bed, her legs tucked against her chest. She wanted to talk. Said she didn't want to depend on other people anymore, she didn't think she needed to. She was already independent. She was taking care of things on her own. The corners of her mouth tightened defiantly. I could see that this was the crux of the phase she was going through. After all, in the past she had never gone to the movies by herself, never had a chance to go for a walk by herself, this rare rose of a girl. She said I didn't have to help her with anything and to let her do it herself unless I was always going to be there. She was slower than other people in finding her own way, but I had to respect her willingness to face adversity.

It was almost ten. What should I do, it's almost ten, she asked, flustered. Don't worry about it, just go home, I said soothingly. What should I do, I have to go home, she repeated, as if she hadn't heard me. It was like watching a drowning man gasping for air. Her sudden panic startled me. What should I do, what should I do. She sat down at my desk and looked at me with helpless eyes. If you don't want to go, don't go. I wanted to make her calm down. I can't, I have to go home, she said, crumpling onto the desk. I was at a loss. So don't go. I can't. I can't.... She started crying softly. Impulsively, I walked over and wrapped my arms tightly around her head. She grew quiet, letting in the warmth. The panic in her heart was no match for it.

4

IF WE'D been playing it cool like a pair of thieves, it was because our grand heist was drawing near. I anticipated, I schemed, I fretted. I had to be prepared for a deadly siege.

She was used to relying on other people. I had a habit of protecting girls. If she was in class at a set time for a set time, I was there to soak it up. In class, I was a show-off. But as soon as class ended, I was out of there. Her long hair trailed over her shoulders. Her elegant clothing gave her the appearance of being around twenty-four or twenty-five. That entire year I went for a kind of misfit look, wearing out-of-fashion jeans that made me look barely fifteen or sixteen.

She moved like a pendulum between school and home. I'd sleep until the sun disappeared below the western horizon, then cut loose from my cave like a charged particle and hit the town. I was a social butterfly. Hindered by shyness, she had refused to socialize. Cunningly, I changed all of that.

Two very different types of people, mutual attraction. And for what reason? It's hard to believe, this something that exists beyond the imagination of the chess game known as the human condition. It's based on the gender binary, which stems from the duality of yin and yang, or some unspeakable evil. But humanity says it's a biological construct: penis vs. vagina, chest hair vs. breasts, beard vs. long hair. Penis + chest hair + beard = masculine; vagina + breasts + long hair = feminine. Male plugs into female like key into lock, and as a product of that coupling, babies get punched out. This product is the only object that can fill a square on the chessboard. All that is neither masculine nor feminine becomes sexless and is cast into the freezing-cold waters outside the line of demarcation, into an even wider demarcated zone. Man's greatest suffering is born of mistreatment by his fellow man.

She agreed to stay over at my place. I was like a little girl finally able to buy a long-coveted doll. At ten in the evening, heading home from private tutoring on Changchun Road, I took the number 74 bus down Fuxing South Road, picking her up along the way. She waved as she stood at the bus stop, an overcoat draped across her shoulders, her spotless white rucksack by her side. A woman ready to elope, was she? She was a vine extending one slender, delicate branch toward my window, hoping I was the sky, not knowing that on the other side, there was no shade, and not much sunshine, either.

Like two sparkling gemstones, we were shakily carried to campus by the number 74 bus. Then I gave her a ride on my bike. She quietly sat sideways on the back. I started singing a song that was popular back in high school, pedaling to the rhythm. It streamed out to the flowers and trees that lined Yelin Avenue, growing more abundant the farther we rode. I couldn't see her face. I was dying to see if it was that of the Moon Goddess herself. "Waiting for the Sun, Waiting for You" and "The Wild Lily Has Its Spring, Too," those were the songs that defined my high-school days. My favorite Sylvia Chang songs—"The One I Love Best," "Flower on the Sea," "Standing on Top of the World," or "She Goes Walking by the Sea"—capture the mood of each of her major eras. "Love Song 1980," "Love Proverbs," and "Little Sister" were Lo Ta-Yu's biggest hits. To my seventeen-year-old self, Sylvia Chang and Lo Ta-Yu were like a dab of concealer, a soundtrack applied to cover up teenage heartbreak. After high school, I forgot the names of the songs and the singers, but I still knew the words by heart—do you?

She said that night she'd wanted to wrap her arms around my waist but didn't dare to, and really regretted it afterward. She told me after a few days had passed. Out of all the various little moments I'd cataloged, that one easily became the core of my memories of her.

"What are you writing?" she asked.

"A journal," I said.

"What are you writing about in your journal?"

"I'm writing about you coming over."

"Why? What did I inspire?"

"Want me to read it out loud to you?"

"Yes."

"'Tonight's the big night. A certain someone came over for a romp in the hay.'"

"That's enough. I don't want to hear the rest."

"Scared?"

"Uh-huh. Scared of you."

We were in the room on Wenzhou Street. I put away the journal. Helped her lay the bedding down. Made her sleep on the bed. I lay down on the hardwood floor next to her.

"If we were locked up in a mental hospital together, would it be any better?" she asked.

"Would we be locked up in the same room?"

"I don't want to be in the same room."

"Why not?"

"I'm scared of you."

"What are you scared of?"

"I'm just scared."

"What's so great about being locked up together?"

"We could live next door to each other. Our beds would be separated by a wall. I'd sit on my bed and talk to you. You'd sit on your bed, too, and we could talk all day long. . . . That'd be so much fun with no one else around."

"What if we ran out of things to talk about?"

"How can we run out of things to talk about? I'd pound on the wall and say I was tired. Then I'd go to sleep. When you wake up, you automatically have things to talk about again."

"Fine. You go to sleep, and I'll write in my journal and wait for you to wake up."

"You're not allowed. You can't keep a journal anymore. I don't have anything. You're only allowed to talk to me."

She leaned partway over the edge of the bed to talk, her face peering at me. I wrapped the covers tightly around myself. When you sleep next to me, I suffer, I said. So come sleep here on the bed, she said. *That'd be even more painful*, I thought. Mischievously and teasingly, she lowered her body onto my covers. Her hair brushed against my face, and her scent filled my lungs. I pulled her head in close, wrapping my arms around her neck. My lips were pressed up against her eyelid. She was so tender. It was an awkward embrace, like black rain pelting snow-covered ground....

5

A HEADLINE in the *China Times* read: TAIWAN DROPS CROC-
ODILE PROTECTION MEASURES; EXTINCTION LOOMS. Nu-
merous readers sent in letters asking what crocodiles were. Never
before in their lives had they seen a crocodile.

"Hey, is this the Earth edition?" asked one reader who called up
the paper with an animal encyclopedia in hand.

"Mmm, that's right," said the editor, taking a bite of a tuna sandwich while answering the call.

"What does a crocodile actually look like?"

"About this crocodile business, please—no more questions about
the article."

"Hello. Is this the Society Page? Are you in charge of crocodile-
related matters?"

"Yes, it is. Trying on my Crocodile brand clothing right now.
Each piece comes with a hefty price tag. Is it official business?"

"Operator, could you connect me to Crocodile Affairs? Which
page is handling that now?"

"You're not the first to ask. You're the one hundred ninety-ninth
person to call today with the exact same question. This newspaper
has authorized a supplement as an official response, since you people
have nothing better to worry about these days."

"Supplement Group. Are you also calling to ask where to go to
see a crocodile?"

"No, I still don't even know what a crocodile is."

"I'm sick of you people who intentionally do not ask the exact
same question. You make it impossible for me to provide a recorded

answer. I have to sit here and have my twentieth serving of crocodile sandwich."

"How am I supposed to know what the exact same question is?"

"Why don't you just start with, 'Can you tell me what the exact same question is?'"

"That makes sense. So what are you going to say on the recording?"

"It's very simple. I'll just record myself saying one hundred ninety-nine times, 'The exact same question is where can I go see a crocodile? Beep. *United Daily News* Supplement Group's phone number is 7-6-8-3-8-3-8. Beep.' The end."

"Hello, is this the *United Daily News* Supplement Group?"

"Beep. Due to the overwhelming volume of calls to the Supplement Group, all of our staff members are currently suffering from laryngitis. We offer you the following recorded message instead. Beep. A crocodile is a human with reptile characteristics, not a reptile with human characteristics. Beep."

"Boring. Beep."

Another article pointed out: "If crocodiles do vanish, there will be no need to protect them." That might have been in the *United Daily News*.

6

IN THE scenario I'm about to describe, which emerged amid all the drama, I was consumed by guilt and fear like never before. I felt like my skin was being grated like a radish—scraped raw, into a pulp. I knew I was capable of the monstrous sin of lusting after a woman's body. That was before she came along, back when it had been limited to a creeping feeling that I should carry my shoes and tiptoe down the street so no one would notice. But then, as I turned a corner, people started running past me, picking up stones and hurling them at a glass house. I knew I had to get out of there before someone with a stone called out my name and ordered me to freeze.

I'd swung around only partway. My shoes weren't even firmly planted on the ground when I was cordoned off by Shui Ling. A stone hit my heart. Then another one or two or three broke through. Their numbers kept growing until it seemed like only a matter of time before every last rock on earth had hailed down on me from the top of Mount Everest.

I don't know when it started, but I naturally began having what you'd call a sexual fantasy. It started back in junior high, after I saw *Valley of the Dolls*. My fantasy didn't follow the original plot, which was replaced instead with one about Shui Ling. Sexual fantasies about her invaded my thoughts, and I sensed that, in due course, I would enter the narrative.

To this day, I've never understood my fear. Where does it come from? I'd been keeping my deviant sexual desires in check for most of my adolescent and college years. I reassured myself that I'd done nothing wrong. It felt like the fear was coming from inside of me. I never did anything to attract it, nor did I choose to be this way. I had no hand whatsoever in shaping the self that was crawling with fear. Yet I grew into exactly that: a carnal being stirring the cement of fear with every step toward adulthood. Since I feared my sexual desires and who I fundamentally was, fear stirred up even deeper fears. My life was reduced to that of some hideous beast. I felt as if I had to hide in a cave, lest anyone discover my true nature.

Ever since I asked Shui Ling *Can we start over?*, I'd become a refugee on the ocean, and in due time, I was drinking seawater. So I decided to confront my desires head on. I would renounce my resistance and hasten toward destruction. I would indulge in reckless behavior until I'd completely exhausted all my past inhibitions.

My days were increasingly flooded with sexual fantasies about her—as I was riding my bike, walking, talking to other people. At night, I spent more and more time masturbating. When I held her body for the first time, it was as if I'd severed the very tendon of my fear, and it hurt so bad that I gnashed my teeth. One form of pain had been brought to an end by another even more violent pain. Like the big bad wolf, I harbored a ferocious desire to devour her body. And that became my new vision.

7

I'D AGREED to meet her after the class on *The Book of Songs*, but in the end, I didn't go. I locked myself in my room instead. She came to Wenzhou Street and rang the buzzer, but I didn't answer. I wanted to be alone, to detach from that part of me that was her and leave it outside, and to go live my own life locked away in my room. At nightfall, I went downstairs and opened the door. There she sat, on her bicycle, staring at me with heartbroken eyes. How did you know I was home, I asked. Your bike was here, she replied. Her eyes were reddening. Are you running away again, she asked me, choking back a sob. I said nothing. She'd hit the nail on the head. Instantly, to subdue her, I acted gruff. Don't get carried away, I said. I overslept, that's all. She said when she didn't see me during *The Book of Songs*, she knew I'd run away again. She'd cried the whole way over.

"Why are you running away again?" she asked me. I'd called her up late the night before to reassure her I'd be there.

"I'm supposed to trust your intuition here?" I dodged the question with a facetious smile.

"Yes." Her reply was stern and resentful.

"Fine. You're right. Your intuition is so scary. Since we've been together, I've been divided in two. One part wishes I could extricate myself from this. The other part wants to help you make me stay. I'm being torn apart."

"When did this start? Does it hurt?" Though her words sounded affectionate on the surface, she was only making accusations again.

"I knew it would be like this from the start, but I never said anything, okay? I've known from the very beginning that we were going to break up eventually. There's no such thing as eternal love," I said hatefully.

"If that's what being with me is like for you, then we should just forget about it." She went for the jugular.

"Ugh. You don't have to be such a drag, you know. Fine. I'm done." For the first time, I was up front about secretly wanting to get away from her. Deeply hurt, she pushed me closer to the edge, grazing my heart. I squeezed my eyes shut and leapt.

The following day. Like a morning lily blooming in a valley devoid of all traces of human life, I locked myself alone in my stinking room, as if enjoying the post-excision, prebleeding sense of liberation after having had a tumor removed. At ten, the time I normally got home after tutoring, she called. Said she was near the number 74 bus stop. Five or six buses had passed, but she didn't see me. I remained silent. It was as if the weight of a gigantic mountain would crush my skull the instant I opened my mouth. I hadn't said a peep when that mountain had already pinned her to the ground and shoved her body deep down into the earth's crust instead. I want to see you, she begged silently. Fine. I opened my mouth.

She sat in her old spot on the edge of the bed. I asked her how long she'd waited for the number 74 bus. She closed her eyes. Tears fell from her eyelashes. Every last fiber in my body felt as if it were being twisted and wrung. I'd wrenched our relationship to the breaking point and watched it split apart. I know I made you suffer. I'll never cut you off again. I spit out the words that were caught in my throat. She let out a laugh, and then, as if she'd finally been torn open, a cry of pain. To paint a picture of our embrace, I'd almost have to use her blood and guts.

8

Two CROCODILES wearing shiny, black, long-haired mink coats walked into a shop, outside of which hung a small hand-lettered pine placard that read LACOSTE (THE CROCODILE LABEL) IM-PORTED CLOTHING AND ACCESSORIES. They began stroking a dark blond mink coat in the shop. They couldn't bear to let go of it, as if they (since their genders remain unknown, crocodiles all take the same form of address for the purpose of efficient communica-tion) were the only ones whom the coat flattered. But the crocodiles weren't eager to expose themselves. They didn't have the audacity to walk up to the counter to ask the shopkeeper to show them a coat, for then they'd have to remove their own coats, baring it all for ev-eryone to see. If such a thing were to occur indeed, what would the shopkeeper say?

"Oh, you're a crocodile." This shopkeeper has seen crocodiles be-fore.

"Robbery, eh? Well, I already paid for security." This shopkeeper only wants to make a buck.

"You're too small. It won't work." This shopkeeper is an expert, someone with ideas and advice.

No one really knows what there is to see when crocodiles throw open their coats. No crocodiles had ever entered the Lacoste store and actually tossed off their coats. These two were simply stroking a mink coat, nothing more. Did they do it because they liked the coat? Or were they stroking it over and over for sheer pleasure?

Who really knew? The average person wouldn't be able to spot a crocodile. Junior and senior high-school students were a dependable audience for crocodile news. After finishing cram school, they would watch the TTV World News broadcast as they ate dinner. College students were the most indifferent age group, having drifted away from newspapers and news programs so as not to be associated with crocodiles. But according to public opinion polls, this demographic had become the most infiltrated by them.

Those forty and up reacted to the storm of controversy surrounding crocodiles like archaeologists to the discovery of a precursor to the Neanderthal man. White-collar office workers claimed they only paid attention to legislative battles and stock prices. Blue-collar workers swore off any of that garbage that wasn't a TV show or a movie, but secretly, they stood at the newsstands perusing magazines like *Scoop Weekly* and *Inside*, while white-collar workers simply bought the magazines and took them home. Thus this demographic had opportunities to supplement their archaeological research.

The crocodiles thought: What was everyone after, anyhow? If that many people secretly liked them, that'd be *totally embarrassing*.

9

HAVE YOU seen *Chronicle of a Death Foretold*? I asked her. It's a film. At the time, there wasn't much sweetness between her and me. On top of that, she wasn't exactly your basic pretty girl. It'd take a lifetime to dispel the lingering specter of my wrongdoings. She nodded and said she had. What'd you think? I asked. Well, she said, it just so happens that I can't bring myself to recount this one part that makes me so mad just thinking about it that I want to punch something. She shook her head, saying she didn't want to talk about it. That meant her emotions were so precious that she didn't want to ruin something by trying to articulate her feelings about it. Because I had moved on with my life, she offered me only the dregs of reconciliation, a cup of black coffee with no sugar, just cream on the side. I'd taken a sip of each, and I have to say, I preferred the coffee. The cream agreed with me about as much as she did.

I asked her to think about how to put it into words and tell me what she thought the next day. The male protagonist searches everywhere for the woman of his dreams. After "selecting" the female protagonist with only a glance, he racks his brain thinking of ways to lavish his riches on her before eventually taking her as his bride. But on their wedding night, he discovers that his bride isn't a virgin. That evening, the half-undressed, sobbing bride is "sent back." And so the bride's family takes her in, and every day, she sends him a letter. In the final scene, the male protagonist, carrying an enormous sack of letters, enters the courtyard, where the female lead awaits him. "The journey is littered with letters...." She wanted me to tell her the story from the very beginning, so that she could enjoy the ride all over again.

This is a metaphor. I can drone on and on about my own love story, which takes place in the short distance between Wenzhou Street and campus. Or I can throw in a few samples à la hip-hop or reggae. These readymades serve as interludes to keep you from getting sick of the monotonous commute back and forth between these same two locations, again and again.

Shui Ling didn't know it, but when I saw *Chronicle of a Death Foretold* and discovered that the bride wasn't a virgin, I followed in the groom's footsteps.

The next day, I slept for twenty hours straight, then got up and wrote her a hateful breakup letter. It was around six in the evening. I wrote facing the window, clouds racing across the open sky like a bay horse in full gallop. I was halfway done when the door buzzer rang. I opened the red metal door. Shui Ling was slumped right next to it. She just sat there, withered. I dragged her over to the stairs and sat beside her, though there wasn't really room for two. She insisted she didn't want to come in. I shut the door behind us. At the rehearsal for the Chinese Lit Department's public reading, she'd made a complete fool of herself and gotten scolded. For someone like her who avoided attention like the plague, it was a major humiliation. She wasn't handling it so well. Didn't utter a word about her feelings, even though I would have given my life to kiss those downcast eyes and lick away those tears.

I can't recall what I said, but I eventually got her to smile. I just so happen to have the gifts of a clown. I knew there was no way I could protect her from the real world or from being yanked around by the tail. That said, I'd still step in and save her regardless. I was such a shitty human being, why not take advantage of her state of disgrace and kick her while she was down? No matter what kind of trouble she was in, I'd run over in an instant to toss a rope down and pull her back to safety. Now that I'd shown myself to be blindly at her beck and call, she was beaming again. But my malice had already reignited. I could have put an end to my ways that night, instead of treating her likc I did. The serial killer in me should have surrendered.

I walked her to the number 74 bus stop, cracking jokes the whole way. I squinted, and the moment I caught sight of the number 74 bus in the distance, I said nonchalantly: I was just in the middle of writing you the letter in which I dump you, and in a little while, I'm going to go back and finish it, so I can run over to your place in the middle of the night and drop it in your mailbox. A few seconds passed, then she recovered. That won't be necessary, she said. And she boarded the bus as if nothing had happened. Later she said that she was ready to turn around and storm off right then and there. As for her cool, collected display of superhuman willpower, it was fueled by a desire for revenge.

It was already a day too late for her to tell me about *Chronicle of a Death Foretold*.

10

FIRST thing in the morning, I put the letter in her mailbox. As if a burden had been lifted—and then dumped into the ocean—my body felt lighter. The letter said that our relationship was over. It was quickly returned unopened, along with a messily scrawled letter that clearly displayed her bitter contempt, as it had obviously been written in a shaky hand. These were the events of April 1988. For about a month, I explored a new dimension of guilt, in which I was swiftly liberated from her influence, and I passed my days alone, silently and uneventfully.

Two days before my birthday in May, I discovered a huge rose in the basket of my Giant. No one was there. At eight that evening, Shui Ling was back again, sitting on her bike downstairs. I said, Today just happens to be moving day for me. She asked where I was moving to. I remained silent, saying nothing. In that incriminating tone of hers, she said I should be allowed to see you in the future. Because in the past, you told me that after we broke up, if could I take it for a month, then I'd be able to deal with it. But I've already taken it for a month, and I'm suffering all the same. Like a cheerful little blade of grass tossed about in the wind and rain, she had explained the entire basis of our relationship. She asked if she could help me move. I shook my head coldheartedly.

She'd exhausted all her tricks and was slow to abandon her manipulative ways. It was almost midnight when she tried to lure me back to her place. In the darkness, I broke down into two selves: the real me, who was ready to sink my teeth greedily into her, and another me who was plotting cunningly how and when to make my escape. As if I could read her mind, I knew from her sticky-sweet demeanor, with its implication that she wanted to fully "give herself" to me, that she'd gained a bit of new wisdom about me during that month. Never before had she used this kind of language. Its veneer was part of a veiled surprise attack on me, one which she herself didn't fully comprehend. Her newfound maturity allowed her to see my final ploy as a mere impasse. But to me, her words had struck a fatal blow, not unlike shoving a red-hot piece of wire up a monkey's ass. It was as if she had ever so lightly brushed up against the edge of a tooth of mine that had been aching unbearably. (What had once been a vague yet screamingly sexual taboo was now my downfall.) In the end, I saw myself with perfect clarity: I had been split in two by some otherworldly force. I was an elusive, two-headed hydra, each head with its own mind. I heard the roar of the beast within me. The question was, which of the two heads was it coming from?

Having come face to face with the real culprit behind my fear, I had a chance to settle the score once and for all. At five in the morning—as this woman was on her knees, clinging to my legs, begging me not to leave her—I shook myself free. It was not unlike casually bundling up a severed limb. Then, with my tail between my legs, I fled.

11

FLED AND forgot—that's how the story ends. I left Wenzhou Street at the end of May 1988. That was my own *Chronicle of a Death Foretold*. The drama that was my freshman year had concluded its final act.

So what can I say? Was I angry? Regretful? Filled with self-loathing? I had to get over my feelings and move on already. It was like drowning in a vat of black tar, the victim of a slow death by suffocation. Best not to let out so much as a fart, since you're not only trapped with your own stink but the tar might overflow.

I don't know how other people endure the violence and cruelty they encounter throughout their lives. There's no way to judge whether fate is playing favorites when it doles out physical disability, murder, and rape, or you're hauled off to the concentration camp. All I know is that I was forced into a corner, and so I violated myself in order to ward off the threat of being violated. I had to sacrifice the real, living, breathing her. To me, she represented beauty in its highest form. And I went and treated her like a piece of meat. It was a mess of my own making, the product of my own savagery and barbarism. But what else was I supposed to do?

No matter what, Shui Ling, I'll always feel your absence. From now on, for the rest of my life, I have to change my ways and pay the price for the crimes I committed as an eighteen-year-old. As long as I'm alive and able, I won't stop talking about humanity and all of its fears.

NOTEBOOK #3

I

ONE NIGHT, the crocodile had a dream. It dreamed that it took a trip with a group of humans. Maybe it was after secretly sending off a payment to a matchmaking agency that organized coed mixers, or after joining the Jinsha Bay Lifeguard Association, which allowed the crocodile to spend its Sundays saving lives while at the same time searching for that someone special. The crocodile packed up chocolate, shrimp chips, dried fruit, chewing gum, playing cards, a skateboard, a Walkman, a point-and-shoot camera, its red lifeguard uniform, and a giant box of saltines. The next day, toting a humongous bag, it went to the bus stop, where it joined a group of young men and women, all of them dressed to the nines. The sight alone made the crocodile euphoric. A grin formed on its snout, which was hidden beneath a human suit, and out came a gurgle (or a snort, a gasp, or a giggle—it was not discernible which). It'd been a long time since the crocodile was this close to humans.

The tour bus let them off on top of a mountain. Everyone pressured the crocodile into buying a pudding pop (why the crocodile, and why a pudding pop, was unclear). When the crocodile returned with the pudding pop, the main attraction was now an array of ferocious creatures—lions, tigers, panthers—at the summit. A few had gotten into the crocodile's bag and were feeding on the chocolate, shrimp chips, and saltines. Meanwhile, a little black panther tugged the red lifeguard uniform out of the bag and scurried off with it. A lion, a tiger, and a different panther, each roughly the size of a truck, stood blocking the crocodile's path. Crouched together in a line, they watched the crocodile muster its courage, every last hair on its body bristling. The crocodile suppressed the tiny, selfsame ferocious creature within itself, and the one within that one, and the one within the one within that one ... and so on. The crocodile called it the lion, tiger, panther propagation dream. But who's to say it was only a dream?

2

FROM THAT point on, life became much simpler. I lived at a relative's on Heping East Road with two cousins, both boys who were around my age. The three of us were locked in a competition to see who could stay out the latest and get up the latest, leaving no time for small talk. One evening in early July 1988—the summer after my freshman year—I was brought to a bustling teahouse by a senior member of the Debate Society to attend a planning meeting for a new student organization. The club charter they'd drafted contained thirty signatures, but after waiting almost two hours, only three people had shown up, with me, an observer, being the fourth. In the end, maybe because the charter was pitiful, or maybe because I was a willing victim, the observer suddenly found herself nodding, agreeing to serve as club president.

During the day, I'd run around attending to organizational duties. At night, I'd go to McDonald's, where I'd buy a small soda and sit and read until closing time at eleven. Rode my bike home. Made about a dozen phone calls to people on the club's contact list. I avoided going home for fear of vaporizing in isolation. During my stint on Heping East Road, I felt like a drop of water in the desert whenever I was alone in my room for long periods of time. I toiled away writing in my journal and breathing, if not much else. The rest of the time, I sought comfort in sleep. My indulgence in sleep was like filling an empty cup until it overflowed. The cup was then exchanged for a glass, which I filled with alcohol. I needed the sleep psychologically, not physically, so I drank beer to force myself back into a broken slumber.

I have vivid memories of reading Pär Lagerkvist's *The Dwarf*, Ma Sen's *Life Inside a Jar*, books like that. I also recall reading "Toward a Solitary Fate," a story by a young Mu Shou San published in a magazine, and then thinking about those three works together. I was living then in a sumptuous double room in a twelve-story luxury high-rise. The room had enormous gold-framed windows, cream-colored curtains, and an executive desk with a dark wood finish. My daily necessities were laid out before me like cast bronzes. Here I was, an impoverished student living in an upscale apartment complex in Taipei and feeling like something straight out of Lagerkvist: a hideously deformed dwarf stuffed into a jar, pressed up against the layer of glass cutting off my senses, blinking (to borrow again from Mu Shou San's imagination) as I clutched my copies of *One Hundred Years of Solitude* in one hand and *Lust for Life* in the other. When a fire is lit beneath the jar, the dwarf's body contorts violently as the flames heat the glass....

That's how I ended up throwing myself into extracurricular activities. Besides, the club kept things colorful in the backdrop. As van Gogh's *The Potato Eaters* illustrates so well, it's all about having your fill and then some, feasting until the last drumstick has been devoured, then wiping the grease off your lips.

3

"CAN YOU tell me when your new inductions are?" That was Zhi Rou's voice.

"Yeah. The moment I saw you, I couldn't wait to join this club." That was the instant Tun Tun walked into my life. Tun Tun and Zhi Rou looked lovely in their matching skirts, like sisters.

"Have you seen our flyer?" Soliciting like a street peddler, I sat on top of a long table with the club's name taped to it, facing the athletic fields. Tables encircled the entire plaza. It was orientation time, and every club was vying for new members, capitalizing on their veterans' talent for presenting a semblance of respectability to hoodwink incoming students into joining, and ideally, forking over the membership fees.

"Oh, I read it just now, when I was standing over there." There was a hypnotic cadence to Zhi Rou's voice.

"Great. Then let me tell you a little about our organization and its activities. We—"

"We already heard it. We were standing next to you, listening to the conversation you just had with that last person. You're not going to go through the same exact spiel all over again, are you?" Tun Tun smiled cheerfully.

"Huh? How do you know I'd say the same thing again?" I refused to back down.

"Fine, go ahead. Let's see if it's the same thing." Tun Tun smiled even more brightly, as if to disagree.

"How's this? We're an empty shell of an organization. Our club president doesn't actually liaise with more than six people. Whatever you do, don't join! The club president hasn't even paid the membership dues. It's been a semester since we officially founded the club, but in actual practice, we haven't even been in operation a month. The club president is *super* ugly. And moody and strange, too. I've known her a long time, and I think she's some kind of freak," I said. "Have you heard this already?"

"You're bad-mouthing your own organization," Tun Tun replied, holding back a smirk. "Don't you care if the club president finds out?"

"I *am* the club president." I kept a straight face.

"Oh my god!" Tun Tun and Zhi Rou cried out in unison.

Zhi Rou smiled shyly, as if this exchange between me and Tun Tun had left her speechless. "Are you some kind of freak?" she finally ventured to ask.

"Yeah, that seems about right, but what kind exactly?" Tun Tun said.

"That's, of course, something you'll find out soon enough after you become a member. As you can see, at my best I'm a freak with wit and substance," I boasted.

"Right, the verbal talent of a smart-ass and the charm of a brown-noser, along with a severe case of nearsightedness!" Zhi Rou broke out of her shyness and joined the repartee.

"Well then, let's get down to business. Have you two ever considered joining a cultural organization with someone like me as the president?" I was beginning to like these two freshmen.

"Never thought about it.... Nope. Someone in a leadership role going rogue, kicking their feet up on the table like a boss when they talk to other people, even standing on top of the table, with a set of pipes that can drown out a vegetable hawker?" Zhi Rou said, her own voice growing louder. She took my chin in the palm of her hand. "You've got the baby face of someone in junior high. And upon closer inspection you are, uh-huh, incredibly feminine." Zhi Rou nudged Tun Tun's elbow teasingly. "Okay, so what were you saying?"

"But think about what this baby face here just said about a college student's lifestyle, what it means to become educated, etc. Sounds like a senior with a few tricks up her sleeve. Pretty impressive. Not only that, but she can take on the two of us complex characters here single-handedly and still keep the bullshit going. She seems qualified enough to be club president." The way that Tun Tun followed Zhi Rou suggested that this little routine of theirs was rehearsed. Unless it was actually spontaneous, and the pieces had just fallen perfectly into place.

Completely captivated by these two girls, I put aside any pretense of niceties. There was something about them, a kind of enviable pedigree. It was a quality I knew all too well. During the three years I had spent at what was known as the most prestigious all-girls high school in Taipei, I had learned to recognize traces of a certain kind of breeding, whether on the athletic fields or in the corner of a hallway, traces that I associated with social class.

"I'm a sophomore. Looking at your info, one of you is studying international business and the other zoology, and you both went to the same high school. Are you two best friends? We share an alma mater," I said warmly.

"Oh! How wonderful. Our big sis-*ter*." Tun Tun drew out the last syllable mischievously, as if she were teasing me. If I had said those words myself, it wouldn't have sounded the same. But the way she gave it an added stress, it was like she was addressing the woman next to me. I realized these two were coaxing me out of my shell. That guardedness was a by-product of my lifelong socialization, of other people labeling me and putting me in a box. Tun Tun revealed that it'd taken them only a glance to figure me out.

"Who's studying zoology? Maybe you were assigned to the same track I was."

"Make her guess." Zhi Rou tugged Tun Tun's hand, interrupting her.

"I think she's the more outgoing one, so she's more likely to be studying international business," I remarked, pointing at Tun Tun.

"Nope. Tun Tun got in through the honors recommendation system. She didn't feel like taking the entrance exam, so she decided to enroll in Academia Sinica's gifted program, and from there, she went straight to the Zoology Department," Zhi Rou explained, pleased that I'd guessed wrong.

"Oh. . . . You weren't on the Providence or Ascension tracks, were you?" I pointed at Tun Tun again.

"Wait, you were in a gifted program, too?" Tun Tun asked me, astonished.

I nodded my head, embarrassed. It wasn't the sort of distinction that you wore proudly. More than anything, it was a source of chagrin.

"We're from Ascension. The gifted group for the sciences is in Ascension," Zhi Rou said excitedly.

"We? So you tested into international business, but studied humanities?" I pointed at Zhi Rou.

"We're from the same group, all right. Zhi Rou switched to the humanities in her junior year. Didn't care what anyone thought. What other people took three years to do, she did in one. Out of the top six examinees in all of Taiwan, she's the most self-directed one." Tun Tun jabbed her finger at Zhi Rou's face, beaming with pride. A faint dimple appeared on Zhi Rou's face. Her dimpled smile was so endearing that the two of us couldn't help feeling a little weak in the knees.

"So we were destined to meet. I like you two. Do you want to have lunch together?" I hopped off the table. My butt was sore from sitting. With a jerk of my thumb, I signaled *let's go*, and the two of them squealed. Without a word, we leaned forward and exchanged high fives.

The October sun shimmered softly. The candy-striped umbrellas over the tables were starting to slouch, like cadets forced to stand at attention too long. The veteran club members clustered underneath carried on, zealously delivering their hollow speeches. The dispersal of the freshmen, who'd just been let out of a tedious orientation, unleashed waves of identical greetings throughout the plaza. The scene was that of a chemical reaction, like a powdered beverage being added to water: The new students were the powdered clumps floating on top—pure and whole, and on the brink of integration. It was a portrait of youth.

It was almost noon. Despite the scores of new recruits, joining a club meant little until membership dues were paid. Most new members would at best show up at a few events or drop by after class to help out. Handing over the reins, I asked my fellow club member to man our booth. I pulled my bike out from the shade, wheeling it over the brightly colored flyers littering the ground. Meanwhile two little devils were scurrying around me, hissing that I was going to get in trouble, and egging me on all the while.

"How is it that one of you went to all the trouble of switching to the humanities and is still studying international business, while the other is so smart that she can pass every stage of the Academia Sinica admissions process, yet she rushes straight into a lab where she'll be trapped all day?" From the get-go, I took advantage of my seniority and dispensed with formalities. We went to a Western-style buffet. I chose a window seat so that I could do some people watching, helping myself to a serving of macaroni and cheese. They sat across from me. Tun Tun was having the honey-roasted chicken legs and on Zhi Rou's huge plate was a small steak.

"It's not like that. Animals are fun. I love Mother Nature. There's nothing wrong with wanting to study living things," said Tun Tun with a drumstick in her mouth.

"Tun Tun made the choice herself. I was forced. The last month before exams, I didn't go near a book. I ran off on my own to a seaside monastery in Hualien. I didn't read a single word the entire month. I totally forgot about this whole entrance-exam business. The day before the exam, I was called in to see the head monk. I was told that my mother had come and wanted me to return for the entrance exam. So I did. When I took it, I placed sixth in the nation. I have a knack for guessing to thank for that. I never thought I'd have such luck. But after earning this distinction, I couldn't bring myself to fill out my application forms. I lay in bed all day until eight, when I'd get up to watch a TV show. Whenever I left my room, my whole family would stare at me dumbly, pleading with and pitying me at the same time. Everyone except my father, who didn't bat an eye. The night before I submitted my application forms, I played forty songs on the guitar. I also made ten paper cutouts of the word *happiness* and ten of the word *Buddha*. Then I put only one school on the application form and submitted it the following day, just like that. No one said a word about me studying international business. In my family, that'd be like singing the national anthem right before a movie. Why would you need to do that? I wasn't going to make them disappointed in me. There's no way I could ever live without them." Though a look of distress passed over Zhi Rou's face, her eyes contained a fierce, hardened determination, and her winsome smile remained.

Tun Tun eagerly seized on Zhi Rou's words. "Ah, well said. 'Like singing the national anthem right before a movie. Why would you need to do that?'"

"That isn't being forced to do something. It's your own choice not to make other people disappointed in you," I said.

"So you're saying that even though I don't really want to study this subject, it's still a choice based on *my own free will*, since my goal is to not disappoint anyone?" Zhi Rou's reply robbed me of any chance to explain further. Her sharpness bordered on cunning. In fact, it revealed a defensiveness that made me back off a little. Even so, I had to admire her flash of wit.

"What would happen if you did disappoint them?" I asked.

"Good question." Tun Tun wiped the corners of her mouth, chiming in. I asked if it was important to her, too.

"You'd be able to live with yourself if your family was disappointed in you?" She shot back, skillfully dodging the question.

"Ever since I started to wise up, my family's been perpetually disappointed in me. Though it hurt them, I shattered their image of me little by little. If I didn't, I'd have to sacrifice myself in order to maintain a false ideal. I've been trying really hard to get over my resentment. It's caused them no small amount of pain," I answered honestly.

"So have you completely broken down that ideal?" Zhi Rou asked softly.

"It's been a challenge. It was hard enough to demolish just one little part. It hurt everyone, including me. To make up for it, I let them form a new image of me. It's been a constant struggle. I'll always feel love for them and have basic needs to be met, so it takes courage to draw the line. But if I don't, my love for them and my needs will become bargaining chips that I have to exchange for my independence. And using those would be like retreating before the battle's even begun." I didn't feel the least bit inhibited telling them about my family. The more I shared, the more open I felt.

"That's what I'd call going down without a fight." Zhi Rou let out a bitter, self-deprecating laugh. "It sounds like that mental disorder where you're afraid that everyone will die if you move even an inch, so then you stay as stationary as possible. It's basically the same thing, no?" Zhi Rou twisted Tun Tun's straw in her hands. I sensed a tinge of self-loathing. Her laugh reminded me of a handsome older woman removing her makeup and revealing her wrinkles.

"It's not as bad as you make it sound," said Tun Tun, shaking her head. She reclaimed her straw and straightened it out. Replacing it in her iced tea, she tried to take a sip. "What Lazi didn't say is that it would be hard to live with your family's disappointment. And we're not even talking about the whole idea of making your kids study international business in the first place. That's actually a tougher barrier than in most families!"

Tun Tun raised her head, blinking. Her tone had darkened somewhat from its gleefulness a moment earlier, but it still ended on the same rising pitch, as if she wanted to offer a spirited response to Zhi Rou's words that sounded somewhere between confident and hopeful. She'd used my words to set up her partner, and when it was her turn to speak, she'd tacked on my name to what she herself wanted to say in an attempt to turn around Zhi Rou's bad mood. She struck me as wholesome and pure on the outside, and optimistic on the inside, preferring not to give away any signs of her true intelligence. There was a pure gentleness about her, like clear waves washing over white sand.

"Hey, who's Lazi?" Despite knowing the answer perfectly well, I pretended not to.

"Why, it's you," said Tun Tun, looking at me in astonishment, as though it were my fault I didn't know who Lazi was.

"Why am I being called this horrible name?" Trying not to laugh, I made a disgusted face.

"Huh?" Tun Tun stared at me, wide-eyed. "Well, I think it sounds good," she said primly, as if the nickname had been a compliment. I was baffled.

"Why not *Zhuozi* as in *table*, *Yizi* as in *chair*, or *Juzi* as in *saw*? Anything sounds better than Lazi," I said.

"It came to me when you were sitting at the booth earlier today, and I decided your name was *La*."

"So why did you add the *zi* part?" I was genuinely curious how she came up with the idea.

"Huh? *La* is the verb *to pull*, so I had to add a suffix to it as a placeholder. I wanted to coin its usage. Other people aren't allowed to use *zi* the way your verbal name does. The suffix *zi* is an attachment, and if you take away the *La*, it has a million different uses." Tun Tun was like an entomologist explaining a new insect she'd discovered.

"Gee, thanks." I gave her the evil eye. "So can I also ask why *La* has to be a verb?"

"Oh, good question." She jabbed her right index finger in the air with a humph. "Chinese people always have all these awful-sounding nicknames like Ah Bao or Ah Hua. But look at the root *La*. It sounds good as a verb—as in *to pull noodles*, *to zip*, *to lend a helping hand*, *to pimp*—"

"Right, and there's also *to take a piss*!" I said.

"Atta girl, that's what I'm talking about! Now you get it!" Tun Tun patted me.

Zhi Rou cackled. She'd been watching our sparring and laughing so hard that she was covering her mouth with her hands. The loyal audience who'd been spurring us on, she was really losing it now.

"So what do you call Zhi Rou?" With a straight face, I proceeded to drag her into it.

"It's a name I gave her during sophomore year of high school. I call her...." Tun Tun's mouth started to twitch as she gestured toward her belly.

"*Duzi!*" I yelled the word, accidentally spraying coffee out with a laugh.

"So if we put our names together, we have *Laduzi—diarrhea?*" asked Zhi Rou sardonically.

Then it was our turn to crack up—Tun Tun most of all. Unable to handle any more, she waved a hand in the air, as if to call a ceasefire.

Lazi. I liked this new name, just as I liked this sisterly twosome (as a unit, they really ought to be "this pair"). There was only one way to describe them—you never really knew whether to laugh or to cry.

4

THE CROCODILE opened the refrigerator. Inside were all kinds of canned goods. According to experts, these canned goods were a staple of the crocodile diet. When the crocodile got home at night, it liked to turn on the TV to see if there was anything about crocodiles on the evening news. Meanwhile, it would sit in a bathtub on casters, scrubbing itself with a sponge. It would reach over to grab a can of food from the side table, then remove its retainer and use its canines to puncture two holes in the top of the can. Shaped like turret shells, its canines glistened in the light and were cool to the touch. Afterward, the crocodile reinserted its retainer. It liked to eat with a sharpened straw that it plunged into the top of the can and used to siphon food. In the water was a green plastic toy crocodile. Leaning over, the crocodile squeezed the plastic belly with both hands. The toy made a squeaking noise and squirted water onto the crocodile's face.

A newscaster in a green suit said, "Before we take a look at tomorrow's weather forecast, let's go to today's report in our special series on crocodiles." The earpiece that had been tucked discreetly in the newscaster's left ear fell onto the desk with a thud. The camera hadn't cut yet to a close-up of the expert appearing on the commentary segment when it paused momentarily on the newscaster still facing straight ahead. The newscaster winked. It was unclear for whom the wink was intended, but it was followed by an embarrassed smile, and the voice of the expert—

In accordance with best practices, and in order to preserve the very essence of our nation, our news bureau has instituted a unified set of provisions regarding the reporting of crocodile-related news, which must undergo a special imaging-technology process so that the results appear in an encrypted form. This is done to prevent foreign entities from intercepting our satellite signals and duplicating our footage by means of current video-recording technology. Since the actual volume of domestic data on crocodiles has grown and the nation has devised new measures to either protect or eradicate crocodiles, this category of highly sensitive classified information must not fall into the hands of foreign states. In this century, all advanced nations have adopted the convention of implementing strategic sanctions, and for this reason, our nation has been unable to access outside signals of broadcasts related to the subject. In the past several years, a great deal of importance has been attached to the issue of crocodiles and their existence. However, each and every citizen, upon receiving news reports, must agree to maintain confidentiality in the event that the domestic crocodile situation reaches a critical state, as we as a nation could very well find ourselves shunned by the international community. This type of response may occur, in fact, at a time when the United Nations is selecting popular tourist destinations for preservation under its UNESCO World Heritage Site designation, whereupon tourists will flock to those locations and a global media frenzy will ensue. Or perhaps our land may become a void on the world map like the Bermuda Triangle, or what is seen as a dark, mysterious place. All communications networks linking to our nation will be severed. No foreigner will dare to set foot in our territory, nor will our own citizens have any means of escape. Should our secrets be leaked one day, it will be difficult to determine whether a diplomatic situation may arise. In the final analysis, our knowledge and understanding of crocodiles is but a microorganism on a fingernail. But in the customary practice of advanced nations, we will safeguard information within the grip of our metal jaws, holding on as if our lives depended on it. At this time, we ask all citizens across the nation to join hands in facing the mystery of the unknown together!

The crocodile sat in the bathtub and listened at length to the news commentary, dozing off three times. Each time, its chin knocked against the side of the bathtub, and the crocodile lifted its head and glanced around in confusion, unable to bring itself to crane its neck to peer at the TV. Someone might see it sleeping in the bathtub, which would be awfully embarrassing. The crocodile blushed just thinking about it. The crocodile clutched the toy and rubbed it against its cheek, pouting. It was deeply distressed. Would this blushing and pouting ever come to an end? Now that it thought about it, things ought to be different since it had been thrust into the national spotlight and made a public figure. At the moment, the entire nation was saying: Why, my dear crocodile, how are you?

5

SEPTEMBER. I'd been living on Heping East Road for two months. My cousins needed to prepare for entrance exams, and I got the hint that I should get lost. I found an attic bedroom on Tingzhou Road. The top floor was spacious, with only a crude toilet, sink, and old-fashioned boiler, plus a narrow slit of a room in which my roommate, a woman with a rather peculiar face, lived. She was twenty-five or twenty-six and worked in a factory. My first impression of her was that she was likely to borrow money from me and never pay me back. She would often knock on my door, then grill me about college life or my romantic history, among other private matters. Then there was this guy who'd come by in the middle of the night and stay over. He was always broke, and he'd walk around naked with a cigarette dangling out of his mouth. Sometimes he'd yank her to the ground and beat her with a whip or a shoe, dragging her outside, all the way down to the nearby plaza. But whenever she talked about him, her face glowed with happiness. He was the only person who didn't hate her, she said.

Living on the top floor meant that it was hot as an oven until nightfall. I'd get home around ten and lock the door behind me. The thought of them terrified me. I envisioned the souls of two prisoners who'd died long, torturous deaths breaking down the door of my room. That feeling of living under the same roof as near-strangers, people who might disappear without ever saying goodbye, was enough to make my home a solitary tomb.

Daytime. The instant the alarm went off, I'd leap out of bed and "go to work" for my club. Didn't wash my face, didn't brush my teeth. I practically flew to campus on my bike as if I'd scheduled an appointment and had to get there pronto to deliver documents or prepare for a noontime meeting. Designing promotional flyers, sending out mailers, organizing the archives, or running an errand could at any time become the most urgent among an endless list of tasks. It was a monotonous game that you took seriously in preparation for the real thing, a means of instilling a strong work ethic. It was a way of finding out what it'd be like one day, when you entered society and the workforce. No more dithering: If you wanted to move up, you had to play the game on a sophisticated level, and make it an exciting contest at that. Otherwise, your enthusiasm would wane. You'd lose your mind. Sooner or later, the sea of utterly meaningless obligations would swallow you alive.

I almost completely lost track of schoolwork. My gym teacher wanted to murder me. I got wind that the drill instructor had been looking everywhere for me and "wanted to see me in his office." I was burying my head in the sand. I was about to fail half or even two-thirds of my credits, which would flunk me out of school. My shift to a value system in which I actually had a life had, in fact, set me on a path to a bleak future: Now I was throwing my life away, just spinning my wheels and keeping busy with no real direction or purpose. My mind consumed with my organization's affairs, I worked to my heart's content until ten in the evening, when I went home. My life started to revolve around work, and my habits gained momentum to the point where they became virtually unstoppable. The minute I got home, I'd crack open a beer and drink myself into a stupor, basically killing time until my alarm went off the next morning.

Chu Kuang. He could see the emptiness hidden beneath my excess energy and enthusiasm. Three years my senior, he was the president of the neighboring student organization. The two of us shared the same office, and his desk was next to mine. His receding hairline revealed a shiny forehead, and the back and the top of his head were similarly reflective. He was heavyset, with what you might call a pear-shaped figure. He often wore the same pair of purple-and-green denim pants with a thin gold belt, like something a nightclub host might wear. Other times he looked like he'd just emerged from the slums, his T-shirt as rumpled as a wad of toilet paper. His baggy, knee-length pants exposed a pair of hairy legs while his sunglasses concealed a pair of puffy eyes.

By eight or nine in the evening, it was just the two of us still "at the office." For the most part, it was an act. Every once in a while, when nobody was watching, I'd look up and glance over at him, and we'd exchange knowing smiles. Then, in unspoken agreement, we'd turn back to our work. Gradually, a camaraderie developed between the two of us nocturnal creatures.

"Hey, what are you doing?" I asked, having just finished folding thirty copies of a meeting announcement.

"Sketching a layout." His organization put out a weekly newsletter. His head was lowered.

"Hey, what are you doing now?" I said facetiously, bored silly. About a second had passed since I asked him the first time.

"Making an illustration." He lowered his head even farther. The tip of his nose was almost touching the paper.

"Hello?! What's that you're still doing over there?" His unresponsiveness made it even more hilarious.

"Why you little!" He mustered the strength to set down his pen and peel his eyes from the page, then stood up. He walked over to me, eyes flashing with anger, and took my chin in his large hand. "Not afraid to die, are you? Gotta disturb me, eh?"

I'd been using him for entertainment. Whenever I stepped on him, some kind of repartee would come of it. Having observed him at work for a while, I had amassed a wealth of data about my counterpart, who had become a screen on which I could project random thoughts. On the occasions we ventured beyond that screen, our conversations were always regimented. The reality was, a taboo had developed. Instead of getting to know each other, we were interacting through caricatures of ourselves.

"You look like shit today." People were sitting between us, and the noontime deliveries of documents were flooding in. "Is that a hole in those lovely skintight jeans? Why don't you mind your own business?" I chatted with a colleague. More documents were delivered.

"Maybe if you didn't rub your eyes when you crawled out of the sewer, they wouldn't be so puffy." Another document came in.

"People who have no eyeballs and lie in a sewer all day need to shut up." I glared at him, then resumed my conversation.

"Keep laughing. If you keep slithering out of the sewer and prying open those bloodshot eyes, you're going to drop dead soon." This time, the document was thrown straight at me. Some people beside him had evidently been trying to talk business as we bared our fangs at each other.

It was the anniversary of the school's founding. I was tied up with the festivities all day long, running around and yelling. By dusk, the crowds were beginning to scatter. I climbed the steps to the second floor of the recreation center, wishing that someone would carry me. People were gathered outside the office door, looking stumped as to what to do. At the foot of the door, his legs stretched out in front of him, sat the vice president of Chu Kuang's club. Sounding exhausted, he announced that we all needed to clear the area. Someone inside was apparently having a meltdown and had shut everyone out.

I pushed to the front and pounded on the door.

"Chu Kuang, open the door and let me in. I have to talk to you." Those words. I had no idea where they came from. Finding them within me was like striking oil. I heard the door being unlocked. The vice president stared at me in disbelief. I ducked through the narrow crack that appeared, locking the door behind me.

I fumbled around looking for a chair, then finally sat beside him on the desk, crossing my legs. "What happened?" I asked gently. The shades were lowered so that we could watch movies in the office, and there was a faint halo around his head.

"Will you go buy me a drink, Sis? And just listen...." Covering his face with his hands, he put his head on the desk and produced what sounded like a whimper.

"Why do you want to talk to me?" I gazed at the soothing rays of the setting sun that trickled in through the window behind him.

"Meng Sheng . . . it's because you know Meng Sheng, too. He's the connection we share," I heard him say. I went out and returned with a twelve-pack of beer and two packs of cigarettes, plus some hot snacks. I sent away the vice president and the crowd loitering outside. The merrymaking still hadn't died down, and the sound of someone practicing the piano pierced the air for an instant before blending into the cacophony.

"This afternoon Meng Sheng came by. . . . He was looking for you. . . . We got into a fight—"

"You and Meng Sheng had a spat?"

"Had a spat? I feel like I could eat the guy alive, tear him to pieces." Chu Kuang lifted his head. A bloodstain ran all the way from the corner of his eye to his nose, and one of his lower teeth had been knocked out. He downed an entire can of beer in one gulp. "Have you ever seen love between two people turn as ugly as this? That's what happens when there's too much masculine energy. The moment he came in and asked 'Where is she?' I exploded. I snatched a metal ruler off the table and started thrashing him with it, but he's not the type to back down. He picked up a metal chair and started pummeling me with it. It was like the whole thing was choreographed. . . . Man, I'll never forget his lightning-fast reflexes or the scent of his sweat." He smiled contentedly.

"You start to fight the second you see each other. Does that mean it's mutual love or bitter hatred?"

"Doesn't Hsia Yü have a poem called 'Sweet Revenge'? I only mention it because I thought you might know it. It's like the title says. Because love goes hand in hand with hatred, and because there's hatred, you're going to fight, and when you fight, you see that there's love. The three become inseparable. Once your sexual frustration reaches a certain point, if you don't either fulfill or rid yourself of your desires, you're going to find yourself deep in the abyss of meaninglessness. And there's no easy way out. In fact, you'll cling even more desperately to the object of your fixation, and when you do, your desires will turn against themselves in full force. I was already self-destructive to begin with, but then I developed a fixation and never found an outlet, which is when it really got scary. One day something set it off, and I grabbed a pair of scissors and stabbed myself. It was when Meng Sheng and I were about to break up. I thought I'd learned to put down the scissors and give him some of my self-destructiveness by then, but there's no cure for it: I still want him. The love I was saving is gone, and whatever passion was left, I gave it away trying to keep our connection alive."

"Meng Sheng told me he saved some guy's life. Was it you?"

"Ha! Is that what he said? So did he tell you all about how he slept with that guy?" He stopped abruptly and slumped his shoulders apologetically.

"Listen, I don't want to step into your dogfight and be ripped to shreds. But if you want to say it, say it. I'm not going to pry. Hearing about your bad experiences won't disgust me or make me think any less of you. Whatever's on your mind, just spit it out. But I have to say, wow—I had no idea you were like this!" I tried to decipher the convoluted expression on his face.

"It's considered pretty unseemly to say these kinds of things to a girl."

"If it's that unseemly, then don't say anything at all. I don't want to hear the censored version."

"Aw, Sis, you're really something special. Really, that's exactly what you are. All the other people I know suddenly tune out or start squirming whenever I bring up that part of our relationship. Most of them have been outright avoiding me. Only one or two people have bothered to stay in touch with me after cringing at my story, which I always thought was funny. Why keep pretending to be a good person when it's obviously that painful for you to show compassion? Anyway, you're a girl, and though you've managed to stomach this much, I feel like I'm making you listen to me describe the calluses on my feet."

"How long have you been in love with Meng Sheng?"

"In all, about four years. That's on my part. For him, it's been off and on for the past five years. Now that I realize he transferred his desire for women onto me, I'm no longer sure if he loved me for more than half a year. He's vile to the core. A worthless sack of shit is what he is."

"Chu Kuang, listen to me. When you're around me, just be your genuine self. I know it's not easy. My feet have a few calluses, too, but I'm not ready to talk about them with anyone yet. Is that okay?"

We hadn't even noticed that it was almost ten o'clock. Outside the recreation center and all over campus, the festival raged on. A heavy metal band was playing, and laser beams shot in all directions as drunken students bid farewell to their desires....

6

WHAT'S written here are fragments from the first semester of sophomore year, the period from July 1988 to February 1989. After the wild boar barreled through the pasture gates and returned to the wild, was it a boar who'd suffered a concussion? With its boar hooves lifted over its boar head, it was a boar skipping through the rain forest, and one that could do a mind-blowing jitterbug at that. It took a merry bath in the river and leaned back against the riverbank, telling itself, "Well, it's a good thing I lost myself crashing through that fence!" Its amnesia was so severe that it struggled to remember what it had said just a second earlier. Meanwhile, ants had covered the half of its body that was above water and were pecking at its cheek.

So I didn't need Shui Ling, then? She'd become the mythical goddess Nüwa—a snail of a woman curled up inside a shell somewhere beyond my recollection. I dove down to a coral reef at the bottom of the sea, a long, grueling journey to a place where all kinds of caves could be found. The reef was a microcosm of deep-sea consciousness, from its pink bud-like tentacles to the moist, black marrow of its skeleton. Whenever I ventured into the wrong cave, the snail woman would emerge from her shell to temper my alcohol-hardened brain, mending the membrane layer where freshly spawned desires were being sundered by a death wish.

A winter's night. I had just finished a paper on Freud for a seminar and was leaving a basement meeting with Tun Tun. The lights were out and a cold wind blew as we biked across the dark campus. Tun Tun said, I don't know how to tell you this, but I have a problem, and although I'm not completely sure what that problem is, I do know that you're the kind of person I can talk to, someone who might be able to help. Her voice was soft and quivering, like the rustling of a lone maple tree in the wind, yet there she was, bravely forcing herself to smile. This girl was so precious, it brought me to shame. What about Zhi Rou? I posed the question with a cool detachment, working my way one step closer to Tun Tun's fears in life. We had almost reached the campus gates. There was no time to get into the details, but she was going through a tough spell, she told me. Is it serious? Is it affecting your work and personal life? It was like this almost every week, her accompanying me to these dingy basements. She was like quicksilver, this kid. It'd been going on for a long time. How was it possible that I could never get past that brave smile and find out what was behind it? My intense affection for her came gushing out. Until that moment, I hadn't realized how much of it was welled up inside of me.

It's nothing. It'll be fine. Don't worry. With overstated confidence, Tun Tun tried to console me. It was just that she'd been at the so-called wall of absurdity for two months and hadn't managed to make it far enough to figure out exactly where it would end. She couldn't fall asleep. She'd been gripped by paranoia. She'd suddenly become afraid of all kinds of things. She couldn't get herself out of the house. She went to class or else she kept busy. The only time I'm happy is on Fridays, when I can come here and see you. I can't stand being alone at night. It was out of my affection for her that I started whistling. I said, Today is my ex's birthday, and after we broke up, I got a package with three little letters in it, but I can't bring myself to open them. I stopped abruptly. So what if these were just kids' problems? Like hitting a patch of broken glass while biking, they could leave you fragile, and unable to speak.

7

THE CROCODILE was a diligent worker. It was so diligent that it was drying a whole bathtub's worth of still-usable one-cent postage stamps. That's the kind of worker it was. It used to work at St. Mary's Bakery, where it stood next to the cashier, wrapping and bagging pastries. After work, it strolled across the street to a gift shop, where it bought exquisite wrapping paper and fancy ribbons. In fact, that was the crocodile's favorite pastime. And courageously, it drew a crocodile design, then stuffed it into the slot in the manager's office door, proposing that the design be adopted on the bakery's plastic bags and cake boxes.

"I heard that in addition to eating canned goods, crocodiles supplement their diet with bread," said customer A.

"That's a minor bit of trivia. I didn't think you'd have heard it, too. Maybe it was in a housekeeping magazine." Waiting in line behind customer A was customer B, who held a cake box with baguettes inside and a wicker basket filled with pastries.

"Oh, does everyone know? I read more details in a cooking magazine. Crocodiles only eat sugar-free bread. They won't even touch salted bread. What nonsense." C was in line after B.

"How could that be true? Their favorite pastry is cream puffs," said the crocodile, who'd been listening impassively to the conversation while wrapping and bagging pastries.

"How do *you* know?" the three customers, along with the girl tending the cash register, all asked at the same time. A was surprised, B filled with admiration, and C indignant. The cashier envied the sheer volume of knowledge the others seemed to have at their disposal.

After finishing work that day, the crocodile didn't return to St. Mary's, nor did it ever set foot in a bakery again.

Though the thought of cream puffs frequently entered its mind, the crocodile could only afford to spend fifty cents on one, so it asked a child at the door of the bakery to go inside and buy a thirty-cent cream puff. If the crocodile didn't throw in a little extra cash, the kid would never do it.

The crocodile was filled with resignation. It didn't say a word to the manager. It was convinced that the manager had long figured out that it was a crocodile and had noted its baked-goods preferences and sold the information to all the local rags. All the evidence was there: A magazine had just leaked the bit about the cream puffs, modifying its earlier story about sugar-free bread. After all, the latest report reflected the conversation that had transpired in the shop, didn't it? Whenever the manager was around, the crocodile chose only sugar-free bread so as not to blow its entire paycheck. After the manager left for the day, it secretly devoured an entire box of cream puffs.

Whenever the crocodile thought about the manager, its skin turned a monstrous shade of green. But now the crocodile was sashaying down the street with its precious, thirty-cent cream puff, cravenly and delightfully taking a giant lick of the filling. It spotted a sign posted on a door: BREAKING NEWS: CREAM PUFFS ARE A CROCODILE FAVORITE! NEW CREAM PUFF STAND AND BAKERY COMING SOON.

Oh no! I can't resist cream puffs!

NOTEBOOK #4

I

TUN TUN. After reaching the aforementioned wall of absurdity she'd told me about the previous semester, she was nowhere to be found.

Zhi Rou. After we met at the club's booth at orientation, she never followed through. She said she was too busy with schoolwork. But really, she wasn't: I knew she was slacking off. Once, she dropped by around noon—basically when the office was at its most bustling—and sat in the far corner, staring at me without saying a word. When I asked how she was, she was all smiles. I raised my voice, trying to show solicitude. A moment later, she'd put on her backpack and wandered off, vanishing into thin air. The next time I ran into her, she'd adopted a more mature hairstyle and there was a conspiratorial grin on her face. She hadn't fooled me, though. I was on to her decadent ways.

I liked these two. And I knew that they liked me. There was no romantic interest whatsoever in that *like*. As for how much I liked them, the two of them were perhaps my very favorites out of all the people to whom that word applied. I liked them as individuals. I liked them even more when they were together. Were I a fanatical collector of figurines, these two would be my most prized pair.

Not only the people I'd forged close bonds with but almost everyone I knew from college appeared or disappeared in the blink of an eye. No one could be counted on to show up anywhere. Our relationships were about as tight as those between one drifting nebula and another.

When I was twenty, these two entered my orbit, and like every other nebula adrift, soon strayed from its center. Yet they came to represent something very important to me. And what was that? The answer is simple: beauty.

The meaning they brought to my life could be condensed into a single image that has stayed with me ever since. On the morning of our school's anniversary, our club set up a concession stand with beverages and snacks to rake in some extra dough. Everyone was doing their own little jig to attract attention, and me, I was sitting there hollering. Out of nowhere appeared the shaggy-haired duo of Tun Tun and Zhi Rou, who had a guitar on her back. Tun Tun had gone for a retro look in baggy white capri pants, complete with suspenders. Zhi Rou was wearing the skirt from her military uniform, which made me smile. She said it was for an occasion that evening, and that she'd add a white blouse for a seamless transition to a formal, elegant look. The two of them joked that they should help drum up business while I was working the concession stand. They sat on the edge of the table, Zhi Rou concentrating on her tuning and Tun Tun riffling through the sheet music. As soon as they were ready, they exchanged a quick glance, then launched into their set. The first song was "Cherry Came Too." One of them strummed, while the other swayed and sang "Oh cherry honey...." A light rain began to fall. After a spell, they stopped to wipe their faces of the ethereal dew that had showered down from the sky like confetti. Life, it seemed, was beautiful. I hadn't thought about it in ages, until one day the sound of pattering rain, along with "Cherry Came Too," entered my dreams.

The Freud seminar ended that Friday evening at ten. Being the last one to leave, I shut off the lights. Emerging from the gloomy classroom in the basement, I was struck by acute waves of self-pity. I scrambled to find a pay phone, then tossed in a coin and called Tun Tun. I hadn't seen a trace of her in more than a month, and I missed her like she was family.

"Tun Tun, is that you? It's Lazi. How have you been?"

"It's nice to hear your voice. Sorry I don't have the energy to go out tonight."

I couldn't bring myself to say anything about my troubles or how much I missed her, as we'd never gone so far as to reveal our feelings to each other. But on that dark night, the two of us, by way of a single coin, were touched by a mutual warmth. That was the moment when the dust settled. Everything was going to be okay.

"How about if I come visit you?"

"Right now?"

"Right now."

"Okay, come over then! What are you waiting for?"

At nineteen years and eleven months old, I'd invested a single coin, and the significance of this act was extraordinary. It was like the moment when a crawling baby learned how to stand up and take that very first step. I was in need, and so I called someone. The instant itself was a blur. I'd wrongly assumed that I, having played the role of protector far too often, was overreacting the way a parent frets over a child getting sick. But no, this was an important turning point for me. For a long time, my hidden shame had made me push everyone away. I'd rejected them before they could reject me. I ran away from close relationships even with the people who loved me. I was a blind man fallen into the ocean. I'd taken the mirror and smashed it to pieces, unable to stand the sight of my hideous, disfigured self. Tun Tun was the first person I'd taken the initiative to call on. She was the one mirror that I was willing to see my own self-pity in.

"Do you want something to eat?" Tun Tun asked.

"I'm starving. What do you have?"

"Milk. Bread. Fruit. Everything. How about if I make you a bowl of noodles?"

"Sure, I'd be up for that. But if I have to help you, forget it."

"How on earth did I end up with this terrible houseguest who can't feign the slightest manners?"

It was eleven in the evening, and Tun Tun had let me in. Everyone else in the house was fast asleep. She came out to meet me, humming under her breath, and it made me feel at home.

"Have you ever hit the wall of absurdity?" She handed me a bowl of noodles and sat down across from me.

"Yeah, a long time ago. When I was sixteen, seventeen. But back then I didn't think of it in those terms." The noodles looked delicious. I started wolfing them down.

"So what happened? Can you tell me?"

I gestured okay one-handedly. "No problem. But first you have to sign a contract saying that you owe Lazi a hundred bowls of noodles." A long, white trail of steam rose from the savory beef broth. There was still one large, tender curl of beef remaining.

"Hey, that beef was actually braised by my dad! Do my dad and I make a good beef-maestro and noodle-chef team, or what?" Tun Tun asked excitedly after a pause, unable to contain herself any longer.

"I don't care if this is processed beef noodle soup!" I responded. Then, becoming solemn, I told her, "It was one night about two or three years ago when my world started to change. I wasn't really sure what exactly was changing, but suddenly, there I was, in an unfamiliar place. I felt like I was being pulled in so many different directions, to the point where I had no idea who I was anymore. I was crying out for help, but no one seemed to hear me. I couldn't imagine my future. I kept waiting for my old world to come back and lift me out of this silent depression. Every morning I'd wake up and see the sun, and cry knowing that today would be more of the same, that the old world was gone forever. It was like, this is how things are now. Welcome to cold, hard reality."

"How'd you get out of it?"

"The wall of absurdity might be gone now, but that was only the prologue. If you fast-forward a little, the relationship between me and the world gets even uglier. The fact is, it's been a constant battle. I mean, absurdity? That's the least of it! You're trapped, so you force yourself to adapt after a while. Otherwise, if you start thinking too much, you'll suffocate. But once you become stronger than your surroundings, the absurdity will come to an end."

"It sounds like the home of a married couple who quarrel nonstop, until someone pulls out a kitchen knife or handgun, and the fighting comes to a halt." She was laughing so hard that it looked like she was trying to swat a mosquito.

"That's really how it is, at least for me. What about you?"

"My whole world wasn't turned upside down in one night, but it's like you said, I feel this silent depression, and I don't know why things have to change. Something is blocking my path, and I call it the wall of absurdity. Honestly, I'm having a total breakdown. Ever since I was little, I've always been successful at everything I've tried. It's probably because my mom and dad let me pursue whatever I wanted, so I had other things on my mind besides wanting to be at the top of my class, or wanting to be the prettiest or most popular. Yet I was naturally at the top of my class, and I got along with everyone, and you could say I've turned out to be okay-looking. Succeeding at whatever I tried made me into a happy, well-adjusted kid. I made it through all the dreadful parts, though getting zits and my period were stressful. You might say I was like a little sunflower in junior high. But back then, life was about jumping through hoops. I always did my homework as soon as I got home from school. Classes were really easy. All you had to do was pay attention in class, and you'd do fine on the tests. So then I had a load of free time. I liked reading *The Big Book of Why* and other science books, and I built and painted my own furniture. The paint you see on my bedroom walls is something I did in those days! It was so much fun, always trying new things. In high school, I got kind of depressed. I was like, how come all we do is study? So I decided to take it easy instead. I didn't want to go home and do my homework like clockwork anymore, so I became captain of all these sports teams. I started a volleyball team and led the basketball team's practices, and organized group outings with all-boys schools. I got into the gifted program at Academia Sinica, and at the same time I was directing all these brilliant performances in drama competitions. After I got into Academia Sinica, I realized that this one guy had been trying to get with me the whole time. Suddenly, doing well in school became less of a priority. Growing up, I felt so different from the girls I knew, though I applied myself all the same. I remember how my older brother had to escort me on his bike when I went out on those chilly nights. He'd be on his bike, and I'd be on mine, and neither of us would say much. I just focused on pushing the pedals, one foot after the other, until we got home. That's what high school was like. It was such a great feeling...." She was smiling as she spoke.

"It doesn't sound like there was any reason you'd change. Do you have any idea what happened?"

"It must have something to do with the college lifestyle, right? It's scary. It's like all this bacteria was already there, but because it was microscopic, you let it build up and form dust under the rug. The college lifestyle is about becoming independent, with no one else around to force you to do anything. So there's this muck that hasn't been dealt with, and because all your arrangements are loose now, you have no one to hold on to, which means you get sucked into the vacuum cleaner and tossed around in it. Your automatic response is to grab hold of something and pull yourself out. My first instinct was to cling to Zhi Rou. I wanted her by my side all day, every day. I even made her sleep over. I was scared of being alone in my room at night. I'd never been like that before. Time crawled by, especially at night, and each second went on for an eternity. I felt like I was struggling to break through the glass wall in front of me. It was agonizing. Having another living, breathing person around made things easier. But then she got frustrated because the homework was hard. She couldn't adjust to college life at all. I couldn't explain what was wrong with me, and she didn't believe me when I said I was a complete mess. I couldn't talk to her about it. I insisted that she do things beyond her abilities and I hung out with her during breaks. I told her she was the only person I'd ever help like that. But our relationship went downhill. She was pessimistic to begin with. She was never, ever happy. Before that, I used to joke around with her. Well, once I went on strike, she became morose. She had no idea how to appease me. When I saw her face, I couldn't take it, I wanted to cry. I had to hold it in, though. There was nothing I could say. After a while, my silence really hurt her. She was tired of bringing me down. One night, I asked her to try to smile a little. I said I couldn't stand to see that gloomy look on her face. So she stood up with a gloomy look on her face and left. She said she couldn't smile. She said she didn't want to see me anymore...." Tun Tun had been gazing at me the entire time, her eyes glistening as she spoke.

"How stupid is that, to hurt each other over nothing. That's so sad. Have you tried talking to her since?"

"She was actually really hurt. I could see it on her face." Tun Tun shrugged helplessly. She squeezed her eyes shut, grimacing. "The moment I saw her face, I choked up. I knew I was wrong. I'd been too needy. I didn't have the strength to make her come back, though. Once, I went all the way over to her house. I walked for half an hour to apologize to her, and I'd even thought of some things to say to make her laugh. When I got to her front door and rang the buzzer, she sent her little sister down to tell me to go away. And that's when I lost my courage. I sat down on her front steps. I didn't know what to do, if I should get up and go home. After summer vacation, I ran into her at school. We both looked the other way and didn't say hi. Whenever I saw her coming, I tried to force myself not to run away, but my feet wouldn't obey, and then my entire day would be ruined. Nowadays I hardly ever think about her, but of course, she's in my dreams all the time. The dream goes on until I say, 'Let's not fight anymore.' But she never responds. She just walks out, leaving me standing there." There was frustration in Tun Tun's eyes. I could tell that her dream had opened old wounds.

"From the look in her eyes in the dream, I know she doesn't blame me. She resents me. There's a rift between us, but she has to learn not to lament for the dead. It's like being struck in the heart with an arrow. It's not about the arrow. The fact is, the damage is done."

I nodded. I could picture Zhi Rou in Tun Tun's dream, the resentment in her eyes. I nodded again. I wanted more than anything to tell her "It isn't so," but it seemed as if those words were intended for myself. I simply couldn't bring myself to say them. All I did was whisper, "She'll regret it." I was caught up in the moment, and the words crumbled inside of me.

2

IF THERE were an encyclopedia on the subject of humanity, the scientific definition of a crocodile would be "a Hula-Hoop (or dead bolt, etc.) optimized for secretly falling in love with other people." Ideally, the encyclopedia's editor would be adept at the use of figurative language, though of course one would hope the same for the whole of humanity someday. Note on Hula-Hoop (or dead bolt, etc.): Once functional, it will emit affirmative noises.

All its life, the crocodile had longed to meet its soul mate. Enough people had gathered to fill a truck, and the crocodile, happy as a pig in mud, was to be the truck's driver. The passengers included the classmates it saw from dawn to dusk, the stinky-breathed manager of the manga shop, the saleslady from the toy department, and the young man in a tank top who heaved the trash into the garbage truck at night. There were only three dentists, while classmates accounted for the vast majority. There was the one whom it fancied who cleaned the blackboard and delivered bento boxes. There was another who would drool while taking afternoon naps. The crowd was growing. When the crocodile pulled up in its secret crushmobile, each of these people with their distinctive traits boarded the truck.

The crocodile had a large wooden trunk, a kind of hope chest. The inside was partitioned like a honeycomb, and each partition was labeled with a name, a list of traits, and the date of first meeting. Inside each partition were the love letters the crocodile had written to its love interests. When the crocodile got home from work, it removed the sweat-soaked human suit clinging to its body and settled in for the night. Usually, it hid in the bedroom ("hid" because it feared the people on the living-room TV might burst in at any moment and discover its forbidden feelings for so many people). Upon opening the trunk, the crocodile kindled the flame it carried for each of its love interests. Whenever it grew sentimental, it blew its nose into a wad of toilet paper, then took out a note card and began penning the next reply in the series of letters from its imaginary lover.

Kobo Abe. The name radiated through the curtains and into the crocodile's bedroom. There was a slight change in the project. The crocodile reassigned all its love interests the alias of Kobo Abe, recataloging them. Most likely it was the crocodile's reading of *The Face of Another* that had given rise to its secret crushes on human beings of all kinds. In the end, the crocodile had to pay its dues to the book that started it all.

Dear Mr. Crocodile: Having received the tape of your first love letter to Kobo Abe, I could thank you until my pubes damn near fall out. I am loath to be included in that Pandora's box of yours. To be desired ought to be a happy thing, but could it be that you remain ignorant of the fact that the torch has been passed to you? The suffering that we, a chorus of Kobo Abes, have undergone is tremendous. Take a cue from the media, and show them where you draw the line.

3

So it was April 1st. April Fools' Day. I waited all day for Meng Sheng to come by, and he showed up at the last minute.

I was in my attic room on Tingzhou Road. He climbed the five flights and crawled through the skylight, clambering over the barbed-wire fence around it. He made it all the way into the attic and knocked on my bedroom door. It was eleven p.m. This was about a year after he'd gotten into the philosophy program at my university. He'd scraped his hand on the barbed wire.

"Hurry up. Come on. April 1st is almost over. If we don't make it by midnight, we'll miss Chu Kuang. You know about our relationship, right? Come with me to see him. Otherwise, if we're left alone, one of us will wind up dead or injured." Wiping off the dried blood with his other hand, he flashed a grim smile, then bellowed, "C'mon!"

Every six months or so, Meng Sheng would appear out of nowhere. The way he would show up, it was as if you were walking down a busy street, and without warning, someone came up and gave you a friendly slap on the back. Ever since I'd met him, I felt as if somewhere in the intricate workings of my subconscious, some part of my psyche (possibly my ego) was constantly waiting for him to arrive, to get the fix that only he could give me.

Meng Sheng led the way as we rushed to the dorm where Chu Kuang lived. When we discovered he wasn't there, we pedaled at full speed to Zhongshan North Road and searched for him along a bar-lined strip. Spotting a pair of legs splayed out on the brick sidewalk, we found him underneath a bench. What made it even sillier was the fact that he'd worn a pristine white pair of jeans and a matching shirt. Drunkenly, he smiled at us.

"Hey, I'm not even late this year. It's only six minutes to twelve," Meng Sheng blurted out. As we carried Chu Kuang back to his room, Meng Sheng said they needed to have a talk and that I should join them. There was a menacing look on his face as he slipped each of Chu Kuang's two roommates a modest banknote, then told them to get out. It did the trick, and as if the message had been imparted with the flick of a knife, they left quickly. Meng Sheng had an imposing manner that implied he could break your neck if he wanted to, and everyone knew it.

I scanned the wall of books at the far end of the room. Wooden shelves had been built to accommodate the window, and the sections were neatly labeled. Eighty percent of the books were in English, and among them were two giant anthologies of fiction and poetry. Each volume had Chu Kuang's name written on it. Though there were four beds in the room, Chu Kuang occupied the space of two people. A three-shelf mahogany bookcase was used to divide the room in half. Cassettes and CDs were placed everywhere except on the bed, which was covered with a blanket. There was a separate shelf for the stereo, which had a medium-size set of silver speakers, and underneath were three rows of vinyl records stored in protective sleeves. Medical textbooks were piled on his desk, on which copies of works by Byron, Keats, Yeats, and other English-language poets were tossed. Books aside, music-related items filled more than half the space of the room. He had hardly any other possessions.

Meng Sheng returned with the green tea he'd made and lifted the cup to Chu Kuang's lips. He rocked Chu Kuang in his arms, slapping his face lightly. Then, kneeling and rolling up his sleeves, he started massaging him with a rhythmic, circular motion that escalated into full-on pounding. Chu Kuang laughed hysterically, pulling Meng Sheng toward him and pressing his forehead against his own. They were like two stones being struck together, the sparks intensifying with every blow. Finally, Meng Sheng pulled away. He sat in a chair and lit a cigarette. Chu Kuang let loose, the tears streaming down his chest. It was a grown man's howl loosed from a cave at the bottom of the ocean. I had never witnessed such a thing before in my life, nor would I ever forget it. As he abandoned himself to grief, the flood of tears seemed inexhaustible, too much for his body to endure, but even so, his weeping persisted with the courage of conviction. Though I was only a bystander, there was no way I could remain detached. My eyes silently welled over. A tear formed in the corner of Meng Sheng's eye, and he coldly wiped it away. It was cathartic for me, and neither of us felt pity for him. Tears, it seemed, had a life of their own. As dolphins hear the call of their shared language and must turn back toward their origins, the three of us found ourselves attuned to a common frequency. It was an experience too profound for words.

"Well! That's enough for one day, isn't it?" Meng Sheng said to me as we all breathed a sigh of relief.

"My thoughts exactly!" I said. I felt as if the three of us were on the same wavelength. We'd experienced a collective consciousness, if only for a fleeting instant. We'd stormed the fortress gates and returned to a place where souls, having no physical form, freely intermingled. In that moment of wonder, there was no distance between us.

"What day is it today, anyway?" I asked, drying my eyes.

"It's April 1st. Chu Kuang and I met four years ago on this day. I broke up with him three years ago, when he got into college. I still saw him after that, but less often. When we split, he asked me to always meet him on the first of April. He said if I missed a year or forgot, he'd die."

"Is that a threat? What, is it ordained by some higher power?" I was skeptical.

"No." Meng Sheng shook his head, rubbing his eye. "Maybe you've never experienced it. To him, I've taken on too great a meaning in his life, though I wouldn't say he's living for someone else. It's not that simple. He's been carrying all this pain and sadness his whole life. He was already like that at eighteen, when we met. One day he decided to take his own life, and I stopped him." He turned to look at Chu Kuang who, having cried himself into a stupor, was now slumped against him. He stroked Chu Kuang's nose. "What a drama that was. I didn't know him before that, I'd never even seen him. This was during my first year of high school, right after I went back. Chu Kuang was in his third year. It was the night of April 1st, and I'd just gotten out of school. I was leaving when he walked past me. For a split second, I saw this young man's face magnified, like in a close-up. There, in that single expression, were all the feelings that had built up inside me that I couldn't express. The face of a moribund man, its lines formed by a lifetime of anguish. Ah, he was the quintessential victim. I followed him to the bus stop and got on the bus. Got to the train station, transferred, took the train all the way to Keelung, and hopped on another bus. I sat next to him, but he didn't notice me. He hung his head and he was in a fog, completely oblivious. After we finally had to get off the bus, he walked to a secluded beach. I wasn't consciously trailing him this whole time. It was like sleepwalking. He had a magnetism, and I was drawn into his rite. I was still far from the water, and a large rock was blocking my path. I moved it out of the way, and the next thing I knew, I was wide awake. Something clicked, and I instantly caught up to him thirty feet ahead. I grabbed his arm and told him: 'Don't die.' And that was the moment he was reborn." He grinned and caressed Chu Kuang's hair.

"It was a stupid thing to say, though. At the end of the day, I have no right to tell other people what to do. Especially after realizing what a head case he was, I got sick of using my own will to control someone else's. Grabbing him by the arm was acting without thinking. Gut instinct. After everything he'd gone through, he'd made the decision to assert his own will. I was the one who wanted him to live, but it wasn't my choice to make. What connection did we have, really, that would justify my saying those words? I've thought about it, and I'd hate to but I'd do it all over again." Meng Sheng put his head between his knees and twisted his hair in his hands. Chu Kuang sat up, gazing at him tenderly.

"Meng Sheng, I trust you regardless. You don't know what death is really like and don't want to find out, so part of you is resisting death. And that part of you spoke up, that's all. You didn't want to let death in. Everyone has the same response," I said. "There's nothing wrong with that!"

"Resisting death. That's what it comes down to. It's like you're on autopilot: No matter how much you hate life, your body doggedly resists death. Even other people aren't allowed to die. You still try to stop them." Meng Sheng scoffed. "What a joke!"

"So then what happened?" I wanted to know how it had turned into this.

"Hey, it's my turn to talk." Chu Kuang's eyes were puffy and red, and he sounded hoarse and congested. "When he grabbed me and said, 'Don't die,' I started bawling like I did just now. I was two grades ahead of him, but he was more mature than I was, in every way. He told me to stop crying and called a cab to take me home. In fact, he handled it like he was the older one. He made me talk about what made me wish I was dead. He acts tough, all right, but he has a sensitive side, too. He appeared at my darkest hour, when I wanted nothing more than to feel exactly that kind of masculine warmth inside of me. Do you follow me, Sis? In his presence, I was a helpless little baby. I'd prayed for him, and now that he had come, I surrendered, willing to do anything he asked. I wished that he would snatch my soul or that I could have his body. Back in his room, he seemed to accept that he held this power over me, that I'd obey him. I couldn't stop crying. After listening, he cried too. He had all kinds of pent-up desires, and I could tell that they were boiling over. It was very real, and very intense. He reached out to me in a way that neither of us had imagined. He reached over, and in one swift yet tender motion, removed my shirt and pants. And without a word, I submitted to him. That hand was shaking with emotion as it caressed me. So I took his hand and wrapped it around my cock. I don't know where that idea came from, but my will to live had found an outlet, which had materialized before my very eyes. What is the human race, anyway, but a multitude of outlets for desires? There's no suppressing the truths that arise from our experiences. Desires teach us lessons, and we have to go forth into the new worlds that we construct for ourselves." Chu Kuang's voice trembled. "When you can't, *that's* when you die."

"The new worlds that we construct." I nodded. I knew exactly what he meant. "But some desires, once formed, are impossible to fulfill, so they become frustrations instead. That's the problem with going forth into new worlds. By having another man grip your cock, you've gone beyond the perceived boundaries of your former world and delved into your carnal desires. You've retraced the roots of self-knowledge, experienced the primal frustrations, and transgressed the perceived boundaries. And you've managed to come back alive." I expounded on Chu Kuang's thoughts, which had stirred something within me. "You've emerged from a primordial state with newly constructed schemata, and lo and behold, you're experiencing a whole new world. Right?"

"Hey, I really like you, Sis. But why do you feel the same way, too?" Having recovered his composure, Chu Kuang seemed embarrassed at his outburst just a minute earlier.

I didn't answer. "So it was just a sudden impulse? It wasn't love?" I asked. Meng Sheng had planted himself at the window and was staring out into the night.

"Later on, it really was love. The happiest time of my life was my final year of high school. We'd go on endless walks at the edge of town. Other times we'd go to a deserted beach and watch the sunset, or make love on the hot sand. I'd recite poetry or read plays out loud to him. He'd brazenly put his arm around me as we walked home. It was an illicit love—a thing so dangerous it refused to be contained, yet made of nothing but sweetness. But it had no future. Eventually women entered the picture. At first, he hid the fact that he'd been chasing women. But his interest in me gradually waned, and I found out. He was shameless, spending all his time with women. He told me straight up that he was going on a date, that he'd come see me when he needed a fix. I loved him too much and let myself be treated badly. Once, he even taunted me by bringing a girl over to my place and making me hide in the bathroom, watching him put the moves on her. I stood on top of the toilet all night, peering through the window over the door until my leg fell asleep and every last detail was burned into my memory. I knew I was damaged goods. So I grabbed a pair of scissors and stabbed myself in the thigh, left arm, and stomach—not deep, though. I managed to not cry out. I had to protect myself from the destructive side of his love. After I took the college exams, he broke it off completely. I was never going to satisfy him. The fact that he still needed a woman already adulterated our love, but being forced to watch the two of them was humiliating. I was living for someone else. I've given up hope that he'll ever love me again, that those dreams will ever come true, and I'm not really saving my love for him. There was a line between us. He was on one side, and as long as I wanted to be on the same side as him, that line was blurred. Meng Sheng was my only reference point." Chu Kuang rubbed his nose. Beads of sweat had formed around his mustache. Though he had stopped speaking, his mouth was twitching. His mannerisms could be comical even when he was upset.

"Chu Kuang, don't you think I'm right? You need Meng Sheng to see you once a year. You're still leaving the line between life and death blurred. All you've done is taken the decision-making responsibility and passed it to him. Isn't that vindictive of you?" Just hearing about these two and their entanglement was draining. Part of me wanted to get up and leave so that I could shut out the panorama of hazardous terrain that had just opened before my eyes, this world of embattled relationships. I wanted to retreat to the solitude of my desert, which, though bleak, was tame compared to this.

Meng Sheng cackled loudly, as if in response to my question. It was two in the morning. We heard the sound of slippers shuffling downstairs in the lobby of the men's dormitory as the giant, broad-leaved trees swayed outside the window, their silhouettes graced by nocturnal melancholy. Meng Sheng had stripped off his clothes at some point and was now strutting around naked, making an ass of himself. Every once in a while, he'd swivel his hips in a womanly manner or, alternately, swing his dick around. But there was more to his acting out than a desire to break the rules or put on a display of vulgarity; it seemed defensive, as if he'd been hurt.

"Whoa! You're not offended, are you? How about if the three of us agree to have post-gender relations? I'm done talking about it. In the end, all three of us have been seriously warped by gender labels. Everybody has, more or less. The only difference is, we're the blessed children of Tripitaka. We'll talk about it later." Blushing, Chu Kuang extended his hand in a gesture of solidarity.

"Hey, we should found a gender-free society and monopolize all the public restrooms!" I was elated at the idea. He didn't have to explain. He too could envision the manual I was writing about my own experiences. I decided to stop pressuring myself to state those experiences explicitly. If I couldn't, I wasn't going to let it bother me. I would speak up when the time was right. With these guys, it was about laying the foundations of trust.

"So, about this problem, Sis...." Chu Kuang, both inquisitive and protective, took my hand. "Making choices versus getting revenge, that's a deeper issue I haven't overcome. When I was eighteen and ready to hurl myself into the ocean, I was in a bad place. That's how my therapist describes it. That ended after I turned eighteen.... We still fight, though. Doesn't take much for us to start an argument, heh.... But when our fights get too intense, I slide back into that bad place...I lose control. For me, Meng Sheng is like this thing F. Scott Fitzgerald described in *The Great Gatsby*: 'A single green light, minute and faraway, that might have been the end of a dock.' Every day, he'd stare at the green light. If it went out, that meant hope was gone. It was his only point of reference. Know what I mean?"

Chu Kuang smiled sweetly. I felt an overwhelming urge to stroke his hair. He lowered his head into my lap, and Meng Sheng came over and curled up behind him. The tiniest beads of moisture formed on the tip of his nose....

4

Preface to *The Secret Lives of Crocodiles*

Based on the research of a central investigator who scaled mountains and forded rivers to locate the nearly hundred-some crocodiles residing across the country, the lifestyle and characteristics of the average specimen are compiled herein. Amid a recent crocodile frenzy, one radical theologian has predicted that no prophet will emerge from among the crocodiles, and that the gods will see to it that they are all cast into a pit of flames. All things considered, it is indisputable that crocodiles—whether they are studied or scorned—warrant closer attention.

Favorite TV shows: *Hawaii Five-o*, *Variety 100*, *The 700 Club*.

Likes: A houseful of lies, lovers' talk, any housework that can be performed with one's tongue.

Toilet habits: HCG brand toilets (with Sujay brand toilet paper).

Wears: Only the finest—Wacoal.

Hobbies: Knitting with wool yarn.

Mottoes: "Those who believe will find salvation." "God loves the common man."

Since it was unemployed, the crocodile went for a stroll. At the bus stop, by the pay phone, was a stack of pamphlets with the words THE LIGHT OF JESUS CHRIST on the cover, the mere sight of which frightened the crocodile out of its wits. Could it be that even Jesus himself was a crocodile watcher? The crocodile mischievously took out a red pen and ripped the first six pages from one copy. On the last page, it drew a giant red *X*, and in one fluid stroke, inscribed the following words: TRUE—BUT DON'T FEEL BAD, EVEN JESUS MADE A FEW MISTAKES! The crocodile placed this pamphlet face-down on top of the stack so that it would serve as the corrected edition. It merged into the crowd that was piling onto the bus, and with a dimpled grin, watched in the rearview mirror as the bus stop receded into the distance....

Nostalghia. A burly man bundled in a heavy coat. He struggles to lift the knitting needles in his right hand toward the ball of white yarn in his left. The classroom is filled with the chattering of school-girls as they learn to knit. In solitude the burly man, deeply engrossed in his stitches, wipes the sweat from his brow. *(The camera zooms out, and the depth of field expands.)* On the second floor are an aristocratic couple dressed in formal attire. The gentleman's hands are folded across his stomach, and the lady has put her arm through his. The sound of the symphony swells, resplendent and exalted. The burly man has grown thin. His coat now fits him loosely as he persists in knitting. Hunched over, he mumbles to himself as the ball of yarn unravels, revealing a white wool scarf in progress. *(As the camera zooms out, the frame widens to capture the ruins of an ancient façade.)* Built for the spectacle and pageantry of sports, the three-story coliseum was at one time filled with the noise and clamor of crowds. On the arena floor is the once burly man, now gaunt as a stick, who, in isolation, has knitted a fluffy white dog. Snowflakes land on its fur coat. That's Tarkovsky.

5

I LIVED on Tingzhou Road during my second semester in 1989. It was right before I turned twenty.

Twenty. I was stuck in a rut and feeling hopeless. I couldn't go on.

Life didn't feel real. My reality was the occasional call from family, the twenty classes a week that kept me glued to a desk, the coming and going of nameless faces in the classroom, taking tests between the ringing of bells, sitting on a table in the student organization offices and goofing around, making plans to hang out with people from my classes. I packed my evening schedule with private tutoring and playwriting workshops. Every once in a while I'd meet people who got me and we'd hit it off. But even so, what good did it do me? Joining the group meant I'd either be the one who mixed things up or I'd get lost in the jumble. In reality I'd always be relegated to the margins. I forced myself to put one foot in front of the other, reminding myself that there was a place for me out there in those moments of happiness, even if I was a different person at home, someone who went to bed shit-faced. It reminded me of a scene out of W. Somerset Maugham's memoirs: My life was extraordinarily lacking in all sense of reality, as if I were watching a different me playing various characters within a mirage. I wanted to be kicked out into reality so badly. . . .

In May, the club president was relieved of her post. By then, van Gogh's *The Potato Eaters* had come to life. The painting shows four gloomy faces under a dim light, figures with dark circles under their eyes, sitting around a table in a cellar, divvying up the potatoes. At the changeover ceremony, Tun Tun and Chu Kuang sat in the front row, grinning at me. Zhi Rou didn't go. I'd latched on to the club for dear life in the year following my split from Shui Ling. I'd fled the jaws of reality and become the painting's central figure—the fifth one, whose back was turned. Whether I was delivering a rambling speech or serving potatoes, I reeked of a degenerative disease of the spirit, the result of having been sequestered for too long. The layer of glass had grown thicker and harder to shatter. Life had drained me.

My twentieth birthday. I was in a bad place, and death was a speck on the horizon. The night before my birthday, I took two years' worth of journals from college and packed them with Shui Ling's letters, a copy of Haruki Murakami's *Norwegian Wood*, and Daddy's credit card, and I took the night train to Kaohsiung. The white light of the station sign flooded my vision as I passed the stop for my home. Inside the train, I felt as if I were being whisked away by the wind, and tears filled my eyes. It was after one in the morning when I arrived in Kaohsiung and lumbered over to the hotel, where I stayed in room 514. The facilities were brand new, the bedsheets were clean, and the carpet was royal blue. There were other amenities—a white refrigerator, a TV, a stereo, a vanity mirror, toilet-seat liners. Splayed out on the bed, I picked up and examined one of the neatly arranged pieces of the ice queen (her name being two strokes shy of being exactly that) and opened it—

July 21, 1988

As you read this, you probably resent me and wonder why I'm writing to you, why I won't leave you alone. Or maybe you're sick of my being evasive and immature. But that won't be the case this time. Just listen. I'm here to confess. Since you think we need to have a talk, it shouldn't be asking too much for you to sit back and listen. In the end, it won't affect you. The only connection between us is the old you, and I can talk to her whenever I want. All I'm asking you to do is open this letter and read it to the end. Someday, when you meet someone who's living in a prison, you can remember how I was once imprisoned by you.

After you left, I was overflowing with love that nobody wanted. You left me standing in the cold, with only you in my heart and nowhere else to turn. I can't say I never thought of running off with whoever was convenient. But I never did because everyone else seemed so inferior. I felt that if I let anyone else into my heart for even a second, it would sully the love we'd shared. I'd never be able to live with myself. I couldn't hate you or stop loving you, and that was only the beginning. It was impossible to hate you, though I tried. I knew there was no hope of running away or winning you back, but I still waited right where you left me. I imagined there was a completely new you who met my needs, that my love was requited. That way, I was never lonely in a crowd. I was just another woman in love, lost in a daydream. My tragedy began when you left. I felt like a child abandoned by her father, facing a hard road ahead.

My love has only grown stronger, leaving me helpless. Just like you predicted, I didn't know what you were to me until it was too late. I wasn't like you: I always knew it was love, that I should love while I could and prepare myself to no longer be able to love. Only I was confused by my attraction to you. The moment I experienced your tender side, I gave myself completely. That's why it hurts so much that your cruel side took my love and never returned it. Though I don't understand how that's considered love on your part, I'm not negating it either. I guess everyone has a different way of expressing their love. No matter how it comes out, it always finds its way to the person it was meant for. I just didn't know—or care—if it would last.

Tell me, just this once, if you still think of me. And let me recklessly, tenderly, tell you one more time: I love you.

Norwegian Wood: "I've lost Naoko! Her beautiful flesh has vanished from this world!" My leaden heart cracked open with sadness, and raging waves submerged the embankment.

NOTEBOOK #5

I

IN 1989, I entered my third year of college. Through the course of my post-heartbreak purgatory, in those eighteen months of being cut off from the object of my desire, I was a blind man fallen into the ocean. I spiraled downward, deeper and deeper inside myself, until I sank to the seabed and slipped into a sinister cave in which Shui Ling's beckoning was the only sound. Sometimes her call grew distant, and other times it drew nearer. Finding myself at the border of life and death, I followed her echo as it led me toward death.

Shui Ling was the only thing I had that was real. That year, my attic bedroom on Tingzhou Road became like a coffin in which I lay awake at night, painfully alone. She was the only one I'd been close to, and now there was no place where my reality converged with the outside world. The look in her eyes, the sound of her voice, snatches of our conversations—those sensory impressions formed a leech that attached itself to me and started sucking my blood. I sealed the leech in a plastic bag and kept it at a distance. But then I discovered white foam spilling over my windowsill. The ocean was depositing its frothy residue, filling my sanctum with wave after wave. To my horror, she insistently lived on inside of me.

That was how I started to see things. Or maybe this was the product of the schema that I'd long been using—unconsciously—to block out the outside world. That way of seeing had gotten me far in this world. But now everything I'd achieved in my first twenty-one years of life—connections I'd forged, status I'd earned, talent I'd nurtured, possessions I'd acquired, and traits I'd developed—were at the mercy of a death wish that negated it all. I'd always been surrounded by people who cared for me, but no matter how much they loved me, they couldn't save me: It just wasn't *me*. I never let others get too close and simply paraded a fake me that resembled their image of me. Sweeping that other me into their arms, they led me in a dance within societal norms, along a trajectory based on a delusion. (Though I couldn't define what I was, I knew what I wasn't.) I was shown the limits, and being confined within a set of walls tormented me and drained me of life, for the real me spanned multitudes, stretching far beyond the bounds of normality encircling ninety percent of the human race.

There was no one I wanted to share my thoughts with. There was nothing I could do to lessen the pain, no source that I could pinpoint. Secretly, though, I did sort of enjoy being a fucked-up mess. Apart from that, I didn't have a whole lot going on.

Who was the real me, then? It was an abstraction that hadn't yet taken shape in my lifetime. Self-actualization became the fulcrum that my survival rested on. Like a convict being hauled off to prison, I handed over my clothing and jewelry, which were to remain locked away in storage, and in turn I was given the key. I would wear the uniform of a prison convict for life, as that alone was permitted. My greatest longing was to use that key, so I could steal a glance into Shui Ling's eyes, which were so full of life.

I'll tell you the kind of person I was. In the eyes of the average person, I was a woman, but that vague semblance was an illusion, an easy category. In my own mind, I was a beast straight out of Greek mythology: a centaur. Like that beast, I'd willingly and madly fallen in love with a woman. Since I'd managed to shake off this woman's affections, I'd succeeded in fleeing from all the desires and fears that came with having someone special in my life. Over the course of eighteen long months, a distant flame had been ignited and passed from one candle to the next across a great distance until it would finally arrive at my darkest hour, illuminating the candle I held before me. Until then, the intermittent flicker of that flame was enough to console me. No matter who I was, no matter how anyone else saw me, no matter whether I knew who I was, somewhere on this planet there was someone who'd completely accept me, who'd been trying to figure me out all along, who genuinely loved me.

And that, right there, was the truth. It hit me one night, under a cobalt sky. It was during the summer vacation of my third year, on the cusp of late summer and early autumn, and I'd just moved to Gongguan Road. The evening air was cool. I was sitting at an intersection of Roosevelt Road and a brick road next to a musical instrument shop. The piano melody of "Thanksgiving" played in my head, putting me in a meditative mood as I took a few soft drags from a cigarette and reflected on the five years that had passed since I'd left home for Taipei. People had come into my life and left without a trace. Late at night, I sat in a desolate corner of the city, dispatching lone smoke signals.

The gears of memory, now warmed, were set in motion: scenes of life with my family when I was little; each of us children leaving home in succession until it was my turn, and this scrawny kid lugged her bags all the way to Taipei; my high school years, filled with secret crushes and the camaraderie of friends who laughed and cried together, later torn apart in the process of growing up. Even if we had prevented that estrangement, our former kindredness would be replaced by a pained silence if we were to meet again. My college years were spent among people who were like oil in water, unable to form bonds. A few friends had broken through my shell and made me less alienated, but I didn't treat them well, and it was my loss. My only salvation—Shui Ling—was as short-lived as a rainbow. What the two of us had was an achievement on par with landing on the moon, then floating in space with zero gravity. Images of all these people flooded my mind. Some emotion of mine—whether love, pain, or sorrow—had been preserved in each of their faces. But there was no escaping separation, which was left to the mercy of fate. One by one, those dearest to me had disappeared, and my memories, which I had so closely guarded, were ultimately of little consolation.

My thoughts were awry. Separation awaited regardless of which way I turned, ready to reduce me to a baby chick shivering in the rain. My eyes welled over to the sounds of "Thanksgiving," and I set my bottle of beer down between my legs. My tears were not those of pain, but of remorse and acceptance. Separation was the thing I'd been dreading the most these past few years, and I'd been in denial that it was a fact of life. Refusing to let go, I'd practically thrown a temper tantrum. What's worse, my attempts to avoid separation had only hastened it. It explained why I'd always been so quick to lash out at those I loved. My realization was akin to discovering the lost city of Atlantis.

In my navy blue sweatpants, I strolled back to the main road. By day, the streets of Taipei were noisy, congested, and putrid, but at night the scene was tranquil. I sat down on the steps of the pedestrian bridge. I'd spent countless lonely nights atop countless bridges, thinking about the people I loved, the people who made me who I was. I knew I'd been here before, on this bridge illuminated in purple. These bridges were all the same, and I'd sat like this before, with my arms around my knees, watching the world below.

The beer tasted bitter. God knows how much I'd drunk in the two years I lived alone, but it was clear I'd been having one long, silent cry. I simply hadn't thought of it that way before. Then it hit me: If I died, what difference would it make to the world? After all, no matter who I was, my death would be no more significant, nor would I be spared from lonely nights. And really, what difference did the world make to me, anyway? With that question, something stirred deep inside me, making my body tremble. It did make a difference. I had needs like anyone else, and sure, one of those needs was a little acknowledgment. But the problem was the way I loved: It was the very cause of my pain.

A second later, I was leaning over the side of the bridge retching. My stomach had purged itself, leaving a sour taste in my mouth. I had to let go of the people I loved. The words came with a mouthful of vomit—in one violent lurch, as if my jaws were pried open and the contents of my stomach were ejected, leaving only the whimpering mess that was me. The image of a tomb flashed in mind, and I knew it contained all that was dear to me. It was shown to me like a geoglyph, a giant symbol of my connections to the universe at large.

I wailed. No matter how loudly I sobbed, the sound was drowned out by the noise of passing cars. I'd taken everyone I loved and killed them off in my heart, one by one. I'd long been tending their graves—secretly visiting and mourning during the day, going out and erecting a cross on starry nights, lying inside and awaiting my own death on starless nights. That was my Atlantis, the kingdom I'd built in the name of separation. I'd never before unearthed so much of myself, and so suddenly at that. Inside the world of my tomb, everyone else was dead, I alone survived, and that was the reason for my sorrow.

It didn't take long to spot the largest sarcophagus. It was the one in which Shui Ling had been entombed, and across the front, it read: This woman is madly in love with me. And then reality finally hit me. I had my old schema (which offered a peephole, really) to blame for my decision to leave this woman, to kill her and preserve her body in this sarcophagus, where she'd stay mine forever. I'd evaded the perils of real relationships and robbed her of the ability to change with time. These two prospects had given rise to my deep-rooted fear of a real separation, which in turn yielded the avoidant mentality that had only hastened it.

That's where I was after eighteen months. I didn't want to see or talk to her, and I'd no longer allow her to set foot in my world. The paradox, of course, was that my love for her would grow. Her corpse would remain in a sarcophagus where I kept her closer than I could in reality. And I continued believing in that unchanging world, which I was at peace with. It was as if Shui Ling simply went on living her life, and it made no difference whatsoever to me.

But Shui Ling was living her life here in the same city as me, there was no doubt about that. So then what?

2

1989. SHUI LING. Gongguan Road. My Romantic Tragedy, round two.

"There—it's for you!"

It was a winter morning in a season identical to the year before. I'd just finished a swimming lesson and was shivering from the cold. On that rare occasion when I'd woken up early, the athletic fields were covered in a layer of dew. I was riding down the sidewalk when a bicycle cut across my path—a letter was tossed into my basket before the bicycle turned and sped off. I almost squealed. It was Shui Ling.

"What are you doing here?" Pedaling fast to catch up to her, I managed to find the warm and gracious tone I'd always reserved for her. I'd imagined this scenario a million times before, and now it was happening. Over the past eighteen months, I'd spotted her on campus from a distance from time to time. Having been burned once, I'd decided to make a break for it if she actually approached me. I was sure that if she started talking to me, I would die. I never expected to stay so calm. It felt as if my tears were absorbed by a giant bath towel before they could seep out, and there I was, as cheerful as ever.

She didn't notice me, and yet she didn't seem entirely focused on riding, either. She stared at the road ahead, pedaling slowly, as if in a trance, oblivious to the sights and sounds around her. Her purple scarf. I was supposed to be the masculine one, and yet her elegance in a simple scarf and jeans left me weak at the knees. I rode alongside her until we reached the intersection. No matter how I tried to coax her, she continued straight ahead. As I waited for her to cross, my now softened heart was wrung by the thought of being involved with her again. I stopped and watched her ride into the distance.

I went home. After intense deliberation, I headed back to campus and sat behind her in class. Unable to look away from her, I stared furtively instead. Her expression hadn't changed. Engrossed in the lecture, she seemed to be off in some faraway place, and it only stirred pangs of misery inside me. I squinted. She was within arm's reach, yet there was a canyon between us. I could practically touch her, but every time I summoned all my strength to sidle up to her, to reach out to her, I imagined myself backing away again and again. All I could do was stare.

She'd been silently resisting me for a while now. She wanted to avoid me, to get away from me. Meanwhile I was trailing her like a spider gliding along a thread. The purple envelope she'd dropped in my basket contained a vaguely sad poem conveying the sentiment that it was meant to turn out this way. And with that, the conflicting forces of attraction and repulsion were set off, desire was piqued in a mix of rapture and pain—and I completely lost myself.

She walked with her head lowered, casting a glare my way a few times. Once we reached the lakefront, she stopped and turned to face me. Her eyes widened. A sudden boldness eclipsed her shyness. "What do you want?"

"I don't know," I replied, feeling at once innocent and prepared to show my old brazenness. I knew I had her.

"What do you mean, *you don't know*?" she snapped.

One moment her temper flared, and the next she'd broken into a self-indulgent smile. She turned toward the lake and sat down on the white metal bench, poking a finger through the yarn of her red sweater. Her face slowly flushed.

"Sorry, I lost control for a second. You pedaled right past me out of nowhere. I wanted to see where you were going."

"You lost control? Tell me, what do you expect me to do when you lose control?"

"If things have changed, fine. But if they haven't, then why can't they be like they were before?"

"No. Not like before." She shook her head forcefully. Her expression was stern and unforgiving, as if I'd done something dreadfully wrong.

"I'm with someone else now."

Those unexpected words came out as she shook her head frantically. For the past three years, every fall had been the same. The wind had swept across the surface of Drunken Moon Lake. The surrounding trees had swayed in a verdant mass as the lake quivered lightly. The vivid sensations of the season had filled my lungs, invigorating me. Last year, and the year before that, I'd stood alone in the middle of an autumn field, a fleck of color, a minute consciousness within the vastness of nature. Now that consciousness was jolted by her words, and it widened in a blur, erasing me.

Like a pair of lovers who'd been exiled to opposite ends of the earth, we'd tearfully embraced each other. But in the end, I was left standing alone on that autumn field.

Her resentment toward me hadn't been evident earlier, but now I understood her pain. If I were to bemoan the fact that she had found someone else, she too would understand my pain. It was the final standoff between two beasts. The bare teeth of one tore into the flesh of the other in an expression of love commingled with hatred. Incapable of licking each other's wounds, the two of us could only stand face-to-face and lament.

And as if that were not enough, the new someone was a woman. The words cut into me, leaving me speechless.

Shui Ling said that just a few days ago, on her birthday, she had been given a ring by that new someone. She had agreed to go out with her and even promised to study abroad together. While I was secretly leaving roses on Shui Ling's doorstep, she was returning home from a candlelit dinner wearing that other person's ring, glowing with renewed desire. Before that, she'd been waiting day and night for a sign. Once again, out of panic, she'd made an impetuous decision and was tied down before she knew it.

She'd waited for me for ten months, she said with a smirk. Her gaze was stiff. After the two of us had been practically inseparable, and after the excruciating heartbreak that had followed, she'd fled into someone else's arms. They were like daggers, her eyes. So she found someone who was *better at intimacy* than I was. But she didn't want a man. That would only mar her pristine memories of me, she said. We'd always be together in her heart, even if she was with someone else. No one could take that away from her, especially not me here and now.

My heart ached. I felt guilty for having put her through such an ordeal. I felt bad for driving her away with my latent self-destructive behavior. Yet out of this morbid, deranged love of hers that pained me to the bone, out of fear of losing the entire significance of our past, she was treating the present me with violent animosity.

God I wished I was dead. This woman had to be part of some hellish eternal recurrence.

3

January 4, 1989

SHUI LING,

Now it's my turn to tell you something. I spent my twentieth birthday all alone. I wanted to die, but that didn't happen. I didn't throw myself off the side of a cliff. I vowed to do it but didn't have the will to follow through. As I stood on the edge, you took hold of my heart, and suddenly I realized that somewhere in this great big world, there really was a you that loved me. For a long time, you and my family were the only ones who loved me, who would do anything for me, but it wasn't the real me. No one loved the real me, and it caused me suffering. You're the only one who knows my pain. I once bared my soul to you. Your love saw past the mess that I was. So in the end, I don't know why I only remember your love hurting me. That notion backed me into a corner, told me there was no place for me out there.

In the past I never understood. Then I had a devastating realization: I'd been shown what was off-limits. I didn't have the strength to die, and the one thing I was secretly living for was the very thing that I wouldn't let myself have. I was headed astray as it was. The secret burned inside me, but because I failed to understand it, I allowed the thing I wanted to elude reality.

So I found my way back. That's right: I came back. I've made a complete turnaround since those days. I want to care for you. I want us to have a real connection again. I used to be afraid of living, and now all I ever feel is the will to live. But just like that, I was released from my mortal fear of what I truly wanted. I wasn't trying to change anything by giving you roses on your birthday. Maybe you think it's silly, but doing that kind of thing only proves that I don't need to stop having feelings for you.

After eighteen months apart, I came back and stood at the wrought-iron gates to your door, calm and collected. I knew you were out and about, that there was no need to chase you down. You were a part of my world, behind its own gates. That's how things were when we were together, when nothing could keep us apart. I told myself that no matter what became of our relationship, I could always return to that sacred place. The thought of it became like a guardian angel by my side, and it seemed as if nothing could ever come between us.

You loved me. I couldn't grasp that, and this inability was at the core of my death wish. I never believed that anyone could love the real me—not even you.

Why didn't I get it? That has to do with my own issues. Ever since I was little and started to learn what it meant to love, I never understood that I had to love me too—otherwise, what was the point? If I wanted to join the rest of humanity, the only solution was gradually to reveal my secret. I would begin to construct what was in my internal blueprint. There was no other way I could go on. For me, it was a matter of life and death, and of pain.

You know that I fall in love with women, that it's how I was designed. What you don't know is how I suffered during that year with you. There's no way you'll ever comprehend how painful it was for me to be alive. My self-actualization was forbidden. That was why I had to leave you.

I once said you were so happy that it made me feel lonely. But the truth is, I was so hardened by pain that you couldn't touch me. Relying on only a lover's intuition, the way a blind man reads a cluster of braille, you reached for me, but your touch was painful, and it broke me down a little more every time. You were like acid on my limestone, unaware of how hardened I was. My sense of self had begun to disintegrate, and so I had to flee. Still, you know nothing of how it transformed me, nor do you realize how I altered your destiny.

For you, being in love with a woman is natural, the same as being in love with a man. You didn't believe in unhappy endings, much less admit that misfortune lay ahead, awaiting you. So you took the agony in my eyes to be part of my tragic disposition, and as in any lopsided romance, you partook of the happiness.

But I'm like a father to you, only younger. A lover with a beautiful soul, nothing special about it. For you, it was an ordinary happiness. I was the one who shouldered the burden when we experienced two discrete halves of the love we shared.

My world is one of tainted sustenance. I love my own kind —womankind. From the moment my consciousness of love was born, there was *no hope of cure*. And those four words—*no hope of cure*—encapsulate my state of suffering to this day. My condition is one that will keep me in shackles for life.

My desires led me to sample a cuisine known as woman, and I got hooked. Confronted with my own inclination, I saw three possible courses of action: (1) Undergo a change of diet; (2) Invent an antidote; (3) Try the old "substitute" trick.

Undergo a change of diet. With this approach, I try to find the will to overturn my fate before even getting involved. I spent all spring in isolation, basking in my desires, having realized it was futile to try to repress one orientation and adopt another. I was able to contain my fears to a certain extent, for a time.

Here's a delusional and misguided hypothesis: If I could just fall in love with a man, it would put an end to the anguish of having fallen in love with a woman by somehow overwriting that earlier consciousness. Falling in love with a man and falling in love with a woman are two completely different things. My attraction to women has materialized, and regardless of whether it becomes a thing of the past, it's a part of me. By the same token, the part of me battling that attraction has been around even longer. It's like taking a bucket of black dye and adding other colors to it, hoping to change black into a different color. You can try, but you'll never succeed.

I'll never fall in love with a man, just as most men can't simply fall in love with another man. Ultimately, a forced change of diet is demeaning. I discovered who I was through not being readily accepted by society. My identity was fully formed long before I was ever actualized, and it wasn't going to change even if I kicked and screamed. When it reached the point where I couldn't take it anymore, I entered a state of denial and started injuring myself. Do you understand what I've been going through?

I was in love with you. I wanted to give myself to you. The benefit of hindsight makes retracing this story even more painful. When Gide left his wife, he told her in a parting letter, "At your side, I have nearly rotted." And then he freed himself to love. It was too late to find a cure: Decay had already set in.

During those six short months when there were feelings between us, I became a monster. That monster caressed you, its paws held you, and its maw pressed against you in a kiss. With its monster desires, it lusted after your body. It took in the adoration and admiration in your eyes, which reflected nothing of the monster's shadow. The experience, every bit of it, brutally scathed me.

I'm unworthy of loving you. I've struggled to find self-worth, but I can't expel the monster's consciousness still lurking beneath my skin. If my self-worth was already wounded, my experience with you only put salt in that wound.

You opened a realm that exposed me. The deeper and harder I fell for you, the more grotesque I felt. The shackles that had been holding me down were removed. But in my mind, the monster's face had taken over. Every night since the birth of this monster, I lay in horror, unable to sleep. I groaned in agony, a patient trapped in a slowly dying body.

I didn't know whether I'd arrived at a final self-discovery or just a bend in the road, but my instinct was to retreat. Arrows were loaded onto a bow and fired fast into the field called romantic love. In a violent, pent-up fury of self-hatred and insecurity, I'd stretched the bow taut. Then, after an internal tussle, came a state of perfect calm. The force applied to the bow was enough to shoot clean through my target, and with a single arrow our fates intermingled in a pool of blood. From there, I resorted to my nefarious ways, chopping you to pieces despite your sobbing and pleading, and savagely tossing the parts in the woods. Your eyes, which shed innocent tears in the wake of horror, never showed anything but unyielding trust in me.

I didn't accept myself. There was no curing the me that had come forth. I'd ingested the poison long ago, and its origins were in the whole of humanity, who'd infected me with their collective chorus. Before I could ever reveal the real me, first I had to remove the label on me that read NEGATED and tear it up.

Before my twentieth birthday, I never believed that you loved me, and as a result, I made a huge mistake. Without a doubt, it was my own wrongdoing. My self-loathing and defeatism made me see the world through shit-smeared eyes. Having only known unfulfilled yearnings, I thought that love was a long shot, that keeping my pride intact was a far safer bet. I didn't think I was worthy of being loved. Though you showed me that you loved me, I assumed it was because you'd never experienced a man's love, that you didn't know the social disapproval we'd face, and that you couldn't tell I was seriously fucked in the head. I thought that in the end, you'd still need a man, that you were just going through a confused phase, and that sooner or later, I'd be dumped so that you could move on to the next shiny new thing.

The only thing left is to survive by means of the old substitute trick. I've tried everything in my quest to replace that source of sustenance. I managed to hide the void from myself, but as soon as my fast ended, I craved it anew. My aching desires, born of a hunger for love, sent tremors through my badly starved body. Having once tasted that sustenance, I'm reduced to a living death without it, tainted or not.

Shui Ling, you probably have no idea that I've spent the past eighteen months in full-on avoidance mode. I don't know how else to go on. I've been throwing myself into busywork that surrounds me with people, then escaping into alcohol-induced numbness, among other diversions. It's a cycle that helps me put one foot in front of the other. It's not much comfort, but it's all I have.

I'm doomed to my fate . . . and I can't resist the temptation to look back. The moment you call, I turn around. That's the punishment fate has chosen for me. You said I'd always be with you, even when you found someone new. How did you not expect me to come back needing you? You spitefully told me the news there was already someone new, that it was me who lost out, and it marked the end of us. What a cruel joke. I left you, this woman, hoping I'd leave no trace of me, this monster, that our connection would disintegrate and be buried in the darkest recesses of your mind, that you'd cross back over to normality—get married, have kids—and live within the boundaries of ordinariness. All of recorded human history, at least, seems to support that basic formula for happiness. How I wish you'd become part of that other world.

When all is said and done, you and I aren't quite cut from the same cloth. Society still considers you a normal woman. Your love for me was a feminine, maternal love that can just as easily be extended to any man. Basically, the only difference between you and other women is that your heart is more open. But me, our relationship left me fundamentally altered. You tore me open and exposed the man inside. That new me has no rightful place within humanity. I don't think you've been cast out. You can still return to that place where I'm no longer allowed.

I came back, but for what? Your choice of someone new is hard to take, even humiliating. In *The Box Man*, Kobo Abe wrote about a man who hid himself in a box wherever he went. One day, this man peeped out and saw another man peeping out from inside of his own box, which aroused the naked woman in front of him. It made the box man feel angry and ashamed of himself. Even if that isn't quite the case here, it should give you a sense of my shame and the extremes I've been pushed to.

In the days that have passed since we saw each other, I've tried to recall the details, but shame hinders me. As I have no image of your new lover's face, the process has been a little like reconstructing the details of a mass shooting.

So I succumbed to the temptation to turn around. And in doing so, I was ensnared in a new trap I never saw coming. My hand is growing cramped and is shaking as I write this. Until that moment, I believed you were still in love with me. It was the conviction that gave me strength when I was ready to die, when I was lost during those eighteen months of separation after the cord was cut. Why did you have to do this now? One of my oldest fears—being dumped for that shinier, newer thing—has come true. I'll never be able to piece myself back together. While I was taken to the altar as a sacrifice, back home a stick of incense was already burning for someone else. What's left of the world I once believed in?

This dilemma leaves me with little recourse but to remove the box around me. It's time I shed my unworthiness, let my feelings of shame and doom die away, and purge my self-hatred. I want to meet your pure embrace. Meaning that even if you were to choose an ordinary life of marriage, I'd still come see you. Like you were family to me. Is that will to love enough? Is it enough? Life is so much more complicated than

I ever imagined, and nothing is as easy as it seems. We meet at the border of mutual attraction and repulsion, and between us is a row of thorns. The two of us (or perhaps three) have been ravaged, yet no one can walk away. Tell me, is love—along with honesty, patience, and determination—strong enough? Is it?

4

LET'S TALK for a moment about the relationship between Derek Jarman and Jean Genet.

Because this country is small and crowded, and life is monotonous, and each day filled with a never-ending stream of media, so-called Crocodile Fever had reached an all-time high. It was now the longest segment on the news, illustrating the public's appetite for information. A high-level alert had been issued in the past few days (the government agency overseeing the hunt had taken out a million-dollar bounty for the capture of the first specimen), so the crocodile had no choice but to quit its job and hide out at home for the time being, living off its savings. It thought about how it had catapulted to the top of the nation's most popular celebrities. Even the president had concluded his inauguration speech with the remark "I hope that one day all of you will love *me* the way you love crocodiles," calling on citizens everywhere to partake in the chase. The crocodile licked its lips, suppressing its secret feelings of unworthiness. It felt honored. In fact, it was seized with the urge to go on national television and tell everyone in the country: "Hey, here I am!"

In 1991, after I got my college diploma, I started reading Hemingway and Faulkner. Sensing that my gifts were yet to be realized, I hunkered down at home to pursue my dream of becoming a writer. After three months, that dream was shattered. I was kicked out of the house. I became a server at a teahouse (which, if you think about it, isn't so bad—Faulkner said the best job for a writer is to work at a brothel since you can write all day and enjoy a rich social life at night, which pretty much describes a teahouse). One evening around closing time, just as the last customer was leaving, an ad was discreetly posted on the bulletin board across the bar:

> NOTICE: Calling all crocodiles! The next gathering is at midnight on December 24th in room 100 of the Crocodile Bar. We're throwing a Christmas Eve masquerade ball....
>
> Yours truly,
The Crocodile Club

When the crocodile discovered the ad, it was so excited that it didn't sleep for days. It had never occurred to the crocodile before that there were other crocodiles, and what's more, they had already formed a club! Could that possibly mean there was a place to go and others to talk to? The thought of it made the crocodile melt a little. As it sucked on the corners of its comforter, giant teardrops welled up in its eyes.

On Christmas Eve, the crocodile showed up at midnight on the dot. At the entrance of the bar, two attendants in white tuxedos were helping the guests remove their coats. Unaccustomed to such amenities, the crocodile shrank back. The attendants asked the crocodile to write down an alias. The crocodile wrote *Jean Genet*, then whispered, "Is everyone here a crocodile?" The attendants nodded. When the crocodile saw that the name next to *Jean Genet* was *Derek Jarman*, it flushed. It wanted to crawl under the reception table and hide.

Inside, the bar was already packed. The space was enormous and the decor sumptuous. The crocodile felt as if it were home at last. *Why did everyone else's human suits fit so securely?* it thought. It had never before dawned on the crocodile that everyone else was just as shy as it was. Suddenly, it imagined a scene: On that cold winter night, everyone was huddling together for a group hug.

In the middle of the masquerade ball, the voice of someone on the sidelines came through the loudspeakers: "We'd like to give a big thank you to the Chemical Trust Corporation for supporting this tenth edition of the Crocodile Club. For nearly half a year, the corporation has been carrying out top-secret research on human suits to benefit humanity's keen and longtime interest in crocodiles. Just a few days ago, it launched a new product, the Human Suit™ 3, designed to meet the needs of those who exhibit latent crocodile tendencies. We hope that each and every one of you will upgrade your current suit for a brand-new one. Now, since this next song is an uptempo dance number and we don't want to see anyone overheat, when I yell *one, two, three!*, I want everyone to strip off their suits."

At the count of *one, two, three!*, the light switch was thrown, and the entire crowd shouted in unison: "Crocodiles!"

A split second earlier, I'd distracted the stage manager and unplugged the lighting console, then hurried back over to the crocodile, whom I dragged out the back exit, its human suit intact as we fled. Moments later, everything came to a complete halt. Panic broke out, and the crowd made a mad dash for the door. With all the neighbors having crashed the party, it created a stampede. I was the one who'd gone by the name of Jarman. From the moment the crocodile set foot in the room, I'd suspected that our guest of honor was none other than the one who'd posted the ad.

Jarman was a British film director who died young. I saw his film *The Garden* at the Golden Horse Film Festival in Taipei. Around that time, a crocodile had arranged for me to hide out in a teahouse basement. The material that crocodile provided and Jarman's cinematic techniques prompted me to write this novel. Upon receiving my degree, I had written: "Woe is me ... I was so close to being able to meet people without having to wear a human suit all the time. Why'd I have to be dragged off?" The crocodile stretched out on some cushions from the teahouse it had strewn across the wood floor. It lay on its back with its feet propped defiantly against the wall.

I waved.

"Everyone wants to get a good look at me ... at you...." Then the crocodile added reluctantly, "Don't you understand that?" Realizing that it had never before been in the company of one of its own, it stammered a little. "But how am I actually different?"

I nodded. "Regarding Genet," the crocodile began, "there was no greater luminary. Raised in a French penitentiary, he lived a dozen lives, always going in and out of prison. In the end, beloved for his artistic genius, he was granted amnesty by Saudi Arabia...."

Mounted in the corner of the room was an 8mm camera pointed at the crocodile. Keeping one eye locked on the viewfinder, I devoured a bowl of hand-pulled egg noodles topped with vegetables. The miniature crocodile in the frame was ecstatic as it delivered its soliloquy. Words streamed out of the crocodile's mouth, faster and faster, like a high-speed film projection, until the very end, when there was only the sound of the film strip flickering.... The crocodile had talked nonstop for three straight days without sleeping. Though I was dog-tired by then, I remembered its last words: "I gotta pee!"

5

AFTER the storm, a rainbow appeared. We stood together on the pier and bid farewell to our sorrows, which by then had sunk to the bottom of the sea. We'd reached the end of the road. As the renewal of desires sent us each searching elsewhere, we embraced the new-found freedom ahead, deeming the last experience a novelty and leaving its messy details in the past. Our desires guided us down a fogbound road marked by one sign after another: a triangle crossed out a circle, which concealed an arrow, which pierced a triangle. Then a right turn onto a one-way street led to a detour in unchartered territory....

I found a black leather-bound notebook pinned to the bulletin board in the Literature Department. The notebook was densely crammed with text, each page packed with the same hasty scrawl. The personal info page revealed Meng Sheng's name, address, and telephone. Seeing his name, I couldn't hold back tears, which damp-ened one of the pages. What was it about our bizarre relationship that made me so sad?

"Hey Meng Sheng, I found your black notebook. I thought I'd return it, so I took a peek inside."

"What? You wanted to see me? Careful, or you'll fall in love with me."

It'd been almost half a year since I'd last seen him. He had a flat-top haircut and was dressed in a wool suit, a cream-colored checked shirt, with a dark green silk scarf draped around his neck, hanging to his knees. He looked stately, aristocratic even. We met at an un-derground bar filled with smoke from floor to ceiling. A foreign act, a band of long-haired metalheads, was performing onstage. The bar's ambience evoked the interior of a primordial cave.

"Meng Sheng, let's not play games tonight, okay? I think—"

"Am I becoming important to you?" He raised his right hand, signaling for me to stop talking. Speaking in a low voice, he stared vacantly at the band.

He'd become mercurial. As I leaned in closer to him, one of my arms was illuminated by the lasers that shone in all directions while the other retained its natural hue. The tiny space was virtually light safe. Our surroundings, including the customers sitting at the other tables, were as hazy as a charcoal sketch. We were sealed inside the bar's gritty atmosphere as the metal band pounded away.

"Do you see that? That big table with a dozen or so guys, all decked out in those crazy costumes? And there . . . that other table with those two women with their heads down? Those people are all genderless. Or maybe I should say, they're opposed to being bound by simplistic signifiers of gender. And see those two other bald guys?" Meng Sheng pointed to the lead singer. "He's the proprietor of this place. I call him Nothing. That's the name of this place. See the scar on his face? That's from twenty-some-odd stitches. He took a fruit knife to himself when he was twenty and made a blood oath: He vowed to cut through the other self that had been handed to him by other people. It wasn't the real him. Then he traveled around the world with just a backpack and became his true self."

"Meng Sheng, I don't want to hear about that. There's something I have to talk to you about." He was sitting on a barstool, hands gripping the edge of the seat between his legs, which were twitching to the rhythm of the music. There was an emptiness in his eyes as he stood up to join the crowd, which had been worked into a frenzy and was now a collective organism throbbing violently.

The bald-headed Nothing was at center stage. Amid a wall of drumming that appeared to be an interlude, he looked over at Meng Sheng temptingly, then motioned with one finger for Meng Sheng to join him onstage. Taking his cue, Meng Sheng slipped off his jacket and leapt onto the stage. The room greeted him with a burst of applause. Then, in unison, the audience began pounding on the tabletops, stomping and shouting: *Bony. Bony—Bony. Bony.*

Meng Sheng grabbed a microphone and unleashed a rapid string of words in English. He remarked that he hadn't sung in a year and was surprised everyone remembered him. Tonight, because he'd come with a special friend, he'd be performing a special song.

The band launched into a ballad. Meng Sheng and Nothing came together in a duet, a soul number. Meng Sheng's scarf was draped across his chest, and he had a seductive glow about him. Turning to face each other, Meng Sheng and Nothing started grinding to the music. Their hips drew closer and closer, until they were almost brushing, and the audience went wild. The two men flicked their tongues at each other hypnotically. Just as the performance reached a climax, the band abruptly ended the song.

"What, you can't handle seeing this kind of thing out in the open?" Meng Sheng asked me through the door of the ladies' room. While watching their performance, I had downed both Meng Sheng's brandy and my own in one gulp. A second later, I bolted to the restroom, my stomach wrenching.

"No, it's not that I can't take it. It's just that my mind and my body are out of sync...." I struggled to get the words out between mouthfuls of vomit.

"Are you okay?" Meng Sheng lifted a hand, considering whether to open the door. "This place is lame. It's totally gone downhill. Back when I was a fixture here, Nothing and I would find girls who were willing to do it right then and there. I even took a crap in the middle of a performance once. You'd have to be nuts if it didn't make you want to puke!"

"Meng Sheng, you've known all along about my issues, haven't you?" Regaining my composure, I sat down on the toilet.

"I took one look and saw right through you." He sat down too and peered at me through the slits of the vent in the bathroom door that separated us.

"I'm screwed, just like you and Chu Kuang. I'm trapped in a destructive cycle and I can't break out of it." Saying those words aloud,

I felt, for the first time, emancipated from the strictures of humanity. I whimpered.

"Holy fucking Mother of Jesus, is that a vote in favor of God's existence!" Meng Sheng slammed his fist against the door. "We come from a long line of deviants throughout history, all with the same final destination in the celestial order: death. But not every death is a life fully realized, nor is there any guarantee you'll make it to the age of ninety. Any history that says I can't live forever is bullshit. Since I was five and as far as I can remember, really, I've hated every breath that I've ever taken. But gradually I started to understand. Do you know what I hate most? It's time. Heh. How can you defy time and space? What does heaven hold for those who do? Hey, we're the chosen ones!"

"It hasn't gotten that bad for me, Meng Sheng. There's still something inside me that's pulling me back from death. It's not just physical instinct—it's a conscious resistance.

"When I turned twenty, that's when things got tough. But it forced me to fight my way out. The universe has a plan for me...." I paused. The weight of shame had been lifted from my lips, and I had never been able to speak so openly before. For so long, there'd been a wall between me and everyone else, and now that it was gone, I felt like crying. "Meng Sheng, as long as there's a woman for me to love, I'll know I'm headed somewhere!" I stopped, and in spite of my best efforts to hold back, tears came pouring out. I couldn't find the words anymore. I was just proud to have broken out of that straitjacket, at least partway, though it made me sad to think of how long I had struggled inside of it.

"Come out. You have my undying respect. Plus I want to give you a hug." From the other side of the vent, Meng Sheng stuck his tongue out at me. "Now it's time to take a celebratory piss." There was the sound of a zipper being yanked down. He relieved himself, whirling in a circle around the lavatory, and sending a woman running out with a shriek.

"Nothing really matters. You have to burrow deep down into the marrow of death itself, beneath the thousands of layers of this mortal flesh that can be peeled away, one after another—your ancestors, your parents, your peers, all the people who are extrinsic to you. And there, buried within, are bodily memories that are at war with your spiritual being, and those memories have to be executed at gunpoint one by one, until there's nothing left except a worthless pile of tripe. That's the abyss of death—and it'll make you relish being nothing but a pile of tripe." There was conviction in Meng Sheng's voice.

"But Meng Sheng, every time I fight my way out, the outside world just blocks my path again. It never gets better. I'm constantly on the border of life and death, waiting for something to come along and push me over the edge."

"Did I tell you the story of the goddess yet?" Meng Sheng sighed. "I was secretly in love with someone you might call a goddess. This was before I met Chu Kuang and around the time I'd just given up my career as a hoodlum and gone back to school. I was in the choir, and she was the conductor. I didn't dare approach her. I knew I wasn't in her league. For a while, I was all buttoned up, and then suddenly, the seven or eight people in our circle were like family to me. When I was with them, I got to experience what it was like to feel normal. They didn't know the other side of me at all. I felt so innocent when I was with them. Whenever one of them brought out that other side of me, I'd feel disgusted with myself. That's how I ended up watching the goddess fall for this other guy, another conductor."

I closed my eyes and tried to imagine Meng Sheng's face and slicked-back hair, those dark, penetrating eyes that could be so gentle and soulful. His forehead was broad and his cheeks angular. His features were so expressive, his face so changeable. As a performer, he was blessed with versatility. I was always taken by his charisma: It was fascinating to watch him be himself. But those handsome looks also kept his despair well hidden.

"Stupid, right? It was never love. Over time, my fixation with her got worse. I never even talked to her, but the fantasy of her grew like a tumor. I looked for her nose, her eyebrows, even the silhouette of her legs, on the face of women I saw on the street. I started to have feelings for every woman. In the end, I betrayed the goddess by sleeping with just about anything that moved.

"It's funny, though. I tried to think about the goddess when I was jerking off in the shower. I tried a few times, but I couldn't do it. Every time, I just couldn't maintain an erection. If I thought about her, this person who'd never thought about me for even a second, I felt like some kind of slimy creature, slobbering all over her image, which is like...." Trailing off, Meng Sheng slid onto the floor.

"I never would've guessed that about you." Standing beside him, I held the door open for a long time. Courage swept over me, and I embraced him, wrapping his head in my arms.

NOTEBOOK #6

I

DURING the period when the crocodile lived in the teahouse basement, it displayed an impressive adaptability. For that alone, it deserved a Golden Horse Award (a Golden Horse because it was the only awards ceremony that wouldn't make the crocodile wear a human suit and take a clear-cut stance) or a darling-of-eugenics award (it would surely inspire the development of a better diaper).

Due to its highly regimented lifestyle, the crocodile didn't need an alarm clock to wake up in the morning. Though the basement got little sunlight, the crocodile woke up at six a.m. like clockwork. It wore a fresh set of brown checked pajamas belonging to the proprietress's son. The sleeves and pant legs were too short. In its hand was a stuffed crocodile it had made from a dozen handkerchiefs wound together and wrapped with one big handkerchief. Every night, the crocodile clung to its toy as it slept.

The crocodile slept in a nook it had carved out among its possessions. When it woke, it would groggily squeeze its eyes shut before scrambling for the toilet in the corner, where it then sat. It took advantage of the hazy light at daybreak to crawl up to the gutter, where it rolled over on its back. Those were the only times the crocodile got any fresh air.

The crocodile had a pre-breakfast exercise regimen: It would leap up and touch the ceiling a hundred times. Fearing the neighbors might detect the presence of a crocodile, it developed a routine that could be performed in virtually any living space. With no canned crocodile food, the crocodile found a hot pot in the pantry and used it to cook up three wildly inventive meals a day.

In the morning, the crocodile would read. It read practically anything that had letters printed on it—the labels on the goods stored in the basement, the stock lists—but what it loved most of all was *Wonders of the World* magazine. In the afternoon, it listened to a transistor radio as it worked on handicrafts. Sometimes it knit wool sweaters, other times it practiced the art of Chinese knotting, and still other times it assembled toy models. It sent me all these things, along with an invoice. Even if I didn't want them, I couldn't refuse.

At night, it watched television (on my small TV set) until ten o'clock, when it crawled back into its sleeping nook. Whenever I told it a bedtime story, it gladly tossed me a coin from its piggy bank.

"Jarman, can I write a letter to the radio station and request a song? I'm a loyal listener!"

"Sure. What name are you going to use?"

"Crocodile!"

"Oh, that won't work. Everyone will track you down for an interview. What song do you want to hear?"

"I want to request my own 'The Ballad of the Crocodile' and dedicate it to Jarman." The crocodile had a peculiar habit: It never looked at me unless it was wearing a human suit. Since it didn't usually wear one in the basement, it faced the 8mm camera whenever it wanted to talk to me. In order to see its expression, I had to look through the viewfinder until I got tired of conversing from behind a screen, a partition that had been erected at the crocodile's request.

The crocodile was a natural-born performer. It simply turned to the camera and said, "A medium of communication, eh? Well, I'll be the first to have done *this*." When I wasn't around, it turned the camera on and talked to me all the same.

"Hey crocodile, where'd you hear the name Genet?"

"Ah, a book called *Baby and Mother*. It said there was a Frenchman named Genet who was an orphan. When he was little, he was locked up in prison, so that's where he was raised. The other prisoners became like parents to him. Later on, when his biological mother came and sought him out, he refused to acknowledge her. The prison had become his home. After completing his sentence, he intentionally committed crimes just to get locked up again! Jarman, are you allowed to watch TV in prison?"

"You can, but there's no way to request songs. Crocodile, do you think you'll ever reproduce?"

"How would I know? I've never met another crocodile before."

2

Senior year was the last time I ever saw Tun Tun and Zhi Rou together. The entire club had gathered before the president's departure, and the location was my fifth-floor attic residence on Tingzhou Road. More than a dozen people were packed inside my little lair playing cards, munching, chatting, drinking, snoozing. We were a lively bunch, carrying on into the wee hours. It was the coziest winter night ever.

The whole time, I watched them at the stereo, deejaying. They were Western music fanatics, these two. They huddled together on the floor, where, under the cover of their spirited discussion of the evening's set list, they seemed to communicate with some kind of tacit understanding. I'll never forget how earnestly they introduced every song, going on and on about its contents and the genre, or sharing little anecdotes. You could hear the excitement in their voices and see a sparkle in their eyes. It was obvious that music had kindled a fierce bond between them.

They didn't mean to ignore the others. It was just that they'd found a warm and fuzzy place within that particular crowd. It was perhaps to be their final musical collaboration, and the last time they got along like they did in the old days.

People were dozing off. Tun Tun was playing a keyboard softly. They hadn't seen each other in some time, and there was a visible awkwardness. They didn't know where things stood anymore. Zhi Rou looked at Tun Tun with those intense, penetrating eyes, then turned to me. With her coat draped over her shoulders, she walked to the window and gazed at the full moon, low and yellow.

Though the years have passed, I still cherish that moment from a bygone era. Even if no one else has given it another thought, the memory is preserved inside of me. Because I was able to witness the last time that things were good between them, the picture I have of those two together heals the sorrow in my heart.

From that point on, my memories of them diverged. Whenever I ran into one of them, she would avoid bringing up the other's name. But in time, I saw that deep down inside, each still harbored a flicker of longing for the other. And so I let my separate conversations with them become entwined in my mind, so that they lived on as a pair in my heart and continued growing up together, chatting away just like old times.

Our natural affinity was profound. We'd hit it off from the start, and even after they went their separate ways, each still gave me her pure, unadulterated trust. No matter when or where, if I was alone and I ran into one of them, she would manage to drag even the teensiest worries out of me, then we'd sit together laughing and joking around. Throughout our casual friendships, I hid how much I cared about them, though their eyes reflected the utmost warmth and tenderness, and their complete sincerity indicated that I could confide in them.

I'd only divulged my secrets to Meng Sheng and Chu Kuang, and so, after my twentieth birthday, I decided that regardless of the consequences, I would bravely approach these girls: I would drop the whole façade of being a protector and tell them how I really felt. So what if my worst nightmares came true—if they spurned me, thought I was lying and didn't believe me, or stared at me coldly as I grew embarrassed and defensive, desperately fumbling for the right words. They had reached out to me and shown that I could trust them, forever changing my world. Now that I was on my way to breaking free of the prison I'd been living in, I was dying to be close to someone, and this was the same feeling that the old me had once extinguished in myself. And so I made up my mind that I would learn trust through a relationship in which lust had no part. First there had to be love and equality, so that the relationship would be built on pure trust.

A lightbulb had gone on in my head: I had to take responsibility for my state of misery. This was a major turning point, my first step in learning to open up. This elementary move may have come intuitively to others, but I had to learn how to get around in the world without the same sense of sight, and my white cane had just found that first raised dome on the pavement.

These two girls matured into beautiful, loving women, each leaving her own messy trail of complicated relationships with men along the way. Though they never saw each other again, both remembered that the first person they had ever fallen in love with was a girl. Emotions may have been pure and genuine in their salad days, but even back then, they'd known that it would never work out. In the years that followed, each started to gravitate toward men, never again exhibiting an interest in women.

One night, I ran into Zhi Rou near the underground entrance to campus.

"Hey, don't you recognize me, Lazi?" Holding a bouquet of flowers, she stood blocking my route home.

"I was wondering who that was! You change your hairstyle at least once a month. I thought, *Who's that standing in front of me, calling my name?* How am I supposed to recognize you?" I said, reeling from shock.

"Okay, enough chitchat. I'm about to run to the recreation center to deliver some flowers. It's for this guy who plays the cello." She winked at me mischievously. "Quick—give me your phone number. I'm guessing that you've moved recently."

I nodded happily, reciting the string of digits.

"You don't even have to think about it! There's an entire column of all of Lazi's numbers in my address book." Chiding me, she jotted down my number.

"What do you want my number for, anyway? You've never called me before." We stood there at the entrance as people came and went around us, like a couple bickering in public. She leaned back against the fence along the road. Since I'd last run into her, her hair was shorter and permed. Her dress, made from a coarse khaki cloth, was loosely cut and hung to her knees, and underneath she had on a pair of striped tights. Even with their flowing silhouettes, her ensembles exuded a comfy, laid-back womanliness—though it also seemed as if she didn't want to be seen as feminine.

"I really did call you before, though. Once it was early in the morning when I had nothing to do and thought of you. And one time recently, it was because my older sister was suicidal right after a breakup. I did my best to keep an eye on her the whole time, but she tried to hang herself twice. Really!" Her vulnerability was so beguiling that she instantly won me over. There was even sadness in her smile.

"Fine. I'll walk my bike and come with you to the rec center, and we can keep talking." Our encounters were always rushed, with each of us checking out the other as we caught up on those odd occasions. This girl stirred the most intense emotions in me. She was like family, and I felt like telling her that she could overcome any challenge, that I completely understood her.

The two of us had a certain rapport. There was an unspoken understanding that we would never cross over into the reality of each other's lives, and our friendship took on a profound weight because of it. Careful to limit our interactions to chance encounters, we felt free to show affection and to speak whatever was on our minds, and those moments contained the makings of a great friendship. Never knowing when or where we'd see each other again, I was moved at our every parting. It wasn't because we found relationships burdensome that we maintained this kind of distance; rather, it was a distinct reserve on her part that guarded her from needing anyone else too much. Because we often shared our most heartfelt emotions, I knew that she respected me, that I was like an older brother to her. We saw eye to eye on the important things in life, but she wouldn't get close to me out of a desire to avoid dependency.

"Lazi, what did you say about how people have to change themselves?" Zhi Rou asked me loudly. She'd dragged me inside the recreation center, where she presented her cellist friend with the bouquet, and now we sat under the portico at the entrance to the Literature Department building.

"Well, it depends on what you're trying to change, if we're talking about breast enlargement or liposuction here."

She glared at me as she searched my pockets for a cigarette, then offered me a sip of her beer. Leaning against a column, she exhaled smoke and said coolly, "Lazi, can you believe that last night I broke up with a guy who didn't understand me at all? Can you believe that I went out with this guy for a full year in the first place? Every Sunday night at eight, he'd turn on the TV, and sit there and watch *Diamond Stage*. Not that it was because of that garbage, but I couldn't stand it. He couldn't sit through anything for even an hour, except a Jackie Chan movie. He thought about only one thing: his chemistry textbook.

"He was smart. He was a fine writer with nice penmanship, and he was good at the piano. But to him these parts of himself were trivial, things he'd do once in a while just to show off. He was not only utilitarian-minded but complacent. Every second of his life was planned out, including the time he spent with me. What he really needed was a wifey. In his mind, that was love. He cared about me. He was never fickle when it came to practical things. After a long day of studying or working, he'd want me there to make love, and as soon as he satisfied himself, he'd fall asleep. I guess that part of him wasn't so developed. Ha!

"When I told him it was over, he thought I was crazy, and as usual he got his way. It dragged on for a long time, Lazi. I didn't want to be alone. I was afraid no one would want me. How desperate is that? Yesterday I saw my sister acting suicidal, and it scared the hell out of me. I wondered if I'd become like that too. I rushed to his house in the middle of the night, climbed over the fence, and took back the letter I'd written him. I cried as I burned it. It was like chopping him to pieces. I feel so much better now that I realize how much I resented him. How did I get this way?" Her voice cracked, and her laugh revealed a mix of sadness and delirium.

I shut my eyes and imagined Zhi Rou, ferocious and agile, scaling a fence. I draped my jacket over her shoulders. Swallowing her breath, she seemed to be weighing things over for a moment. In her two years at college, she'd already been with three guys. Zhi Rou was a complex woman and a gifted artist. Within music circles, she'd developed a reputation as the best female guitarist on campus, while the theater crowd was enthralled by her acting. For her, performing onstage was the opiate of university life. During her time in the spotlight, she'd grown more sophisticated and womanly, and yet she seemed to be eternally changing. No matter your sex, it was hard to resist those bewitching eyes. I couldn't help recalling what Tun Tun had said:

Lazi, Zhi Rou is such a mystery. She'll get tripped up over the stupidest little problem, but she's in her own league in every other way. The depths of her soul are unfathomable to me. She's like fire and ice at once. Back in high school, I never would've imagined that I'd ever be in a relationship with her.

Neither of us seduced the other. It just happened at the time, and we fell in love. Deep down, we both knew where things stood, that this was different from a friendship. We didn't care what it was or see anything wrong with it. Every day I'd get so excited about our next meeting. We were just kids, curious. In the beginning, there was no chemistry. I was a mediocre student. People thought I liked to have fun. She came across as quiet and hardworking, always at the top of the class. I was intimidated. I wanted to enter a biology contest, and I knew she was good at experiments. Out of nowhere, I found the courage to ask her to enter the national competition together. It was crazy of me. With the deadline fast approaching, she said yes.

Then, one day, during our experiment, the two of us were reading the scale together, and I said to her, "You have beautiful eyes. The instant I looked into them, I knew I'd been saved." I always wondered if I would ever fall in love, but after I looked into those eyes, I couldn't wait to see her again. I practically skipped the whole way to school. I'm so grateful to her for opening me up.

On the eve of the big competition, we stayed in the dorms at National Cheng Kung University, down south. We squeezed into the same bed, and both of us were really nervous at first. I was scrunched on my side. We didn't dare to brush up against each other. Finally, I couldn't take it anymore, and I asked her, "So...exactly how far away are you?" We both burst out laughing and slept peacefully after that.

The next day, sure enough, our experiment won first place. After this long struggle, we were victorious. We jumped up and down, screaming, and celebrated by uncorking a bottle of champagne that we drenched ourselves with....

Zhi Rou took a gulp of beer and puffed on her cigarette. She looked so tough that I had to chuckle. Then she grew solemn. "Lazi, there's something you once said that I've always remembered: 'Only healthy people are capable of being in love. Using love to treat an illness just makes the illness even worse.' I realize that's exactly what I did: I used love to fight illness, and it ruined me. I have to change my ways. I can't be like that anymore.

"It happens all the time. I don't think you know what I'm talking about. Guys, girls—everyone wants something from me. I don't even have to try. No matter who it is, sooner or later, I start wondering how long we'll be together. By the time things get serious, it's already over in my mind. I made up and acted out the whole thing from start to finish. It was actually my decision.

"I keep making myself fall in love so that I have someone to worry about—someone who's mine, who's real. I don't know how to live without it. I'd have no will to go on....

"Do you know what I mean? These past few years, I've been sleeping late and rushing off to class. I'm stuck in a daze all day, so then I leave, taking a stroll across Fuhe Bridge on my way home. But whenever I cross the bridge, my mind is trapped in a fog, where I never meet a single soul.

"It scares me, and I don't know where this is heading. Sometimes I imagine myself walking over the edge of the bridge and into the river. Then I snap out of it and hurry to the other end of the bridge so I can be with the special person in my life at the moment.

"If no one fills that role, I'll keep drifting in that fog.

"What problems have I ever faced in my life? There's a void I can't get away from no matter how I try: The void is inside me. Love has actually made me richer through the experience of pain. But it's not even the kind of problem that takes center stage—it's more on the sidelines.

"I have a huge existential void, and no one can make me happy. When I'm with a man, I see the beauty of a woman's soul, and I wish I were free all over again. But I can't be with a woman, either, because then I fantasize to death about men's bodies. Argh, this guy and I deserve each other—we're both demeaning ourselves!"

Zhi Rou couldn't hold her liquor very well. Her face had turned red and her breathing was heavy. One moment her face conveyed such horror that my heart ached and I was rendered speechless, and the next moment, it was lit with innocence and joy. Her eyes were tantalizing. I wasn't put off, nor could I judge her. My only fear was that she might strip off her clothes and try to seduce me. I could imagine Tun Tun whispering in my ear:

Within a few months, she'd switched over to the humanities track. We'd try to sit next to each other. Every day when I went home, I'd get some jokes ready. I learned that she was into music, and I realized that she was probably the only one in the whole class who knew much about it. In high school, she didn't listen to pop. I started listening to U2 so I could talk to her. I'd go home and translate the lyrics so I could learn them. Our breaks together were the most magical times. I'd make her laugh, then sing the songs she'd shown me. I spent afternoons staring endlessly into her eyes. . . .

Once, when everyone had gone home and we were the only ones left in the classroom, she told me she wanted to give me a haircut. The sun had just gone down, and it was only a sliver of bright orange on the horizon. So I sat there obediently and let her cut it, feeling the touch of her fingers. I can still remember how it felt. We realized at once that we both wanted the same thing. So I said, "Hold on a second." I shut the door and the windows and turned off the lights, and then after that...we shared our first kiss.

I glanced over and lifted a strand of hair from Zhi Rou's rain-soaked head. Her face was so beautiful when her hair was wet. Somberly, I told her, "Zhi Rou, there's something I've been wanting to tell you. It's something I told Tun Tun not very long ago, but I've been hiding it from you this whole time. Back when I told you I had my heart broken, that was actually about a girl. I lied to you. I'm so sorry!"

She froze for a moment, then turned to face me, regaining her sobriety. The absolute tenderness in those eyes still melts my heart whenever I think back on it. With hardly a second thought, she stroked my hair and said, "It must've been tough for you, huh? Do you feel better now that you've said it?" Unable to lift my chin, I nodded. "What is there to be sorry about? It's like leaving out the single stroke of a pen. All you have to do is change *he* to *she*, and it's the same. Besides, after all the crazy shit that Tun Tun and I have done together, it's hard for me to go around telling you what to do."

Crouching in front of me, she gazed straight into my hurt-filled eyes with a sincerity that burned into my memory. "After I switched over to humanities, Tun Tun and I fell head over heels in love and became inseparable. She was basically living at my place, a big house in Taipei I shared with two of my siblings. We were family, but with everybody doing their own thing, we acted like strangers. Tun Tun and I would sleep, play guitar, listen to music, procrastinate, bathe together.... She was with me before and after class, helping me with homework. Ten minutes after class ended, we'd huddle on the stairs. Back then, she spent all her money on me. She was talented at illustration and gave me cards she'd made herself. She was good at handicrafts and gave me a million little knickknacks she'd made. And almost every day, she gave me a rose.

"Things were still going strong between us before the entrance exams. I really loved her, but with her clinging to me, I was afraid of going insane. How do you slow things down? Then I started to realize, we were two women! I couldn't think clearly anymore. I was suffocating and needed to get away, so I didn't tell her when I ran off to the temple in Hualien. I didn't even care about the entrance exams anymore. When I closed my eyes every night in Hualien, I saw her eyes burning with passion for me, and I'd try with all my might to extinguish them.

"By the time I returned, we were already done for. I found out that Tun Tun couldn't handle being without me, and she'd already found a guy to console her. When I ran into them together, I was devastated. But we'd still talk. Every so often, we'd call each other and she'd complain to me about how two different guys were into her, and how stressful it was to have to decide between them. Then I'd tell her about my current boyfriend's big, long—"

"That's bullshit!" That ironic jab was directed at the last part. It was my way of affectionately teasing her. My eyes welled over as I listened.

It was beginning to pour now. Zhi Rou and I joked around for a while, shielding ourselves from the rain with my leather jacket. Roaring with laughter, we sang in unison at the top of our lungs, and the sound carried into the dark, wet night. We stumbled arm in arm as we left campus. I took her home on my bike, crossing Fuhe Bridge along the way. Muttering nonsense, she lifted her face to the soaking rain.

After everything, when we got to the door, she came on to me. "Can I give you a kiss?" Her feelings seemed awfully genuine.

"The privilege is mine," I told her.

3

THERE are some sorrows so great they are unspeakable, taking hold in the body and leaving a void after the fact. There are some depths that love can never again reach. The mind anoints every fossil with significance in an attempt to preserve it—but in time, they all invariably turn to dust.

Man's greatest sorrow is the loss of what was once his greatest desire.

When Shui Ling and I saw each other again in 1989, she was histrionic. I'd become a menace that might gobble her alive, hack her to pieces, or otherwise mangle her if I came anywhere near her. Her body was apparently ready to convulse and cry out "No!" as it threw off my hands and dodged my stare. I could tell she was repulsed by the thought of me. In order to deter the risk of my encroachment, she spared no harsh words, criticizing my every word and deed, and attacking without warning, without cause. But she saved the final blow for her own feelings toward me. Beset with a disease in which I was the toxin, she turned hostile.

She was afraid that I'd leave again, that those wasted years would be like a bridge rebuilt, only to collapse a second time. Neither of us had been willing to face the fact of how little weight was required to trigger that collapse.

She had tied me up with wire and left me to die. But when all was said and done, she wanted me to die in her arms. So before entering my dreams every night, she yanked the wire tight to make sure I was still there. Vowing never to let me go again, she made me promise over and over that no matter how bad things became, I would never abandon her.

Yet I was not allowed to see her, nor was I allowed to be a part of her life. My loitering outside the lecture hall was met with reproach. Any trace of me in her everyday life was perceived as a threat. There was a murky chamber reserved for me in her soul, where I waited and waited, for all of eternity. . . .

Late at night, her hands would dial my number. She didn't know whether I was home or not, whether she was having a conversation with me in reality or in her imagination. Her willpower had begun to wane. She claimed to be sleepwalking, and so we were back in touch.

She'd regressed. Lying in bed in her white pajamas, she lifted the receiver like a woman possessed. Alternately cheerful and petulant, she wasn't aware of having betrayed her own neediness. To her, things were the way they used to be when it was just the two of us. She had convinced herself of this—as if no one had been hurt in our breakup, as if she hadn't started a new life, as if she weren't conflicted, as if she hadn't found someone new. The calls went on into the early hours of the morning.

So I asked her why she resisted me, why she was afraid of me. I asked her to make a choice. I wanted to know whether she still loved me. I told her not to repress her desires. Choking back tears, she nearly had a breakdown. Dejected, she told me she couldn't look at me. She couldn't see us together. She hated that I thought she didn't love me. She didn't want me to know her reasons, God forbid I run off again. . . .

She'd always had a mad streak, but in her hour of weakness, it became an affliction. She was unable to sleep. She couldn't wash her hands clean.

And I was powerless. I tried to remain level-headed about her state. But I couldn't be near her. She was volatile. Driven by psychosis, she had come back to haunt me, and I awaited the worst. Our sadomasochistic dynamic had given rise to a host of new miseries, and I eagerly took a swig of love's poison.

4

NOVEMBER. The harshest part of winter. It was our last happy memory, like a condemned man's final shot of whiskey.

She agreed to see me just once, saying we should go to a bar and get smashed together. We were at the front entrance when she bolted. I trailed her faint silhouette down Heping East Road. Then, out of nowhere, she turned to face me. In a flash of brilliance, she proposed that we write the final chapter of our history at National Tsing Hua University.

We decided to camp out by the pond on campus. At the dormitory, I finally met her best friend, Zi Ming, who had been at her side through the trials and tribulations of the past few years. Zi Ming was earnest and forthright. I immediately felt as if I'd known her forever and was grateful that this person existed. I could sense the strong familial affection between them, and it comforted me.

Viewed from the hillside, the water's surface glistened. Next to the clear pond was the new physics building. There were no signs of human life anywhere. The scent of dew-kissed grass, pure and fresh, filled the mountain air.

The natural beauty cleansed our spirits, and our troubles back in the city faded away. We were open with each other. It was then that the warmer, simpler Shui Ling of the old days emerged like a dainty white bud, untouched on the mountainside—if a bit puerile and wild. Tears of longing came to our eyes, and she opened her arms to me.

I buttoned her up in a snug-fitting coat and spread out layers of clothing to serve as makeshift blankets. I tucked her in. Her arms were wrapped around my neck as she said to me, You know, we might die together like this....

5

"TONIGHT I went to a salon near my house and had my long hair chopped off."

"What did you do that for?"

"I just felt like it. But let me tell you a secret: I'm sick of myself. Heh heh. It's not like you two love my long hair and I'm disappointing you . . . right? Short hair looks sharp. It makes me look capable and efficient . . . career-oriented (ha ha). I just don't want you guys to think I'm some fragile 'hothouse flower.' Yeah. . . . Even my friends are mad and saying that I ruined it. None of them like you."

"So what did *she* say about you chopping off all your hair?"

"She was upset. We fought for a while. She cares about little things like this. She said she's told me a million times, but I still do this . . . or I shouldn't do that. What about you? What do you think?"

"I'm kind of sad, but if you want to cut it, cut it. I remember when you had short hair in high school and you looked good. Like a little sailor. It's been so long since we last saw each other. I can't believe I'll never see you with long hair again."

"Ha! I was just messing with you. I still have my long hair."

The whistling sound of the ocean air in Penghu. Waves pounded against the shore, washing everything away. I'd burned myself and then fled to Penghu, where I sat in total isolation all night on the embankment, hearing all kinds of noises.

My first phone call that evening was to Shui Ling's friends' place. They said, She's drunk, she's been bawling and flipping out because of you. A crying mess. They had to stay away from her. They said it was impossible to talk to her. She was in a stupor. Shui Ling, I'm calling from the phone booth behind the seawall. I'm right by the water....

"Last night I had a dream, but it was a bad dream. I don't want to tell you. Okay, if you help me write my final paper, I'll tell you....

"I dreamed there was a black dog approaching my house. I was scared, really scared, so I hurried to lock the doors and shut the windows. I pushed a bookshelf up against the front door and I heard the dog scratching against it. I was terrified, so I ran to my bed and threw back the covers—and oh my god, there it was, the black dog, with its shiny black fur and huge eyes. I screamed....

"I also wanted to tell you that I saw *Hans the Hedgehog and the Princess of Sweetness and Cherry Pie* on public television. After the prince and princess marry, they live in a castle in the woods. But every night as the princess sleeps, the prince leaves the castle. He doesn't come back until dawn. He tells her that he goes hunting. So the queen tells the princess to hide the prince's coat. The next day, waking early, the princess discovers she's been asleep in the woods. There's a hedgehog by her side. The castle is nowhere to be seen, and the prince has turned into the hedgehog. Because he doesn't want the princess to find out that he becomes a hedgehog at night, he runs off into the woods and never returns.

"The princess is determined to track down the prince. Even if he never changes back into a human, she still wants to spend the rest of her life with him, so she roams the country for ten years searching for him. Then one day, in a run-down shack, she finds a hedgehog. She leans over and kisses the hedgehog, and the hedgehog changes back into the prince. Then the prince and the princess live happily ever after...."

"That's not how it goes. Haruki Murakami says that in the end, the king and the imperial guards all burst out laughing."

The murky seawater seemed bottomless. Two motorcycles veered down the paved slope. Four members of a gang had pulled up beside me, only three feet away. The roar of their bikes already fearsome enough, I turned pale. They swung around and left.

Why didn't you tell me you were running off?

Shui Ling, I have burns in two places. They were blistering, so the doctor scraped them off....

You burned yourself, didn't you....

It's so cool and lovely in Penghu....

You went too far.

Sobbing. The ocean was weeping, too. Our love was still mutual.

"Tell me how you think I'm different from her."

"You're better-looking. She's a little heavier, heh. But I feel comfortable with her. I like it when she touches me. It's like we're just having a little fun....

"I'm scared of you. If you did that, I'd be completely disgusted by you.

"Oh, come on. We don't have to talk about it if you don't want to. I was worried you'd be like this. I don't know why I have to take jabs at you, either. I'm afraid of stabbing you into a pulp, until there's no more blood left. I could stab you to death and not even know it."

"So you have to take jabs at me to make yourself feel better?"

"I'm afraid I'll open the door and let you in. But I know you're sleeping outside, and I can't bear the thought of not letting you in, so I tell myself to open the door so I can prod you with a long, sharp object."

"I don't care. I can't tell you not to be with someone else, so of course I have to say that I don't care. There's really nothing I can do."

"I know."

"You're into someone else. You're not into me."

"I'm not into you, silly. I love you."

Out at sea, the cobalt blue lights of a distant patrol boat were flashing. Water under the bridge, as they say. There was a growing cacophony inside my head.

"I feel so close to you right now because of our past together. But you're acting strange and distant toward me," Shui Ling said.

Blow after blow. She was messing with my head. Spare me, Shui Ling. It's killing me. How am I supposed to keep from falling apart?

So I burned myself. I burned me, and I burned her, and I burned the life I hated so much. I could see the glow of warmth from a nearby log cabin.

"I feel bad for you." She caressed my wounds. Her embrace was a farewell song—long, agonizing, and tearless.

6

OVER THE next two months, it happened again . . . and again.

I came back from Penghu, my strength already sapped by the grisly battle between two wounded, dying beasts incapable of licking each other's wounds.

There was no doubt that Shui Ling was avoiding me. It wasn't because she didn't love me. It wasn't because she needed space. It was because she feared that she'd smelled blood on me. She'd been deluding herself, saying our love hadn't turned into a hunk of maggot-infested flesh when really she'd been living life to the fullest, taking this hunk of flesh that was me and kicking it out of the field of vision of her reality. She'd moved on to the next relationship, and with greater exuberance. No phone calls, not a word from her, while I wrote her letter after letter. Though I knew my love song's days were numbered, I was determined to keep singing until my voice gave out. I was intent on starving myself while I saved my rations for her.

Stupidly, so stupidly, I assumed that she no longer felt a thing for me, that she refused to crumble, that there was nothing more to it. Clinging to the belief that we'd always be together in her heart, she began to rationalize her course of action.

Underlying that rationale were hysterical tendencies. I waited as Christmas Day passed. I waited as the New Year passed. She acted even more detached, declining my requests to meet until the chill of her indifference froze me to the core. She was entirely unconscious of it, and there was nothing I could do.

"Sorry for bothering you this late. I just wanted to give you this journal in person. Like I said before, if you don't want me, I'll give you my journal and go.

"This journal from freshman year is the only thing I can give you. I'm not your everything anymore, so even though I want to love you now, all I can do is give you the old me, the one you once loved." I was in her room, kneeling at her bedside. I hadn't slept for days, and my voice was small and quivering. It was the day after New Year's.

"I don't want it. I don't want it." There was a stunned look on her face at first. Lying in bed, she shook her head vehemently, as if unable to endure this unexpected shock. She twisted around to face the other way. Her voice was hoarse. She didn't dare peer at me clutching my diary against my chest.

"I thought maybe the answer was in your heart this whole time, and you just couldn't bring yourself to say it out loud. You've been silent toward me, and all this waiting has taken its toll on me. You left me hanging with a question in my heart. Whether or not you admit it, the answer is no, right?" I was indignant.

"Okay, okay, you're right! You're completely right. I've left you hanging!" Rolling over, she glared at me. Her eyes glinted angrily. Tears ran down her face, forming two jagged streams. "Why don't you understand me at all anymore?"

"I understand, all right. I understand that because you loved me too much, you've completely changed who you are. I understand that even if I started beating you to death, you wouldn't tell me to go. If the facts were laid out, you'd still run. You can barely make it through the day. I understand all too well that you're scared of me. Tell me it's not true."

She grudgingly nodded.

"Because things were getting worse, you cut me off. Three people have had to suffer, and one of us can't take it anymore. I don't want to keep injuring myself, so now I have to make you reject me." I spoke as if I were the one holding all the cards, but in reality, I was the vulnerable one, the one who was begging for mercy.

"Fine, I will. I've realized some things during this time, and it's because you made me. But I had to refrain from saying too much. I was dying to talk to you, but I was always afraid that the slightest peep could make you run away. So I had to think long and hard about how to make sure you'd understand completely." An expression wholly unfamiliar to me—one of rigid determination—spread across her face.

"After you came back, I thought I was treating you really, really badly, and at the same time, I didn't know what I was doing. I took the love that I should have given to you and turned around and gave it to someone else. I opened my heart to other people, and meanwhile, I mistreated you. It was like I was debasing myself...." She began to bawl.

"You don't know it, but I have"—she paused, summoning her courage—"I have a lot of love for you! But not this you—the you from freshman year. I don't know the exact difference, either. Sometimes I just know my love is for you, and that's when I want to run back to you and give it all to you now. I want to love you well. But we've already become distant strangers. What else am I supposed to do? I have to rely on old memories in order to get along with the new you. I can't even tell you how much you've changed."

Hunched over the covers, I choked back sobs.

"Why did you have to come back? I'd already found the perfect spot for you in my heart. Why did you have to ruin it? All I wanted was a way to love you for the rest of my life!" Now that she was agitated, I knew the theatrics were under way.

"I *have to* jab you. I don't want to be close to you because you'll taint the memory in my heart...." Her stare, brimming with hatred, said that she no longer knew me. "I won't let you. No one can. It's mine alone. You abandoned me and left me out in the cold. All I have left now is the you that I created, and it's the best you there is...."

She let out a condescending laugh, as if to say a prayer for me out of pity. "I beseech you not to shatter it." She sounded histrionic.

She'd shared emotions I had no idea about—so profoundly and lucidly, so poignantly, so beguilingly even! This woman was like a nautilus in her intricacies. She'd been harboring her love for me like an oyster cultivating a pearl. Yet none of that pleasure was to be mine. What was I supposed to say?

"How would I taint it?" I asked timidly, my heart sinking.

"I don't want to see you. The two of us have to stay pure. We have to." With her patronizing tone, she took a subtle swipe at my pride and sliced off a piece of my heart.

"Don't be sad! I'll always have your purity. I thought you left because that wasn't what you wanted. Zi Ming said the only reason that someone dear to you leaves you is because they love you and you'll always love them. That's how it works. A long time ago, I decided I would always love you. My love is that deep. It's funny, because I completely changed who I was in order to be more like you. You left your mark on me. Did you know that?

"But then you came back. You faced the issue of *sex* and didn't want a platonic relationship anymore. You weren't always like that, but not me. I just didn't want to shatter the image of you that I hold dear in my heart. Then I'd really be left with nothing, and I'd hate you!" Her eyes, her expression, her voice all conveyed a rather tender form of cruelty. At last, I was meeting her destructive side head-on.

"I've grown up a lot. I'm not a little girl anymore. I'm talking about sex here! I was never against the idea of doing it. Anyway, she's really pretty. When I'm with other people, a physical relationship just happens naturally. But it wasn't like that with you. It wasn't because you're a girl. It wasn't because of sex itself. And it wasn't because I didn't long to be intimate with you. It was you. . . ." Her eyes hardened. This conversation may well have been her most audacious moment.

"We shouldn't talk about this anymore. There's no way I can make you understand. You don't know how badly I've been wanting to talk to you." This was the final act in my humiliation, and it had unfolded to my surprise. It was like the removal of a parasite that had been lodged in my flesh. Though the experience would make me infinitely stronger, I also had to cry out in pain.

"I know I treated you mean. But you were so intense. Don't you know that? You turned my world upside down. I'm where I am now because you led me here. All of this is your doing. How could you have abandoned me and left me out in the cold?" She was holding me. Consoling me.

"It's not that I didn't want to mend things with you. When you and I were together, I told her three times that I didn't want to see her. If you hadn't been so afraid of commitment, and if you'd prom-ised not to leave me, you and I would have been together for the rest of our lives!" She wiped away my tears, and with the piousness of a devotee, she planted kisses on my eyes.

"I love her too, and she treats me well. It's a totally new relation-ship where I can practice the things you taught me. She's always there for me. There's no reason for me to hurt her. But that's not what this is about. It's about you. There's no way I can imagine spending my life with you. You need to go out and find that person in life who's going to love you!"

The grief that had been long dormant in her now awakened, her crying descended into wailing. I could feel the pain she'd been going through.

"I can't find that person. I can't find that person you're talking about who's going to love me. I only have you."

"You can. I know you can. You're wonderful...."

Her voice softened. Her eyes were red and swollen, and she was exhausted from crying. She wanted to listen to me talk as she lay there. I told her I was going to Europe, that I'd be her shelter, wait-ing for her, and when that time came, she could bring her children with her, since she always wanted to have a child of every color in the rainbow, a perfect, happy family.... She fell asleep with a sweet, in-nocent smile on her face. Every now and then, half asleep, she'd take my hand, and make me tell her that I wasn't going anywhere.

It was the last time I saw her. Her long, soft locks spread under-neath the covers, her pale blue kimono pajamas, her slender, well-proportioned figure, her mildly weathered skin, her distinctive light scent, her beautiful tear-stained face, those two piercing eyes that were now shut, and those hands that couldn't bear to part with my journal. Happy New Year.

Those were the things I took. I gently turned the doorknob and closed the door behind me. Stepping into the light of dawn, I left once and for all. Realizing I'd forgotten my glasses, I walked the streets like a blind man early that morning, trying to feel my way back. I wanted to go home. Home....

NOTEBOOK #7

I

THERE are many important images in my mind that were captured at strange twists and turns, during the passage from one stage to the next, accumulating a weight I never expected. But I never did say goodbye or thank you to all the people in those images. With a stiff upper lip, I stood back and watched as they slipped out of my life.

2

THERE are three people I have to write about in this journal. These three are from my final year in college—a stage of my life I call the eruptive phase—and all of them profoundly shaped who I am today. Each had distinguishing qualities that influenced my life's direction, and I saw in each of them a certain majesty. During that time of intense bonding, it was their influence which made me realize that romantic love was not the only thing that brought an individual closer to others, nor was it a matter decided by fate. There are other, essential experiences that ought to come first, for one must be capable of being touched, of embodying the innocence that forms the basis of compassion ... and of showing a heart that cries out in pain that genuine suffering deserves no less than the dignity to go on living.

Meng Sheng. Half born of malice, half of goodwill. Half sincere, half put-on. This freewheeling lunatic became a close friend of mine after Shui Ling and I went our separate ways for the second time. To this day, I've never understood what his true motive was—because while he saved me from my self-destructiveness, he also pushed me toward total depravity.

I was determined to transform myself into a real girl. At Tun Tun's encouragement, I made a big decision: I wasn't going to fall in love with another woman. This time, I was going to make a clean break with the past and pursue a normal happiness.

For my entire life, I had been inherently attracted to women. That desire, regardless of whether it was realized, had long tormented me. Desire and torment were two opposing forces constantly chafing me, inside and out. I knew full well that my change of diet was futile. I was a prisoner of my own nature, and one with no recourse. This time, however, I was determined to liberate myself. Convinced that it was possible to change, I went about it all rather nonchalantly, and during that phase, I basically behaved as if I had sold my soul. I felt no personal attachment to anyone. Nothing fazed me. Once I shed the overwhelming burden of my sadness, I felt as light as a feather. In my mind, I had been given a mandate: I would live as I pleased and let myself do whatever I wanted.

And so I became dissolute. In my total hedonism, I explored all possibilities, however transitory. I went out every night and hung out at restaurants, clubs, bars, a new friend's place. At the same time, I invited the advances of men, resorting to the most blatant and dubious means to lure them.

Meng Sheng was among my partners. My feminine clothing, speech, manners, and hair tossing were plainly intended to attract a man, and he was perceptive enough to notice my transformation. Yet he didn't ask questions, and instead he adopted a chivalrous attitude toward me. Every few days he'd see me, and I'd be waiting for him, as if we were dating. In my heart I was hoping I'd find a guy to fall for soon, yet Meng Sheng treated it like a big joke, like we both knew it was a charade. Only much later, when I recalled the look in his eyes and the words he said, did I realize that no matter what his real motive was, he had tried to love me.

"Hey, if you don't meet the right guy, you can always call me up," Meng Sheng said. He dragged me to campus on my birthday, saying that in honor of the occasion, he'd take me out for a celebratory round of drinks.

"Meng Sheng, do you think I'm changing in order to find a man?" It was the first and only time in four years that I'd spent my birthday with someone. In fact, when Meng Sheng suggested it, I felt grateful.

"I don't buy any of it. You people are ridiculous, wasting your energy trying to improve yourselves. What good does it do? You all think I don't try hard enough, and that's why I'm such a failure. But what do you know? In order to save my own life, I had to muster a hundred times the strength that any of you have. Hell, I can't even exert myself anymore! Do you know how psychology defines 'help-lessness'? I like you the way you are right now, being like, *Who cares?* and seeing how bad it gets. The best is when things get so bad that I actually feel something. That's when I reach self-understanding," Meng Sheng said, laughing. He'd written me a song as a birthday present.

"Seriously, though, don't die before me. If you did, I'd be even more bored than I already am. You have to go on living for me." He solemnly placed his hand on my shoulder, his emotions genuine, and we bonded in a profound moment of mutual understanding. Then, he added, "Really, you should let me make love to you just once. It'll be your birthday present."

"Okay!" I merrily agreed. In that instant, we abandoned all inhi-bitions and sentimentality, yet it was anything but an act of de-bauchery. He wanted to give me a gift that was hard to come by, pure and simple—and what I got was the experience of absolute trust.

A campus patrol car passed. We lay naked, hidden in a patch of tall grass, and the entire time I felt wild and free, not self-conscious in the least. Suddenly Meng Sheng let out a howl.

"You have to stop hurting yourself! You're not okay at all!" He practically exploded. For the first time, I realized that he was in pain, that my tragedy had become his own.

With that revelation, a hole was blown through the earth's crust. That reckless lunatic felt sorry for me, and I truly loved him. Numb to my own feelings, I never saw it coming. Faraway sounds drifted toward us. The charade was over. It was no use.

3

Tun Tun. She was the first person I went to whenever I needed help. If I learned anything about life during college, it was to turn away from my shattered ego and move on, and I owed it all to her.

"Tun Tun, is it okay if I come over to your place? Shui Ling and I had another falling out, and I feel vulnerable right now. I don't want to be home alone!" My cry for help came at eleven p.m.

"Sure, hurry up! I'll be waiting!" The sound of concern on her end came through the line.

On the taxi ride over to her place, all kinds of memories drifted through my mind. My bond with Tun Tun was a safety rope whose resilience had been proven every time she'd been there for me over the past year. The countless late-night talks. The countless times I'd been feeling down. I remembered the warmth of her room, and the sound of her voice and her laughter. She'd been by my side at so many crucial moments.

I'd been burning myself before I left for Penghu. Tun Tun unexpectedly rang my doorbell as I was frantically packing my bags. As always, she listened intently while I opened up about my feelings and experiences. With her sagacity, she tried to guide me away from despair toward broader horizons, toward hope. She'd come over to tell me that she was taking a leave of absence from school to cure her insomnia. In spite of her own troubles, her innate humor, optimism, and wit were there to pull me through.

She accompanied me to Songshan Airport and told me to come back to Taipei in one piece. I passed through the ticket gate, then turned to look at her. Her face betrayed her heartfelt worry. She was the one person I could let into my sanctum, and there she stood, urging me to cross over into her reality as she waved goodbye. Shui Ling, Meng Sheng, Chu Kuang, Zhi Rou—everyone else was a mirage. They were on the same side as I was, while Tun Tun was on the other.

"Tun Tun, I've been lost all these years. How come it never gets better for me? No matter how hard I try to improve my life, everything falls apart. There's a saying: 'By the time a man celebrates his creation, it has already half turned to dust.' I always end up back at square one. This is a hateful, dog-eat-dog world."

"You must be tired. Why don't you lie down and rest for a while? When you wake up tomorrow, the world will be different." Tun Tun's room was downstairs, and the rest of her family had already gone to bed. She tiptoed out to pour me a glass of milk and slice some fruit.

"Are you going to move again?" she asked me.

"Yeah, I'm going to look at places tomorrow. I really need to do it tomorrow. If I keep living there, I'll go insane. All I can think about is whether she'll call or write or knock on my door. I've had enough. I have to get a grip. I keep checking my mailbox and picking up the phone. It's the only way I can make myself stop!"

"You should make me your real estate broker. Every few months, when you move out of a place, I can bring in a new tenant and collect a commission."

"Why don't you rent me out, too? On the ad you can write: Special lady to keep you company at night. Available Sundays."

"That won't work because you won't use protection," she said, grinning. "You'd better memorize your current phone number tonight. Last time you had to get in touch with your old landlord about your deposit, you asked me what your old number was, and it was only the day after you moved!"

"How's your insomnia? Are you up all night working on handicrafts? Or chopping asparagus? Peeling oranges? Mending fishnets—"

"Right, and embroidering satchels," she finished. "Taking a leave of absence was the right move. I keep a strict regimen. I get ready for bed around eleven, and before I go to sleep, I do yoga. When I lie down, if I feel lonely or sad, I'll recite the Great Compassion Mantra. My mother taught it to me. Then my mind winds down, and soon enough, I'm asleep. My dreams are weird and funny. I take yoga classes by the teachers' college on Mondays, Wednesdays, and Fridays. Yoga is awesome. I have to keep working my way up until I become a guru."

"How is yoga different from Buddhist practices?"

"Yoga is liberal. It's not anti-sex. Sex is actually a technique in yoga! The anti-sex aspect of Buddhism is just a slant that was adopted later on. The Buddha was never anti-sex. Oh, it's so great, Lazi. I want to do yoga with A and set up a learning center with experts who can teach people how to achieve orgasm. A true orgasm is like being at one with the cosmos."

"Nice! You're going to be on TV one of these days. What about zoology, then?"

"Ugh, that's a headache. Science is fun all right, but it's also boring. You spend all your time reading incredibly dry material. I remember you said it was like moving bricks. Science is about plowing through it all until you reach the one interesting point. How is biology going to help us to understand man's nature? But because I got in through the recommendation system, the department chair loves me to death. The other day I went to the office to talk about my return, and we had a talk about my insomnia. He turned into a bodhisattva. He had such compassion in his eyes, like he was afraid I would start crying at any moment. He was so fatherly toward me. Lazi, I could have seduced him in a second. He totally likes me," she said excitedly.

"That's great. Seducing the department chair sounds like a blast! Just don't get pregnant," I said with mock seriousness.

"Don't worry, I know of sixteen different types of contraception. I even taught my mother a few!" she said proudly. "Lazi, we don't need to study. Why don't we start a business instead? My dad bought me a Singer sewing machine. I've been sitting at it every day. I love sewing things. It builds character. I made a purse for myself and a pencil case for a student that I tutor—"

"No kidding. Sewing builds character?" I didn't know how to respond.

"Look. Aren't these pajamas nice? Lazi, I can make some sexy sleepwear for you, how about it?" Tun Tun gestured toward the white silk pajamas she was wearing. They were well made, thin, and form-fitting. On her slender figure, they looked refined and elegant. Suffice it to say that Tun Tun had turned living into an art form.

"Forget it. They're too tight. My legs would look like pork hocks!"

"Suit yourself. Last week I had a dream where Zhi Rou and I were sitting in a classroom for military training. You were dressed in a green tailcoat, and you entered our classroom and motioned for me to come out. You said, 'Hello, tailcoat here! Let me give you this book as a gift.'"

"See? Your dreams understand me. They even dressed me in a tailcoat!" I teased her.

"So what do you say? I can sew some things on the machine or by hand, and you can sell them. We can be creative entrepreneurs. Hey, I never told you this before, but a fortune-teller told me that the DIY route would be my road to riches. I just read in the paper about a cosmetics company that's holding an open call to offer training to the next generation of makeup artists. Part of me got really excited and wanted to sign up. God, why did I hold back all these years, when I've been free to do things that are fun?"

"Working is nice for a while, but in the long run, it turns you into a pile of shit-covered garbage. I'm sure whatever we do will be a success, as long as you're involved."

"Yay! I feel the same way. Together we can achieve anything."

It was almost one in the morning. We were both starving. Her family's house was near the night market. We headed out for a bite to eat, walking side by side, cutting through the dingy, desolate back alleys of the market's scattered stalls.

"I remember back in high school, we were a bunch of misfits, always having fun. There was something going on every day. We were part of a community. Now life's all about being tied down by a man. Falling in love is all there is to do, and there's no going back. It's all Zhi Rou's fault. She dragged me over to the other side, and ever since, there's been a constant stream of people coming over...."

"Doesn't sound too cozy. Tun Tun, what's going on with the guys in your life?"

"With guys?" Her voice squeaked as she glanced at me. "Not much. There's maybe three or four, but it's mainly still A."

"The rest are just there for reference?"

"What am I supposed to do if they come to me? It's like Luo Chih Cheng's poem: 'I never knew so many stars secretly adored me.'" She couldn't resist a wisecrack.

"I'm so proud to call you my little sister. You're up there with the Li Tang Hua Stunt Team. You can flip a man with your bare hands as you head-butt another."

"And with a kick of my leg, I can spin around a skinny one." She struck a pose to demonstrate. "Ah, it's an age-old problem. Lazi, if I could take A's brains, B's money and apartment, C's upper body, and D's lower body, and put them all together, I wouldn't be at the supermarket picking out fruit."

"Someday you'll find someone who's the total package. Right now you're sowing your oats, and that's not a bad thing. Life is a process of awakening by degrees, in depth and in scope. At its most profound moments, you experience wholeness. That's what this one philosopher wrote," I said, comforting her.

"When I celebrate my twentieth birthday, there's one thing I really want to do—go swimming in Drunken Moon Lake!" she said.

Back in her bedroom, I started to feel lonely again. Tun Tun said she wanted to play guitar and sing for me. Tun Tun, her guitar, and her singing. I never knew what beautiful memories those three elements could evoke....

The first image that comes to mind is the time Zhi Rou and Tun Tun sang and played music together in the rain. To me, it's the most evocative memory, the very definition of bliss. It's followed by the first time Zhi Rou and Tun Tun performed as a band. I presented them with a bouquet of flowers, hardly able to contain myself. The show was at seven p.m. in the courtyard in front of the cafeteria. There was no elevated stage, just an audience of students gathered around them, their anticipation building. Tun Tun had a shirt tied around her waist. In her slim-fitting jeans and tank top, she had the fierce air of an avant-gardist. She was the lead singer, leaning over a keyboard as her high-pitched vocals brought a song with English lyrics to a howling climax. I was exhilarated. Only then did I understand the core of my friendship with Tun Tun—that maybe I wanted to be just like her, that maybe she was my favorite person in the whole entire world. . . .

"Tun Tun, I want Shui Ling. . . ." My mood sank.

"And I want Zhi Rou. . . ." She sounded childlike.

"Tun Tun, will you play that song 'Cherry Came Too' for me?"

"I can't play that song, I can't stand it! Me and Zhi Rou's favorite band used to be the Smiths. They're these five guys. The lead singer and the guitarist act like a couple, where the guitarist is the father and the lead singer is the mother. Their lyrics are ironic, like 'I'd like to smash every tooth in your head.' There's one that goes, 'Manchester, so much to answer for' in this callous, unfeeling tone. They grew up there, and it made them who they are. In another song he's walking on the beach and he meets this girl who only wants to hook up with him, and he sings, 'But she's too rough and I'm too delicate.' *She*'s the one who's rough, and *he*'s the one who's delicate. . . ." She hummed it for me, beaming.

"Tun Tun, how could you possibly not go after her?" I mustered the courage to ask that taboo question.

"Don't even start. How am I supposed to approach her? Lazi, in the past two years, I've become a woman. Nothing's the same anymore. I'm not pure anymore. I can't face her now. I just want our sweetest memories to stay in the past. That was probably the one time when it was totally pure. She's the only one who made me live fearlessly. . . ." Her voice grew weak. I patted her.

"Lazi, I have complete confidence that you'll get through this rough patch. Human beings are endowed with both yin and yang.

When you become too dependent on one, the other becomes inhibited. You have to let both sides develop fully. That way, you'll have the ability to love anyone, as long as you harness your yin and cultivate more yang when you need it. You give up too easily. With a change of perspective, will things still be the same? You need to develop your feminine side!"

"I wish I could fall in love with a man, but there are too many beautiful women."

"You can ride an ox all the way to Beijing, but it's still no horse, right? Women are beautiful and mysterious, aren't they?" She clicked her tongue. The two of us sounded like such pigs whenever we indulged in talk about women. Once we got started, neither of us could stop the buffoonery.

"Tun Tun, I'm hungry." Shamelessly, I turned to her.

"I bet you are. I have to conduct photosynthesis just to feed you," she said teasingly.

"I'll have to write a story called 'My Sis: The Plant Who Nurtured Me.'" We were cracking up.

That night, she let me sleep in her bed while she slept on the floor. Her comforter was soft. I'd never felt so safe in my entire life. On that occasion, I avoided revealing to her the true depths of my pain. Though it was killing me, I kept my heartbreak hidden. My will was broken, and I felt drained. There are times when affection between family members is so deep that emotional burdens become too much to share. When the boundaries are nearly nonexistent, who has the heart to impinge on the other?

All I could do was lie there beside her and go to sleep. Things were looking up for me as it was. I had to get up early the next day. There was an apartment hunt for me to get excited about.

4

XIAO FAN. This woman, five years older than me, came into my life and took me to an even more desolate place than Shui Ling had, tearing my youth apart before suturing it back into one piece. From that point on, I had a face that was whole again, a face covered in stitches. While she managed to reconstruct my entire visage, I can only describe a few fragments of her. Yet those fragments add up to an important chapter. And there, where the stitches were, the pain still remained, lacerating my flesh....

"Yeah, when I was sixteen, I was tricked into leaving home. My mom took me to the bus stop. Some friends and I had to take the Zhongxing Line to Taipei for high school. My mom stood in the ticket line, smiling and waving. The bus started to pull away, and my mom was caught in the crowd. Her eyes flooded with tears as she was pushed to the front of the line. She was crying helplessly. At the time, I didn't realize what was going on. I just felt bad for her. Only years later did I finally understand."

I can still recall the first time we met. We were volunteering at the same organization. In the evenings, between shifts, we'd all get bento boxes and eat together. I'd developed a reputation as something of a ham, so I had to inject a little melodrama into my story. One of my female colleagues sat in a far-off corner, eating in silence. She listened attentively, smiling at us. Once in a while she'd chime in, and when she did, it was always with something witty that made everyone laugh. Suddenly, she turned to me and said, "*Tricked* is the word for it, all right. I was about that age when I left home, and I've been in Taipei for ten years now. I used to go back to Taoyuan every time I had a long break. Home was where this squabbling old couple lived, and I was obligated to watch TV with them every so often. That's all there was to it! In fact, after being tricked into leaving, I eventually stopped going back."

And with those words, we had officially met. I sensed she was much older than me but on the same wavelength. She knew what I was talking about. I started to feel intimidated.

"Is your blood type A?" I unwittingly engaged in small talk.

"Do I look like I am? No one ever guesses I'm type A based on first impressions. What makes you think so?" I'd taken the initiative, yet there were no signs of awkwardness or aloofness on her face, and the way she answered me was friendly and relaxed.

"Your neediness."

"Neediness? What about my appearance makes me seem needy? Hey, what you're saying is kind of unusual. No one has ever told me before that I'm needy. As far as I know, my friends really wish I were a little needier, especially my fiancé. Tell me more. I'm really interested."

"No, no, there's no basis for what I said. It's just my gut feeling. You look like you're independent. But did you know that first off, you come across as warm and feminine? My next thought is that you seem neat and organized, like you do everything thoroughly and methodically. On the outside, you act like you don't need other people. You can get things done quickly and well on your own, but at the same time, your mannerisms make you seem sensitive, like you pay strict attention to every last detail."

"You're right about that. I like to fight my own battles. Whenever I encounter an obstacle or a setback, I turn to others to figure out the solution. You don't have to comfort me or anything. I'll listen calmly, then I'll go and get the job done on my own. Even with my fiancé, I don't talk that much about my feelings. . . ." Then, half jokingly, she added, "You know how I talk to him on the phone? He calls me and says, 'It's me,' and I say, 'I know.' He asks me how everything is going, and I say everything's fine. He says, 'I'll let you go then,' and I say, 'Okay.' And that's it." There was a tinge of sadness in her words.

"Maybe because you project the opposite, you have a type-A kind of neediness that's hidden, since you rarely need to express it. It lies dormant and stays intact. I have a friend I've known for years, and she puts all her needs out in the open and doesn't spare any details, so I've come to recognize these things. Your neediness comes out inadvertently. You never exercise that part of yourself, so of course you're not conscious of it. You're just overly independent. Why not let yourself be needy once in a while?"

"Where do I go to find that part of me? I forgot how to rely on other people ages ago!" she said.

5

XIAO FAN was the most desperate woman I'd ever seen. Despair was in her past and in her present. Everything about her screamed despair. Because of her despair, I loved her. Because of her despair, I was shaken. Because of her despair, I was overwhelmed, and because of her despair, I left her. Her despair was her beauty.

I secretly looked forward to seeing her during my weekly shift. By day, she worked at the offices of the Youth Corps. By night, she and her fiancé and a few friends ran a bar. Every Saturday at six p.m., we'd work together. The two of us made a good team. By the time her shift began, she'd be overworked already. She often arrived looking thin and pale. Naturally concerned, I'd stare at her out of the corner of my eye. She smiled at me. It was a tired smile.

She'd ask me why I was sitting next to her, and I'd say because you're smart. She'd also ask me why her. I'd say because you're so beautiful. She said maybe you don't know that I have nothing to offer you. I said doesn't matter, other women don't want me. She said you can't handle me. I said let's cross that bridge when we get there.

She sat on my bike, waiting for her fiancé to pick her up. I insisted on giving her a lift home. She didn't think I'd be able to move with her on the back. I got on the bike, and we went for a ride. She was so light. We ran a red light and made a sudden turn. And with that, she became a little kid screaming in delight. She said she'd never ridden so fast before. We rode up a giant bridge, taking the steep lane for motorized vehicles. All around us, cars were zooming past. We were on the only bicycle. I was drenched with sweat. It was a dangerous and slow journey, and she was behind me, shouting go, go, go....

Her capacity for happiness was limited, and yet she seemed happy. She always seemed happy. Her happiness was natural, infectious. Having been endowed with an intuitive understanding of others, she knew how to give and take. She was the epitome of graciousness. The art of courtesy, as she so ably demonstrated it, was a musical instrument in the hands of a virtuoso.

As I carried her on my bike, her weight became my own, and for a time, she was a part of me. During my grueling ascent of the bridge, a cool breeze encircled us. The surrounding riverbed was visible beneath the limpid waters, and the twilight sky was a gentle pink. To our left was the sun, tiny and round, its rays forming striations of color.

Xiao Fan and I inhaled deeply. All was peaceful. I let up on the pedals, slowing down as much as I could. I wished the bridge would never end. With her close behind me, I could tell that her breathing was irregular: She'd gotten overexcited. I had seen this day coming, when we would drop the façade and find ourselves at a loss for words. In a calm and matter-of-fact tone, she asked whether I'd still see her if she quit her job. She was older and worldly-wise, sober and heavy-hearted.

I could see into the depths of her soul. I knew her type. Insight was my natural gift. Just go on managing your bar. I'll come see you. Doesn't matter what time you get off, I said. A flock of white pigeons flew overhead, and in that instant, having been shown a glimpse of absolute freedom, I found courage. I wanted to fall madly in love. I already knew I would take the love in me that no one else wanted and give it all to this woman. All my memories of Xiao Fan and I together were to be captured in this single bleak picture.

She knew I was secretly in love with her. She knew my demons. She knew I was trying to figure out the inner workings of her soul. She knew that I understood her, that she could trust me. She even knew that I would vanish; I could hear it in those words on the bridge. I could tell that she was not one who was easily moved, but that I had moved her. She hid too much. She begrudged my absence before things even began. Her feelings for me were complicated.

During the lowest point following my split with Shui Ling, I disappeared for a month. Didn't report for duty. Didn't get in touch with anyone. I was at home, incapacitated. Out of the blue, I got a phone call. It was Xiao Fan's soft, courteous voice on the line. I heard her say, "I don't know why I'm calling you, and I really don't know if there's any point in me calling you, but I just wanted to make sure you were still alive." (At this point, I was certain that she was crying, and that she was stifling the sound.) "So it's just for my benefit, okay? You haven't shown up for work all month. I sense that something's going on with you, but I know very well that I have no business telling you what to do. You always have to have your way. You're always looking after me, and whatever it is I need, you're there to offer it. But you never tell me what's going on inside of you. Something bad happens, and you hide at home, alone, wallowing in misery. So tell me, what can I actually do to help you? Or should I wait for you to feel better on your own and show up for a shift with a smile again? You make me feel so helpless." Her voice betrayed a nasal congestion from crying, and she seemed to be struggling to maintain her composure as she spoke.

On the most intense night of all, I finally went to the bar to find her. I was already drunk, but she didn't ask questions. She just sat with me and kept me company, telling me all kinds of anecdotes about what had happened while I was away and what was going on in her life. I laughed as I listened. I laughed so hard that my entire body shook violently. Tears of laughter streamed down my face the whole time. With firmness as well as understanding, she looked me straight in the eye. I stared back as she rattled on. Through my tears, I was laughing hysterically, and I thought about how I had always longed to be loved like this....

The alcohol kicked in. I vomited everything up in the bathroom. I told her not to worry, that I didn't want her to see this disgusting side of me. After I threw up, I came back and hid in a corner of the room. I lost control and burned myself. I thought she wouldn't notice, but when I looked over, she was standing at the bar, watching me as she poured a drink. There were tears welling in her eyes.

6

SIX MONTHS later, I moved into Xiao Fan's apartment. She took me in like a stray dog. The months that I lived with her were, in all my four years, probably the only time I was truly happy. They were like a dying man's final glimpses of the world.

I was haunted by despair, pain, confusion, and loneliness, which threatened to drag me out of a world filled with the promise of the future and engulf me at any moment. For the time being, I was wide awake and living each day to the fullest, marking the dawn of a new era in which I was truly living the good life. This newfound ardor was all Xiao Fan's doing, and like a moth to a flame, I reveled in it, allowing the desires that had once been dammed to run recklessly wild. I loved her ferociously. And in my total abandon, I relinquished all self-respect. I stooped to a new low.

Xiao Fan was the only woman I ever made love to. Of all my memories, my memory of her is the single most beautiful. It should be evident by now that I can't conceivably depict this woman. In writing this much, I've already condemned myself to failure and done her an injustice. It amounts to nothing more than a sham, and I've gritted my teeth trying all the while. There's a raw passion that still lives in my blood, still courses through my veins. The mere thought of her fills me with enough desire to send me into a mad frenzy. Yet this memory is also the saddest and most painful of all, for I never really knew this woman's heart, and I never would.

7

"XIAO FAN, what's wrong? What happened?"

I'd been waiting for her in my room. The lights were out, and I was lying in bed when I heard the sound of the key turning. I bolted out of bed. It was midnight. She walked through the door, her face deathly pale. She went into her room and changed her clothes. She came back out, emotionless. She went into the kitchen and started to boil water. I followed her around anxiously, and every now and then, she gave me a wan smile. She sat down at the dining room table and stared ahead blankly. She looked haggard. Usually when she got home, she'd knock on my door and we'd chat. But that night, she was out of sorts, zombie-like. I had the sinking feeling she'd been dealt a severe blow, and my heart started pounding.

"What are you looking at?" she demanded, sounding amused and tired at the same time. It was as if she'd suddenly realized she had an audience.

"I'm looking at you, trying to figure out what happened." There was a hint of indignation in my voice.

She was silent. "Stop looking at me," she said sulkily.

She stood up, then shook her head and sighed, glaring at me. She poured herself a glass of milk in the kitchen, then headed straight to her room, slamming the door behind her. I heard the lock turn. Not another word.

This was her way of handling things, setting up a zone that I wasn't allowed to enter. In the few months we'd lived together, we'd spent hundreds of hours talking. I'd gotten to know her well—so well that I more or less knew how her mind worked, and if I closed my eyes, I could imagine how she would respond to a situation. She was generous that way, letting me analyze her. But there was an off-limits zone where she hunkered down in need of solitude. She was like someone who carried a gun everywhere she went, taking it to bed with her, even when someone was sleeping beside her.

I pounded on her door impatiently. In that act of ignorance, I threw away my self-respect. I barged in. Whenever I intruded on her privacy in this way, she'd put up with it for a while before kicking me out. The absurdity of my logic notwithstanding, I couldn't bear the thought of her suffering alone, so I'd go to her door begging, and sit there waiting.

"Would you please leave me alone?" The door opened to reveal her sitting on the bed. In the dimness, I could see her head hanging low and her hair dangling over her eyes. Her voice hinted that she was trying desperately not to lose her patience.

I watched her calmly and said nothing.

"Well?" She stared up at the ceiling, doing her best to keep her composure.

"Did you have a fight with him?" I had to ask.

"You should be used to me not talking about it. When *you* don't say anything, that's when it's time to worry." She turned and looked squarely at me as I sat down at the foot of the bed.

"This is a natural cycle. People have to slow down and do nothing for a while. There's no point in being active. That's just how it works. You have to lie there and do nothing for a while. You can't sleep because you have nightmares, and you wake up feeling even more tired than before. I knew you were outside my door. In the back of my mind, I knew that I should open the door, but I couldn't get up. Whenever I think about the past, my head starts spinning, and I can't focus or remember well. Then I start thinking about death. This hasn't happened in a long time. God, I wish I were dead!" She ended with a cynical laugh.

"Why don't you lie down and get some rest? I'll sit beside you and keep you company." I helped her under the covers.

"Just now, in the car, the two of us went completely berserk. He wants me to marry my boss. As soon as he said it, I tried to get out of the car, but he grabbed my hand and wouldn't let go. He flew into a rage and slammed the car into the median barrier. I clawed him with my nails and broke free from his grip, and got out of the car and ran back here. Ah, it's been ten years of this. I've been trapped for ten years. What have I done to deserve this? Though we've been together this long, he won't marry me. I don't even know the real reason why. Isn't that ridiculous?

"He was two years ahead of me when I got into junior college. We were in this die-hard group of seven people from the same club. We've been together ever since. The year we graduated, we decided to get engaged. Then, one day, he went missing. Not even his widowed mother or his little brother knew where he was. There was no news from him for a whole year. On the wedding date we'd set, I came down with hepatitis. It put me in the hospital for three months. I lost about twenty pounds, which is why I'm this skinny. During that time, I bawled my eyes out and didn't talk to anyone.

"Then I got a job at a company. It was because of my mother that I accepted the boss's advances. She liked him. He was much older than me. He was a mature, considerate man—with a lot of money. He could help me provide for my family. He was like a father, the way he'd cook for me. He was so kind to me that I felt guilty because I didn't love him one bit. He's continued to pursue me this whole time that I've been engaged."

Xiao Fan sighed as she took my hand and started playing with it. I ran my fingers through her hair. By sharing her experiences, she'd brought the two of us closer. And since I could apprehend her feelings at that very moment, I felt relieved.

"He reemerged a year later, and I learned that he'd gone to Mount Dongbu to teach at an elementary school. After jilting me, he didn't say a word. He just met up with me every day and went to grad school as usual, as if nothing had happened. I couldn't reject him. Do you understand? That liver disease nearly killed me. I was terrified. Then I realized how weighed down my heart had been. But after that, even though he'd come back, I didn't know how I felt anymore. I felt empty. I thought if I just worked and worked, I'd save up enough money to buy my parents a nice house. But I never imagined he would leave me again.

"One night, when he was taking me home, he put a ring on my finger and said, 'This is to make up for my past behavior—oh, and by the way, weren't we planning to get married?' Ever since that night, I've been living in a continuous state of anticipation, waiting for the day to come. The past is repeating itself, but even as I wait, I have faith. Is that great or what?" She stopped abruptly. Her question was directed at me.

"Are you tired? Don't you want to rest for a while?" I couldn't refrain from planting a kiss on her forehead.

She continued as if she hadn't heard me. Whenever she told stories, she exuded an allure beyond her twenty-six years. Her beauty sent undulations through me, riveting me, taking hold of me. It was not a sensual beauty but one born of wisdom, perhaps a moral beauty. Her words showed that her fate was out of her hands, that when karma began to flow, despair was only natural. She understood the workings of destiny, the forces that had come to define her. She had seen all the world had to offer and was entirely capable of playing the hand she'd been dealt. And still she managed to retain a sensitivity that allowed her to penetrate the deepest aspects of human nature. That was why she and I got along so well. I was amazed at how she responded to me by treating me the way I treated myself. It was due to her social maturity.

"Just look at us and tell me if we're a good match. We never tell each other what we're thinking. Whenever we go out, we don't talk about anything except our day-to-day needs. We have to be around friends whenever we're together. That way, we can act wild and crazy and say stupid things. I doubt he really thinks about anything. He isn't self-aware like you and I are. He just goes and does things. Sometimes I don't know why we're together. Whenever I feel down, I can talk to you, but I could never talk to him...."

I got under the covers and lay down beside her. She climbed out to put on a movie—a tearjerker—in the background.

"I've always been a loser. For as long as I can remember, I've been hopeless at everything. I envy people like you. You and him both. You guys are self-confident and successful at everything you do. You're both so free-spirited. You can go anywhere and say to yourself, Now I want to go here or there. You guys are amazing. In the past, I felt like I was amazing too because I was with him, so then I hid behind him, where it was safe. I don't know when I started to accept my place, my permanent inferiority. Wherever I go, it's never because I want to go there, it's because I'm following the amazing people around me. I'm too enamored of your amazingness!" The last part came with a bitter laugh.

She rolled over and timidly wiped her tears. I'd never seen her show such grief before. The look of anguish on her face was unfamiliar to me. She almost never cried. That gentle exterior concealed her true mettle. Despair was a fire inside of her, steeling her, incapable of immolating her, and so she was neither fragile nor self-pitying. She was resilient to the point of ruthlessness, toward herself as well as others, so much so that the love I gave her was stepped on, even trampled on.

Because of despair, she would never submit to anyone or anything.

Curiously enough, her grief caused me profound agony—physical agony. I felt sharp pangs inside me. My entire body grew hot. My heart was palpitating. What I experienced was not mere physical torment but full-on sexual arousal. What I hungered for was her naked body. I was practically throbbing. . . .

I pulled her close and kissed her eyelids, her back, her neck and shoulders. She was stunned, and her body tensed. Wordlessly, she yielded to it. The vibrant sounds of music filtered through the shadows, and the curtain wafted gently. The dusk light formed a layer of camouflage as the occasional car passed. There was a palpable sensation in the air. Pulling herself free, she rolled over, sulkily telling me not to get her worked up. She said no one could handle the burden. She said it wouldn't be fair to me. I wrapped my arms around her from behind and turned her over to face me. I held her tightly in my arms, and from there, plunged headlong into the throes of passion....

Her scent has been ingrained in me ever since, and I can still recall it at any given moment.

"Look at me. Now tell me, what do you want me to do?" she asked devotedly.

The reason Xiao Fan accepted me was because I didn't reject her. And because it wasn't love.

8

AFTER the Crocodile Club incident, everyone caught Crocodile Fever. Once the citizens' bureau confirmed a firsthand sighting, crocodile-related news went from wild and wacky conjectures to the fruits of legitimate scholarship and research. Crocodile coverage took the place of "DIANA JOINS BRITISH ROYAL FAMILY" as the lead story on the front page, bumping Diana to the full-page special-feature slot previously occupied by "WILL HUMANS EVER EVOLVE?" On any given day, individuals set out in every direction with one urgent mission: to hunt down crocodiles. There was an unspoken rule that crocodile-related information was to be exchanged only in private. No one mentioned it in public, lest crocodiles be frightened away. Everyone was on high alert as they searched for the slightest evidence of a crocodile, remaining convinced that crocodiles had no idea humans were on the lookout for them.

Various crocodile experts had begun to crop up. Every day in the papers there was a new crocodile-related article written by a PhD. A tenured professor signed on to host *Focus on Crocodiles*, a TV program that featured leading authorities on genetic engineering, developmental psychologists, officials from the Ministry of the Interior, and legal scholars. One such genetic-engineering expert, who had obtained the cells of crocodiles for research purposes, argued that crocodiles and humans were two distinct species that could, through the processes of evolution, form a new type of human, forecasting an eighty percent chance of a hybrid species through mating.

From the standpoint of the developmental psychologists, crocodiles were an aberrant species. In accordance with their discipline's understanding of crocodile families, their research indicated distinct differences from humans at every stage of development from birth to puberty as well as in maturity, though details had yet to be ascertained. There was a general consensus, however, that up to the age of fourteen, crocodiles adopted a homemade "human suit" before running away from home. While exact causes remained unknown, scholars cited societal attitudes as a factor in crocodile mutation, suggesting that there was no means of preventing an increase in the number of emergent crocodiles, which would ultimately contribute to a broader societal trend toward a full-fledged crocodile ecology and genetic mutation.

The legal scholars asserted that in order to protect the native civilization, traditions, and social order of the past five thousand years, advance revisions of labor laws, property laws, marriage laws, et cetera, were needed to restrict the crocodile race to designated occupations in the tourism and service industries. Additional taxes were also proposed lest crocodiles drain societal resources, along with the enactment of explicit measures to prohibit marriage between humans and crocodiles. An official of the Ministry of the Interior made a televised announcement that the Alliance for the Protection of Crocodiles was growing in popularity and holding daily demonstrations in Taipei to pressure the federal legislature to meet its demands for crocodile protection statutes. The alliance also advocated the legal creation of crocodile ecotourism zones to prevent extinction. The ministry official reiterated that the constitution contained a provision ensuring crocodiles the right to exist.

One month later, the Bureau of Health and Sanitation published the results of a secret study. According to the bureau, which tracked a Crocodile Club event on December 24th attended by sixty active members, within a month, five percent of those in attendance had experienced a dermatological problem—their skin had turned red in places and sprouted dense patches of black specks. The body hair of those subjects was examined under a high-power microscope, revealing the presence of tiny ova-shaped specimens. A bureau spokesman issued the following conclusions: The tiny spawns were the product of a toxin secreted by the crocodiles; as an oviparous species, crocodiles produced spawns, which were agents of reproduction; a new organism was produced not through sexual intercourse per se but through the discharge of a spawn that entered the human body and transformed the host into a new crocodile.

People were stunned. A huge uproar ensued.

The Alliance for the Protection of Crocodiles and the Anti-Crocodile Coalition (known respectively as Pro-Croc and Anti-Croc) held a televised national debate, with three networks providing joint prime-time coverage at six p.m.

"As controversial as research on crocodiles may be, there is no doubt whatsoever that crocodile spawns are not pure human beings. Because they are 99.9 percent different from humans, or those of us who constitute the majority, they are abnormal. Is everyone here willing to accept the risk of mutation as a product of social intercourse? Are you prepared for a future in which we, as a society, are completely transformed into crocodiles?" Anti-Croc asked.

"But Anti-Croc, you've never even seen a crocodile before. How can you start talking about what kind of influence crocodiles will have on the future of society?" Pro-Croc said.

"Oh, don't tell me that crocodiles don't have enough influence on society as it is. Haven't there been eyewitness sightings of crocodiles? The phenomenon of deviant crocodile spawns is an established fact. How else has society become this unstable? I can just imagine how crocodiles look with their human suits on. What horrifying creatures, with those specks growing all over their red skin. Just the thought of something that looks like a human producing spawns makes me sick," Anti-Croc said.

"But even if crocodiles emerge from human beings, that doesn't mean we all harbor the same potential to become crocodiles. The actual chances are slim. What makes you think otherwise?" Pro-Croc said.

"Crocodiles are not humans," Anti-Croc said.

"According to you, all crocodiles should be preemptively thrown in jail, just in case you have a child who might become a crocodile.

What if you suddenly woke up one day to find that you'd turned into a crocodile, what would you do then?" Pro-Croc said.

"That would never happen. I would discipline my child or I would turn myself in. And you?" Anti-Croc said.

"Actually, we have a collective goal, which is to protect crocodiles and to allow them to subsist naturally. But because society poses a threat to crocodiles, we need to provide some safeguards for them, which is why we've compiled a registry of crocodiles so they can be gathered in designated tourism zones, monitored and protected in the event of a large-scale disaster, and serve as sample specimens, as a practical measure to prevent public interference," said Pro-Croc.

The following day, the Bureau of Health and Sanitation and federal law-enforcement authorities issued a joint statement: "Effective today, we have designated this month as National Crocodile Month in order to give crocodiles nationwide an opportunity to turn themselves over to the registrars of the Bureau of Health and Sanitation or the National Police Agency, to whom crocodiles must provide their names, which will be made public. Scheduling of treatment and a pledge of compliance will also be undertaken at that time. Any late registrants who are discovered will be subject to penalties, which will be administered separately."

NOTEBOOK #8

I

ON HOW to love well: Instead of embracing a romantic ideal, you must confront the meaning of every great love that has shattered, shard by shard.

2

SHUI LING lived on in my heart. Like a pendulum swinging toward me, memories of her surfaced from the darkest recesses of my mind, blurring with reality one moment and vanishing like a dream the next, leaving stillness in their wake....

December 16, 1989

Shui Ling, it's my second day in Penghu. I waited until the most spectacular moments of sunset were over, then headed to the balcony of my hotel room with my journal and a clear, sober heart. I wanted to sit at a round white table, inspired by the fast-fading colors as the darkness enveloped the sky. With the last remaining sliver of orange light on the horizon beyond the murky waters, I found myself unable to witness the end of a thing whose beauty was never realized.

The sea shrouded in blackness, the stirring sounds of night, and the ocean breeze—elements of an all-too-familiar scene, aren't they? I saw the dimly lit sea yesterday, and that's when it sank in. But here I am, gazing sentimentally at the green light reflected on the water's surface, savoring what time is left before it goes out.

Every time we spoke, I bungled the opportunity. My words ran amok. My most volatile parts surfaced. I tried to tell you in a letter but gave up trying to finish. I tossed and turned all night, unable to escape the awful din inside my head. I couldn't get out of bed or make myself clean the house. I couldn't put a pen to paper. That's the state I was in for two months. I didn't tell you, but I was worried about myself.

I ran off to Penghu. My defenses weakened, I watched helplessly as my brigade was decimated. But still I pushed forward with the flag raised high, flapping in the wind, refusing to surrender.

December 28, 1989

You punished me by making me wait. What was I willing to wait so long for? I waited for a breakthrough in honesty, for you to say that your love for me had an ultimate meaning. I was in desperate search of some sort of connection.

In the end, it wasn't love. We could love, and love would leave us, or we couldn't love, and love wouldn't leave us. That was the ultimate meaning. Blessing or curse, there was no escaping it. All I could do was learn to play the hand I'd been dealt, knowing that the profundity of my life experiences would rest on my ability to formulate a plot.

I waited for you though you weren't the one, and succeeded only in hurting and debasing myself.

January 3, 1990

On holding grudges. According to the Dalai Lama, one pursues the noble life not to depart from this world but to accept those who will depart from it. And so I vow never to revisit my journals from those days.

This pain has left me feeling worn and empty—unable to refrain from these effusions, unsure of how to mend the gaping hole in me, unable to reach the place that Haruki Murakami described: "Six years during which time I'd laid three cats to rest. Burned how many aspirations, bundled up how much suffering in thick sweaters, and buried them in the ground. All in this fathomlessly huge city Tokyo." I don't know how to dig myself out of the rut I'm in, and the pain, which comes in paroxysms, tears away at my mind.

April 19, 1990

Shui Ling, this separation has to be. Four months later, I'm in a completely different place. I thought long and hard about romantic fantasies and shattered loves. I cried for days on end. I put all the time and energy I had into finding closure, making sure that you'd never again be a part of my life. I wanted you to fade into the past so that I could mourn. So I gave myself a bloodletting, replaying hurtful words from our time together over and over in my heart. Our breakup was not the most beautiful memory, but this time, it was the best.

Passion alone is never enough. That was my biggest lesson. As a first year, as a third year, and even now, I could never give you stability. Love, however beautiful, always comes at a great cost to the future, don't you think?

Unhealthy love is two people stoking a shared fantasy of desperate beauty, weaponizing passion and desire. Real life is filled with twists and turns, changes, recurrences. Before you even know it, you've become a deluded romantic who denies the consequences of time or destroys the very thing that they love. It's funny how the only time I'm not hypersensitive is when I'm breaking up with someone. Then again, we brought out the ugliness in each other, as if hatred was the seed of our love.

I don't want to be close to you again. Our fighting knows no end. I want you to shatter the illusions I created, and go out and love someone else. Don't love too much but don't fail to love, either. Love prudently. Love realistically, just enough to treat someone well. Though you don't love me anymore, relationship or not, I want you to be well now and always. I want you to love someone else, even if it hurts me.

Part of me has been secretly hoping that good things do last forever, but it's time to renounce that hope. I looked across the water, and as my tears fell, I told myself: "You can't hold on to a beautiful thing forever—not in your memory, not even if you keep loving it. If you tried, it would only die in your possession. Beauty must be free to run its course." I decided to free you from my heart in a gesture that is nothing short of poignant, for beauty belongs to no one and must be relinquished to the eternal.

The deeper you love, the deeper your compassion grows and the more you realize that the other suffers just as you do. When all is said and done, human civilization is ugly and cruel, and the only thing to do is to raze it to the ground, and that's because kindredness is the one true constant between you and anyone else. The best way for any relationship to end is with the sentiment *I wish the best for you, and I am grateful for what we once had together.*

July 13, 1990

Shui Ling, tonight I'm moving in with Xiao Fan and starting a new life in which reality comes first. I look forward to leaving fantasy behind and keeping a grip on reality, with all my thoughts and feelings intact. I've never been as close to or further from reality than I have in the past six months of loneliness and misery. I learned the hard way when my ideals collided with reality, but each exists for a reason, and at least I now know why.

In confronting my desires, I felt sorrow and regret over my former, unrealistic ways of thinking, but I was also moved and inspired. After having come so close to ending my life, I came back, my will to live completely reawakened. I faced reality, where I would learn to live again, this time boldly and fearlessly. My body was screaming at me, telling me that life was a gift. The agony of the past few years, like the conflict between the real me and the one everyone knew, is gone. I even feel a little sorry for my old self, so feeble and self-pitying. It seems I've finally come around to living the life I've always dreamed of.

3

After that perilous night, I went on living in the room next to Xiao Fan's. She always brought work home. Every morning, she'd drag herself out of bed, exhausted, then open my door a crack and peek in. I'd open my eyes to greet her. She'd come in and sit on my bed, and we'd goof around like little kids. I'd put on a wake-up song (like Don McLean's "American Pie" or Dan Fogelberg's "Leader of the Band") and stretch, while she'd pour herself a glass of milk and make me a cup of coffee. Then we'd sit down at our little dining table and eat breakfast. As she read the paper, I'd sit there and interrupt her, asking random questions. She had to keep up with the news for her job, and I'd try to make her laugh so she couldn't get any reading done.

She normally wore contact lenses, which made her look sober and aloof. Breakfast was the only time she ever wore her thick-framed glasses. Behind the lenses, her eyes were two tiny dots. She looked endearingly simple and honest. The best was when I could tell that she found my teasing funny and annoying at the same time. On those occasions, she lived purely in the moment, which made me happier than words could ever describe.

Then she'd head to her room to get ready. She was like a free-wheeling bachelor who was being forced to masquerade as a woman, and her brilliant execution of a feminine style didn't stop her from making fun of her own clothes and makeup. Once, while wearing an evening gown to a cocktail party with her boss, she stepped on the skirt and tripped as the two of them were dancing. She laughed about it the whole way home, then boasted to me afterward. Like me, she could be flippant about appearances. But she just didn't give a damn how she looked, and in that respect, she was ballsier than I was.

I'd sit on the carpet in my bedroom, smoking in silence as I waited for her to leave her room, transformed into a woman who fit in. Suddenly, the chasm between my reality and hers would become painfully apparent. Then, as if she didn't want me to see her in such a state, she'd slip out the door.

My ear was constantly up against the wall of her room, listening for any movement—the phone ringing when she and her fiancé made a date, her light footsteps, the sound of her gingerly closing the door. Day after day, I'd hear the door shut, and I'd be separated from her anew. She slipped into another dimension that I had no connection to, one in which she belonged to this other man.

As I drifted off to sleep, I'd hear a key being inserted into the front door lock and turned. The sound would trickle into my dreams, waking me. Like a goalkeeper, I knew instantaneously if she'd made it into the entryway. From the time she left the house to the end of the day, I sat in the dark, waiting for her. Apart from the few classes I couldn't skip, or when I absolutely had to go out, I spent most of my time at home. My once hectic social life ground to a halt. I ended my complicated, dodgy relationships with various men. I didn't do anything except sleep, then sleep more. I didn't even read books. The dormancy made me restless, and I put all my energy into writing in my journal. Whether I was sitting or running around or lying down, my mind was filled with things I wanted to talk to Xiao Fan about. In my heart, I talked to her all day long. The sheer volume of these conversations was too much to contain. They were practically oozing out of me, incapacitating me. My body had entered overproduction mode. Its mostly unsaleable products were piled in a warehouse, and the warehouse soon had to be demolished.

My long slumber came to an end when the sound of the key rescued me. I sat up straight in bed, then crept over to the door, peeping out through a crack. It was easy to tell whether she was in a good or bad mood that day. When she was in a bad mood, she'd stand at the shoe rack grimacing before forcing a vague smile in my direction. That was her way of preparing to unleash the trials of her day. Then, from behind that shrewd, capable exterior emerged a pure innocence. She had the face of a ten-year-old girl, it was that adorable. Xiao Fan was so thin that her cheeks were sunken, but whenever she smiled, her dimples would appear. I often had an overwhelming urge to pick her up and give her a big squeeze. She was so angelic that I'd forget she was five years older than me, and engaged.

Other times, before she'd even gotten dressed, she'd talk to me through the crack of my door, animatedly and rapidly unloading a massive stream of information. She'd talk about her crotchety old colleagues at work, or how she'd take advantage of the times when no one else was in the office to make long-distance phone calls to friends on three different lines at the same time. Or how she'd managed to plow through a huge pile of work, or how in the middle of the day, some shady madam had dragged her to a beauty salon to help settle a dispute. Or she'd mention any good music they'd played at the bar, or interesting customers she'd met, or even how her old boss K was hanging around the bar one night, pestering her....

She talked nonstop. She'd talk while getting dressed, while getting ready for bed, while straightening up her room. I'd listen enthusiastically and contentedly before starting my day. I'd eat the breakfast she'd made, then take a shower. Sometimes when I was in the shower, she'd pull a chair up to the door and sit there, going into excruciating detail about a movie plot. In spite of being completely captivated, I was impassive. I'd be silent for so long that she'd jokingly threaten to break down the door. Listening to her talk about movies was the greatest pleasure of all, not just because of her eloquence but because the only time that she shed her self-consciousness and guardedness was when she was wrapped up in her feelings about a movie. In those relaxed moments of openness, I could observe and experience her as she authentically was, soaking up her brilliance. But the occasions when she was uninhibited were few and far between. Whenever her mind wasn't encumbered by some major problem, I felt relieved, if only for the time being.

Before bedtime, she would read quietly in her room, and I'd sit nearby in the living room to keep her company. I'd put on some background music in my room. Occasionally she'd come out and sit beside me. She'd watch me until she was sleepy, then turn out her light and climb into bed. Her bedroom door was directly across from my reading spot, and she left it open so I could check in on her, since she had trouble sleeping. A little while later, I'd go over and see if she'd fallen asleep, then tiptoe inside and tuck her in. I'd gaze at her before leaving, gently closing the door behind me. Then I'd go back to my room and get ready for bed, or I'd stay up all night reading in the living room, keeping watch as she slept. On nights like this, it felt like we were best friends, or even lovers.

But alas. Alas, our conversations always avoided one part of her daily regimen. She refused to discuss *him*. It was as if he didn't exist. She went to increasingly greater pains to keep the two of us in separate worlds, compartmentalizing her life into two distinct halves. It was her way of adapting to the new instability that arose when I came into her life. Even as I watched her from the living room while she slept, that other person known as her fiancé was likely waiting downstairs, and once the lights in her window went out, he'd start the engine of his motorcycle, then take off. But alas, these things Xiao Fan and I both knew.

4

EVER SINCE Shui Ling turned me away with a wave of the hand, I didn't know what kind of affection I needed. All I knew was that I needed a woman who wouldn't run away. Every time I fell in love with someone, they never met my basic needs—meaning, I never should have fallen in love with them in the first place. Knowing this about myself, I didn't expect much from Xiao Fan. I simply hoped to cherish our time together and to care for her. The most important and only thing left for me to do was to concentrate on loving the one I was with. Xiao Fan just happened to be there by my side, and that was why this privilege had been bestowed on me. With the click and turn of a key, the happiness inside her was mine to be had.

Or maybe, just maybe, she wanted to love me, but what she gave me was a love with too much pride.

That's the kind of person she was. As far as intimacy went, she no longer had any desires or fantasies. What she had instead were crippling fears. She not only realized that she couldn't afford to pay the price but she refused to. All of her energy went toward upholding the responsibilities of another intimate relationship, and so she refused to take up the same kind of romantic involvement elsewhere. In forgoing any further intimacy, she dispensed with romantic involvements altogether. She had come to experience everyone as an intractable burden. Her worst nightmare was to be loved. That was why, at the core of her passion, there was fear. She had rejected love and taught herself to live without intimacy.

It was too late for her to fend off my encroachments, which confounded her. Even if she did accept my love, she didn't process it or know what to do with it. Her only response was a passive guardedness that prompted me to commit more severe encroachments. In the end, things fell apart and she withdrew from me. As long as I treated her this way, she would remain impervious to me and frustrate me whenever necessary. Our relationship entered a vicious cycle, and living under the same roof, we were fast headed toward a standoff.

She let me give myself over completely, then prevented me from falling madly in love with her by forcing me to love her in a rational, controlled way. She didn't want the soul-baring embrace of intimacy. She wanted to admire me from afar, and it was enough for her to know that I'd always be there. That distance partly served to help her make sense of me. She was so impervious that she couldn't tell how much I needed her. Even if she could tell, she'd never be able to give me what I needed. Instead, she'd drop hints about how little she had to give. To make matters worse, she'd sometimes give me the exact opposite of what I needed, so that there was no point in expressing my needs. She constantly had the upper hand. That was her way of protecting herself from me—by giving herself an out—and protecting me from even greater pain.

It was plain to see that in needing her love, I was doomed. It didn't matter how she saw herself or how she loved me: She was too proud. She was so set in her ways that I stopped wanting her.

Because I couldn't stop loving her, a single directive took over me: *Never, ever let her hurt you.* I had to lock up my love and leave it to die. I had to repress my desire for intimacy, or else she'd never let me near her again. Our dynamic was shameful, and it reflected the worst in us. I could lend her my ear, but that was about all. Even though I wanted badly to listen to her endless chatter and answer her every beck and call. And even though I'd come running if she needed me.

We'd signed a perverse unspoken contract. Due to some greater good, we were each unwilling to part with the other. At some point, I developed the savage conviction that she would never truly love me. Or perhaps it was the sheer intensity of my love that caused me to fiercely resist her. At my weakest and neediest moments, I avoided her. Otherwise, she'd start messing with me. During those times, I told myself that the problem was in me. I could no longer balance her out as I once had. I was backsliding. She cut me off completely to punish me, and so I stopped craving intimacy. It was all based on a frightening dysfunction: lack of trust.

In the end, our conflict erupted in an argument.

"Can I come in?" She leaned against my bedroom door, trying to feel out the situation.

"Come on in. Didn't I say my door was always open to you?" I replied calmly, lying in bed.

The night before, she had come home and locked herself in her room without saying a word, without knocking on my door or leaving hers open. Having learned my lesson last time, I tried not to worry and instead left my door open all night so she could talk to me if she felt like it. The note that I stuffed through the crack under her door read:

Xiao Fan. If you're not in a good mood tonight, that's fine. I just wanted to say, no problem. If you need a little time out, don't worry about it. So if you've locked yourself in your room because you're going through a hard time or just have stuff to deal with, I understand. At times like these, you can handle it on your own. You say that if I approach you, it'll make you pull away. There's no way I can give you the sense of security that you need or make you open up to me, but maybe you'll come to me one day. I still don't know if I should give you a hug, or ignore you and give you space.

I just wanted to tell you how I feel. I was worried that I wouldn't be able to talk because I have a sore throat. For the rest of the night I'll be with you—over in my room, patiently waiting for you, waiting with a smile.

The next day was Sunday. At eight in the morning, I heard her door open. I waited, but she didn't come to my door, so I went out there. She was in the kitchen, boiling water for eggs. Her expression seemed normal, as if nothing had happened, except for that strange veil of detachment. Cautiously, I asked her what was going on, and right away, she replied coolly that it was nothing, that it had nothing to do with me. Then she went about her business.

I didn't ask anything more. After hitting a brick wall, I felt dejected. I turned and headed back to my room, where I fell asleep with the door open. I slept until the sky turned dark. I'd inadvertently slept for more than ten hours.

"Why did you sleep for so long?" She sat on the floor near my door.

"I don't know. It just happened. I probably needed to."

"Did you know that you've never slept this much before when I've been at home? Whenever I'm here, you're asleep. It must be because of me." There was some guilt in her voice. Her face looked even paler than usual.

"It's just me. Don't think about it too much. I solve problems by sleeping."

"What kinds of problems? Are you still thinking about what you should do about me?"

"No, I'm over that. I don't need to do anything about you, I just need to deal with myself."

"Did you make up your mind? It worries me to see you this way." She sounded dismayed.

"I couldn't make up my mind. If I could, I'd be fine. In the end, I can't leave you. I want to be there for you, to take care of you, but I need to look out for myself first. Otherwise I'll become a burden to you."

"Take care of me? What do you mean, 'take care'? How are you taking care of me? I don't need your sage advice. You never even say what you want. You just wait for other people to make up their minds, then you accept it and feel like you've been left empty-handed. I've watched you live aimlessly and grow more dissatisfied by the day. I don't know what to do about you."

"Is it really that painful? Maybe it'd be better if you didn't pay attention to my aimless existence. That way you wouldn't have to watch me suffer."

"Oh, is that your latest decision? What else am I supposed to do? Hold your hand while you throw your life away?" Stone-faced, she stood up abruptly. Then she turned on her heels and left. The door slammed behind her.

I froze in terror. My mind was spinning. The realization cut through me: I'd hurt her feelings. A second later, I stumbled to her door and pounded on it, hollering for her to open up.

"Xiao Fan, open the door. I was wrong. I won't say anything like that again. You put me in my place. Please, open the door!"

I heard the lock turning. I stormed in. Xiao Fan sat on the floor, looking devastated. I noticed traces of tears on her face. She didn't see or hear me. There was a faraway look in her eyes, which were almost black. Her hair was a mess. Her appearance startled me. Gathering myself, I braced for the worst. This was divine punishment; it was what I deserved. Strength was a part of her character, but at that instant, she'd suffered a shattering blow, and she was letting it all show. Because of my love for her, I was about to be shattered, too, if I didn't harden myself.

"Xiao Fan, listen to me. I'm not going to let you go, even if it kills me. We're friends for life!" I hugged her with all my might. She responded slightly, touching my hair.

"You dummy! You tossed aside what I had to give. I saw. You threw it away," she said weakly, offering a pained smile.

"It wasn't what I needed. Even if you weren't secretly trying to push me away with it, I'd still have to say no. If I started to need or rely on you, and you didn't reciprocate, I'd die from having this tenderness for you. I'd resent you. It would change everything between us, and then I'd really be left out.

"I have to learn not to need or rely on you so that I can give you what you think you need, but I haven't been doing a good job of it. Sometimes when I wait for you to rely on me, you throw me this chilly look that's devastating to me. It feels like we're in a boxing match, and you just landed a knockout punch."

"Whatever it is you want, just tell me!" Her voice was filled with sadness. She caressed my face.

"I finally understand what you meant when you said, 'You can't give me what I want.' It wasn't because you didn't want to give me anything. I told you the best way to pay me back was to let me take care of you, but I realized you can't give anybody anything. I've been trying in vain." I glared at her.

"I understand, all right. You wouldn't take me as your lover if your life depended on it. You ask too much. Your expectations are too different from how I love, in that you have a lot of pride. You can only love someone who's more arrogant and difficult than you, though you probably don't see it that way. But I'm the exact opposite. I can only love without holding back, and that's not what you need. We're not well matched when it comes to give and take. You might need me, but you don't understand why I'm in your life. Maybe someday it will all make sense!" I managed to get it all out in a single breath.

There was a helpless look on her face. "I don't know why it's like this, either. In the beginning, I didn't treat you this way! I feel like I have to reject you and force myself not to feel anything, or else you'll just keep sliding further into the abyss. But every time I check on you, you've already slid further, and I can't help you.

"I gave you a chance before, and this time, I'm trying my hardest. Just now I felt like running away so I wouldn't have to see you all the time. That's my gut feeling. When it gets like this, I end up denying that I've ever gotten anything from you. I don't want to run away, though. Maybe I should give it another try and see if I can still have you around somehow." She sighed.

"Thanks! Thanks a lot! You should just pretend I'm your building superintendent," I said.

"No! I don't want you as a superintendent!" She shook her head. There was tenderness in her eyes.

5

TRAGEDY lurked in our relationship. Xiao Fan and I had relied on our mutual understanding, supporting each other and weathering crises. Yet things had deteriorated and taken a turn for the worse.

The following week, Xiao Fan's fiancé finished grad school and enlisted in the military, based in the south. Xiao Fan grew visibly uneasy, fearing that because of her fiancé's sinister, warped nature, anything could happen. She was in a strange mood that week, and I knew it was because of her fiancé. Realizing how close she was to the grave she'd dug for herself, she was all nerves. Day after day, I watched her, feeling the chasm between us. Living in the ancient castle she shared only with him, she wouldn't be poking her head out anytime soon. She didn't realize that she had sealed herself off. Though it hurt, I stayed out of it and simply looked on. She didn't even notice me.

One night, I waited for the sound of the door until three a.m., but she still didn't come home. That had never happened before. I went into her room and opened the window facing the street, and a cool breeze entered. I stood there for a few hours, counting the cars passing by, and every so often, I'd call one of her friends. Then, out of nowhere, a car pulled up directly below. I just wanted her to come home, and I was about to shut the window and return to my room when I took one last glance at the car. I could barely make out two people huddled inside. I sensed that they were locked in a long, passionate embrace: I knew that her fiancé had returned. I forced myself to keep watching and watching. I'd been waiting for the ax to fall, and now a bloody limb hit the ground with a thud. I knew it was over. My heart a lead weight, I quietly returned to my room and sat down at my desk. Xiao Fan came up the stairs. She didn't say anything, and only glanced guiltily at me as she passed. I tried my hardest to act normal. She had no clue how I felt.

It's hard to explain the horror I felt in the split second I witnessed them together. In actuality, this man had always existed in my life and in my heart. He was responsible for creating the close bond between me and Xiao Fan, and I'd accepted his role a long time ago. Xiao Fan was never to be mine, and though I'd accepted it, the circumstances that had once been far-flung and thus under control were paraded before my very eyes. I'd had a rude awakening. From that moment on, my world with Xiao Fan was fundamentally changed. She'd left me with a scar that revealed my sacrifice had been in vain, with the realization that I'd become subservient.

I kept my mouth shut. Didn't say a thing, didn't try to argue. It was all because of my festering wound, and I knew it. I just kept living under the same roof as Xiao Fan, trying my best to smile when I saw her each day, and it felt like I was treading along the ocean floor, expelling air bubbles in lieu of words or emotions. It marked the beginning of the end for me, and I silently awaited the day when my languishing body would breathe its last.

I spent every minute and every second of the day crying. As I was walking, riding the bus, talking to other people, in class, during tests, in my room, in my sleep, as I dreamed, every single moment, in my heart I was crying and no one knew. At all hours, from inside of my chest came a sob, a distinct wail that only I could hear. After two weeks of bawling like that, I didn't shed another tear. Life returned to normal, but I was rarely at home, where I'd likely run into Xiao Fan.

Two months passed. The time had come for madness to beget a complete unraveling, and it came precisely the day before my college commencement.

That evening was one of the rare occasions when I returned early to the apartment. The phone suddenly rang. It was somebody I didn't know, telling me to hurry to the hospital to see Xiao Fan.

She'd had an attack of acute hepatitis. One of her colleagues, who'd taken her to the emergency room, said she'd repeatedly asked for me.

Riding in the taxi, I felt a mix of bewilderment and cool detachment. My heart's desires were about to meet their doom. A knife was held against my throat. The moment of decision had arrived. If I had any residual feelings for her, I would stay at her side until the bitter end, no matter how degrading it was.

I entered the emergency room. It was painted a cold, dreary shade of green and filled with the overpowering stench of medicine. I immediately spotted Xiao Fan. She was lying on a stretcher in the hall outside the internal medicine ward. Her eyes, dark and puffy, flooded with tears at the sight of me. Before my eyes, she had become feeble. She sobbed helplessly, her tears surging out from some inexhaustible source. She had come undone. Then and there, I told myself never to forget that image for as long as I lived.

That image. It took me to a more profound place than I had ever known. God, how can I even explain? It dawned on me what Gabriel Marcel meant: I could write an entire book based on a single moment of silence. This was that moment of silence. In witnessing this woman's breakdown, I was pulled into her destiny, and my fate became forcibly intertwined with hers. Observing her breakdown, I broke down. I lost myself. Yet there was something to be learned from the bond that was forged between us, though at the time, I didn't realize it.

With that breakdown came a total collapse. The weight of her sorrows came down on me, crushing me. Having asked to be responsible for her, and having ventured into her darkest depths, I finally shouldered the burden of my own desires. Unceasing tremors of all kinds—tremors of love, tremors of desire, tremors of hate, tremors of pain—coalesced inside me. It became perfectly clear that I'd always carried this image of the real Xiao Fan in my heart, and now it had materialized before me.

So there I was, a complete outcast who'd had a collision with cold, hard reality. It didn't matter what kind of person I was inside, how I yearned for a bond with Xiao Fan, or if my desire to love her had been my undoing: The world didn't care. It was nothing personal. Even the woman right in front of me was telling me no. There was no right or wrong here. In the end, the world didn't owe me anything, not even half a chance. That was the hand I'd been dealt in life, and while detachment was enough for me to withstand hatred, extricating myself from the jaws of suffering called for enough detachment to exercise cruelty.

"Today I got a letter from him. I've waited four years for this and now it's happened. He sent it from training camp. He said he's decided not to marry me. Another woman is already five months pregnant with his baby . . . one of our schoolmates, younger than us. He said he was penniless and never worthy of me in the first place." Xiao Fan gripped my hand tightly. Her hair was soaked with tears around her temples, and her cheeks were sunken. She was so emaciated that she no longer looked like an adult. With those words, she turned away. "He did it on purpose. He got her pregnant on purpose. His mother just came to see me. She said a few hours ago he was sent to a hospital . . . a firearms accident. It was all deliberate. . . ." Turning her head back again, she buried her face in my hands. "He's still alive. Can you check on how he's doing for me?" She lifted her head. Her eyes, full of trust, now locked with mine.

"Sure, it's just that there's something else I have to do before I can go." I looked away.

"But . . . aren't you going to go? Just when I really need you. . . . Isn't that what you wanted more than anything?" She brushed away tears, her voice innocent and frail.

"Xiao Fan, listen to me. This has been going on for a while, but I've never had the courage to tell you. I haven't been doing so well these past two months. I'm barely getting by, and I can't go on like this. I can't play the same role that I played in the past. Things have only gotten worse. I can't open up to you. I can't even share the same space with you. I honestly feel like screaming at you. If I have to endure this drama of yours, I'll explode with resentment.

"This isn't who I am. I don't want to suffer. Love should be a beautiful experience. If it can't be saved, then I don't want to love anymore. I have to shut down. That's how I am, and I'm not blaming anyone. I need to get away from you and your drama. I'm sick and tired of it. Do you hear me? I need a break!" I managed to keep my cool. I had no idea where those words came from.

"I know." That was the only thing she said. A burden was lifted from me. And it would always be, forever after.

6

At one in the morning, Chu Kuang came to see me. He wheeled his bike so we could walk down Roosevelt Road together.

Taipei in June. It was late at night, and while the bustle on the streets had died down, a certain feeling still lingered in the air. The fiery red blossoms scattered on the cotton trees had multiplied overnight. Illuminated by the streetlights, they were almost radiant. This scene along Roosevelt Road had long become familiar to me. Every year, I anticipated the first red blossom and counted the days until the last had wilted. The tree-lined road was my earliest memory from freshman year. It was where the upperclassmen greeted us when we first arrived, and where heartwarming songs were sung in the darkness after the lights in the classroom buildings had been shut off. To this day, I can still remember so many faces....

"Gazing at the cotton trees?" Chu Kuang asked me thoughtfully. He was wearing white wide-leg jeans with a turquoise short-sleeve shirt. His usual stubble had been shaven off. Tonight, there was something different about him, as if he'd been transformed into this squeaky-clean new version of himself. Chu Kuang's life was a constant drama. He seemed to have passed through a different chamber of hell every time I saw him. His ever-changing mien and the stories he told made it impossible to tell how he was really doing.

"Chu Kuang, whenever I take the bus to campus and pass the cotton trees in bloom, I get the chills. It's like my heart's saying to my ex, 'Look, the cotton trees are blooming again! It's been four years.'"

"You know what I think? Ever since that one night five years ago when Meng Sheng took a dump under the cotton trees by the campus entrance, whenever I see those cotton trees, I want to say, 'Hey Meng Sheng, look! There's your shit!'"

"Chu Kuang, what's going on with Meng Sheng these days?" I asked as we sat down by the campus entrance.

"That's exactly what I came to talk to you about, Sis. Meng Sheng has vanished from my world." His face grew flush, and there was excitement in his voice. "Seven years passed in the blink of an eye. You might say I had an awakening. He was like a stain that washed out after a good rinse, and my clothes are nice and clean again. I don't know why, but I felt like I should tell you. The drama's over." Amid his newfound maturity, his old innocence appeared to resurface for a second.

"Well, you don't have to convince me. I'm happy for you, Chu Kuang." I couldn't resist squeezing his hand. "How did this happen?"

"Last month, when I was riding my bike, I got hit by a taxi, so I was taken to the hospital and my leg was put in a cast. I was bedridden for a week. During the crash, I had an out-of-body experience. For a minute, I felt as if I was lifted out of my body and looking straight down at myself. The past few years flashed before my eyes like a movie, and everything became clear. Then I reentered my body. The second I felt pain, I knew that Meng Sheng had been excised from me.

"I couldn't move for the entire week after I got my cast. It gave me a chance to sort out the past, which is how I arrived at the conclusion that I wasn't in love anymore. I used to be fickle, but now I'm ready to commit to someone. I realized that love is the one thing I've been searching for all along."

"Chu Kuang, do you think it's true that love never dies?"

"Sis, I think you and I have both been through a lot." He placed his hands on my head affectionately. "I honestly hope I'm experienced enough to impart a few words of wisdom." He contemplated this for a moment. "I'm pretty sure it's not true for you right now, or for me in the past, but I believe it's true for me today."

"But when you decide to love someone, how do you keep thinking of commitment as a choice, when you're closing yourself off to opportunities that might lead to even greater happiness? And if you continually demolish your old internal structures, then how can you preserve enough of yourself to keep the same relationship alive day after day?"

"Right now, I have a plan in my mind, and I can use that as a guide, but it's not something I can describe." He scribbled on the ground for a while, then murmured, "If it's really love, it'll work out."

"Have you ever really loved anyone?" I asked earnestly.

"Sis, I love someone now!" His eyes lit up. "There's an eighteen-year-old sailor who's been pursuing me for the past two years. He's in the naval academy, and he's always at sea, but we meet up every so often. I haven't seen him in a while because Meng Sheng made it hard for me to love.

"I toyed with this little sailor, and he only fell harder. All of our arguments are caused by jealousy. He gets mad if I don't need him. After my accident, he was huffing and puffing on the outside, but I caught a few glimpses of true love shining through. In the end, I was the one who was taken in—by his sincerity.

"Now we're living together in a log cabin in Danshui and being supportive of each other. I told him that from here on out, it's for real. If he doesn't grow up, I'm gone. I told him there are only two things: equality and honesty. I understand you, and you have to try your hardest to understand me. There are other people in my life too, you know. We're open about everything. If you don't love me anymore, fine. I'd rather know than have it hidden from me, even if it kills me. That's how it is. I feel like I could be with him for a long, long time." We turned onto Xinsheng South Road as he spoke. The streetlights cast a soft, gentle glow on his face.

"Chu Kuang, don't you think if you guys are both too masculine, there'll be a serious conflict?"

"It'd be hard to live together if he were a different man. But with us, we each have a husband and wife rolled into one!" He beamed with pride for a moment. Then his expression quickly faded. "Sis, I came all the way here to tell you something I feel strongly about: You haven't been honest with yourself. You're not ready to love someone if you can't even admit your feelings and needs to yourself."

"Look at that big building over to the side—all the windows are lit now. When I was a freshman, only five of them were!" I turned and faced Chu Kuang. "I'll remember what you said, Chu Kuang. I appreciate you looking out for me all this time. I hope you take good care of yourself in the future." Chu Kuang hopped on his bike, and I waved goodbye.

7

DEATH EXPERIENCE #1

A certain part of me has died as I've learned to leave behind the qualities of my youth—the overanxiousness, oversensitivity, and self-consciousness, not to mention arrogance and idealism, that diminish with life experience. I was a late bloomer, but at long last, I lost my innocence. Like anyone else when they're young, I harbored lofty expectations but lacked the self-knowledge to comprehend my own passions and vices.

DEATH EXPERIENCE #2

I no longer think of myself as an unhappy person—quite the opposite. Admitting that I have problems is a mode of optimism, since every problem has a solution. Unhappiness is a lot like bad weather: It's out of your control. So if I encounter a problem that even death can't solve, I shouldn't care whether I'm happy or unhappy, thereby negating both the problem and the problem of a problem. And that is where happiness begins.

(from *Suicide Studies*)

8

GRADUATION day. No one came to my commencement. I zig-zagged through the flocks of graduates in their black caps and gowns. There wasn't a single person on that huge campus I wanted to see. I just ran around in circles, with no idea where I was headed. There was a sudden downpour in the afternoon, and in the panic that ensued, the crowd dispersed, going home or sheltering in nearby buildings. Yelin Avenue grew deserted as the rain pelted down, leaving a magnificent sheen on the surface of the road and not a soul to be seen under the open sky. Freshly invigorated, the flowers, grass, and trees took center stage. I walked down Royal Palm Boulevard alone, in full regalia. The wind and rain were wild, and there I was, taking it all in, with hundreds of pairs of eyes staring at me from indoors. I stood under the giant palm tree in the plaza at the campus entrance, getting drenched until it was nightfall and my eyes were swollen and aching from the rainwater.

I went home. I got a strange call from Shui Ling. She'd graduated exactly a year earlier.

"It's me!" Her voice was small and wavering.

"Hey!" I replied.

"Do you have three minutes to talk to me?" she asked timidly.

"Sure!"

"Let me tell you a secret. . . . Today I went berserk. This morning my mother, father, and grandma were all telling me to wake up, but I stayed in bed and ignored them. I didn't get up or go to work. Don't tell anyone, but I was going to go to your commencement today. Hah. So finally my mom and dad got mad and left, and only my grandma and I were home. So I got dressed and tried on different outfits, but I couldn't find one nice enough. I wanted to look my best for you. Suddenly the phone rang. It was *her*. She said, 'Why aren't you at work?' I thought about saying that I was going to see you, but I couldn't bring myself to do it. And that's when I lost control and screamed 'AHH!,' and I hung up the phone and started throwing a fit. I was yelling at the top of my lungs. My grandma ran into my room and grabbed me. As I was screaming, she had a heart attack. She fell to the floor and said she was dying.

"I was so scared, I ran and got her medication. Then the police came. They said the neighbors had called. I tried to stay calm as I sent them away. My grandma was on the floor, asking for a doctor. I said I'd wait for you to take me to the hospital. Then I waited by the phone. I kept dialing your new number. For half an hour, it rang and rang. You lied to me. You said I should call you before I went crazy, but you weren't there. . . ."

I hung up the phone and closed my eyes. All I wanted right that instant was to find Meng Sheng.

Meng Sheng. Someone told me they'd seen him a lot recently in an abandoned security booth near the rear entrance after sundown. I rode around campus all night, searching for signs of him. When I found him, he was near a tall brick building in that area, curled up in the corner of a phone booth by the door, shooting up.

I immediately recognized two signs of a full-blown addiction. His eyes were not only bulging but glassy and bloodshot. The skin on his face looked as if it had been partially gnawed away. His shorts were wrinkled, and on his feet, covered in mud, were a pair of canvas shoes that were falling apart. A gray coat was draped over his shoulders, revealing his bare chest underneath. His torso was wrapped in thick layers of bandages.

I took his left arm and examined it, tracing the length of his veins. The skin was riddled with tiny needle-insertion marks. I took a few steps back and squatted on the ground. I lit a cigarette and took a few slow drags. Silence filled the air.

"Hey, congratulations, you nabbed yourself a diploma! Me, I

dropped out a long time ago." He forced a cackle. "So, how about it? How does it feel, seeing me looking like a coward right now? It doesn't matter what you say, I really am a weak man. I've been reduced to making a mess of myself like a three-year-old!" There was a strange wickedness in his laugh. His entire body shook as he coughed.

"Shut up!" I shot him a stern look. Sulkily, he reached over and motioned for the cigarette. "How'd you get that wound on your chest? Tell the truth. I didn't come to hear your bullshit."

"What'd you come here for, then?" he sneered. "This...this is from last week when Chu Kuang stabbed me, that fucker. He used this beautiful dagger I gave him. It cut through the skin, but didn't puncture deep. I had to see a specialist. Why not send me to my maker once and for all, and save everyone the trouble? I was sent to the hospital, and they operated on me and saved me. Look at me now—I'm permanently scarred!" His laughter reverberated inside the booth. "If you want me dead, no problem. Just give Big Brother a ring and he'll have me lying soundly in my grave in a matter of days. It's that simple. If I've got any brains, I'll run. Then, when you receive word, you can be the star-crossed lover who rushes to my side, only to find me dead."

"Nonsense. Last night Chu Kuang came to see me. He said he was just in a car accident. He's over you. He has a brand-new life now, and he's happy. I saw it for myself. He's a different person now," I told him indignantly.

A sinister smile crossed Meng Sheng's face. For a long time, he didn't reply. "He hasn't changed. There have always been a lot of different Chu Kuangs inside of him. You can't tell because you've only known the Chu Kuang that's more or less stable. There's a dominant Chu Kuang who can focus and interact normally whenever he has to. This past year, he stopped going to his psychiatrist. It was a gradual process, but one by one, each personality split off into its own domain again. Now there isn't one that dominates anymore, and he switches depending on who he's talking to."

He continued as if this were a funny anecdote. "I got to know his transformations well. There's nothing wrong with how he's been recently. This way, he doesn't seesaw so much, since every part of him can come out and take a breather. Everybody gets a turn at being king. That's where he's heading, and he'll probably outlive us both. I was the only one who got along with all of them, you know. I just find it fascinating."

I was quiet. "Meng Sheng, will you still die with me the way you asked me to four years ago?"

"Not anymore, my dearest bride. I wish I could, but it's impossible now. I didn't love you at all then. Four years later, my masculine side loves you, and my feminine side loves Chu Kuang. But how can I truly love anyone when in the back of my mind, I've already given myself to a goddess? Isn't it incredible? It was all in the master plan." He closed his eyes as if he were imagining it. "Not only that, but death no longer holds the same meaning for me. I'm stronger now. Whether I live or die, I'm doomed all the same, so there's no need for me to court death. That's a weight no one can carry. I'll just wait calmly, and whatever happens, happens."

"But if that's how you see it, Meng Sheng, then your world is perpetually coming to an end. Love is dead, hope is dead, faith is dead. I would never stand by and watch the people I love suffer. It would kill me. Every second of existence would be painful. My mind would scream that Judgment Day was near. Is that how you live? I'd be at my wit's end if I didn't force myself to stop or turn back. I have to save myself from myself. If there's no need to court death, like you said, why put yourself through all of this?"

"You have to get over this whole idea of *me*!" He stood up. Leaning against the wall, he started to gag violently.

Leaping away, I hopped off the steps. Standing in the plaza, I looked up at the sky and wailed until my throat hurt.

"Meng Sheng, you really want to die!" I hollered at him. Though I couldn't help crying out, there were no tears in me. "You're even more pathetic than I am. Why don't you go love a little? Why don't you ever put yourself out there and try to forge a real connection with anyone?

"You just stand back at a safe distance and act like it's all a joke.

Has it ever occurred to you that maybe this goddess, in her heart, loves you? That maybe not loving you is her way of loving you?" I shouted at him hoarsely. My words seemed to come from an unfamiliar voice.

"Just shut up. I don't want to talk anymore. This is pointless. . . ." Gripping his head in his hands, he thrashed around violently.

"You're not a coward at all. You're brave in a hundred ways, but you're a coward in one, which is in love. Maybe it's true that pain is an unavoidable part of existence, but some things are close enough to perfection, and they're right in front of us. They've been there all along, you're just not willing to admit it.

"Have you ever thought about how much Chu Kuang needed your love, no matter how badly you treated him? The smallest gesture meant the world to him. You can't walk away from or deny all that. I think you're afraid of being truly loved. . . ."

Meng Sheng let out a sharp cry, cursing me as he banged his head wildly against the blue pay phone.

I fished a small banknote out of his bag and ran to the rear entrance, but the gate was locked. My head was spinning. I scrambled up the brick wall, scraping my hands on the shards of glass littered on top of it. The full moon came into view as I made it over, and just then, I was reminded of how in Truffaut's *The 400 Blows*, the boy breaks out of prison and runs to the sea, and that final close-up of the expression on his face.

(Freeze frame.)

9

It was the last hurrah of Crocodile Month. Starting at noon, TTV continuously displayed a news ticker that read: EXCLUSIVE! FIRST-EVER ON-CAMERA PROFILE SENT TO US BY A CROCODILE! TUNE IN FOR A SPECIAL BROADCAST AT SEVEN.

Seven o'clock arrived. Each and every household turned on their television sets. CTV and CTS showed animated films.

An announcer declared the start of the broadcast, then the title appeared: *Last Words of a Crocodile*. The camera shook as a figure in a white paper mask leapt out of the way of the shot, yelling at the crocodile to hurry up and get ready. (Note: That was the director, and his name was Jarman.) The white paper mask was gone, though a white-gloved finger remained in the corner of the frame. (Note: The camera hadn't been turned on properly.) There was a shot of someone carrying a piss bucket up the stairs, closing the door behind them.

The scene cut to the seaside. A bathtub was floating in shallow waters. Someone wearing a white mask was reclining inside, their body cloaked in a white robe. The bathtub was lined with holes into which bouquets were stuffed. (Note: That part of the video had been lifted from *The Garden*.) It was followed by footage of someone sitting on the toilet, then standing up and peeling off a bodysuit. Then the monologue began. The camera panned across piles of goods that had been packed into a basement.

"Ho! How is everyone? I'm a crocodile. I'm probably the only real crocodile out there. I've waited for this day to come. You've all been looking for me, and I can't believe your warmth and enthusiasm, I really, really like you guys.

"To start things off, I wanted to tell everyone about a variety show that held a contest seeking the answer to a riddle. And the riddle was, 'What is friendship?' Though I wrote a hundred postcards on friendship and sent them in, they still didn't pick mine. Then I called the *China Times* with a tip, saying I'd discovered a crocodile. The response has been so overwhelming that I've had to take a step back. I've been lying low, wondering if it was just a passing fad. But the truth is, I couldn't be happier!

"This is a bodysuit that I sewed for myself because my skin has been green ever since I was little. My mother said it would scare the other children. There aren't any red patches on my skin though. Also, I have bad teeth. They grew in jagged, so I have to wear braces. I think that's it. Oh my goodness! And I'm totally oviparous. I can show you—" *(Jump cut.)* "I hope everyone will continue to like me, even if I stay out of sight. Oh my goodness! I can't eat cream puffs anymore, and I'm living in a prison like Genet. Oh, that's right—I want to perform a bit of 'The Ballad of the Crocodile.' Do you all mind?"

The camera cut back to the seaside. The crocodile sat in a wooden bathtub with a burning torch mounted to its side. A finger abruptly entered the frame, pointing at the bathtub as it drifted out to sea, and suddenly the entire bathtub erupted into flames. As the camera zoomed in slowly, the image on the screen dissolved into a sea of fire. . . .

Note: As Jarman said, "I have nothing more to say. . . . I wish you all the best!"

TITLES IN SERIES

For a complete list of titles, visit www.nyrb.com or write to:
Catalog Requests, NYRB, 435 Hudson Street, New York, NY 10014

* *Also available as an electronic book.*

CAMARA LAYE The Radiance of the King

GIROLAMO CARDANO The Book of My Life

DON CARPENTER Hard Rain Falling*

J.L. CARR A Month in the Country*

EILEEN CHANG Love in a Fallen City

EILEEN CHANG Naked Earth*

JOAN CHASE During the Reign of the Queen of Persia*

ELLIOTT CHAZE Black Wings Has My Angel*

UPAMANYU CHATTERJEE English, August: An Indian Story

NIRAD C. CHAUDHURI The Autobiography of an Unknown Indian

ANTON CHEKHOV Peasants and Other Stories

ANTON CHEKHOV The Prank: The Best of Young Chekhov*

COLETTE The Pure and the Impure

JOHN COLLIER Fancies and Goodnights

CARLO COLLODI The Adventures of Pinocchio*

D.G. COMPTON The Continuous Katherine Mortenhoe

IVY COMPTON-BURNETT Manservant and Maidservant

BARBARA COMYNS The Vet's Daughter

BARBARA COMYNS Our Spoons Came from Woolworths*

ALBERT COSSERY The Jokers*

ALBERT COSSERY Proud Beggars*

HAROLD CRUSE The Crisis of the Negro Intellectual

LORENZO DA PONTE Memoirs

ELIZABETH DAVID Summer Cooking

L.J. DAVIS A Meaningful Life*

AGNES DE MILLE Dance to the Piper*

VIVANT DENON No Tomorrow/Point de lendemain

MARIA DERMOÛT The Ten Thousand Things

DER NISTER The Family Mashber

TIBOR DÉRY Niki: The Story of a Dog

ANTONIO DI BENEDETTO Zama*

ALFRED DÖBLIN Bright Magic: Stories*

JEAN D'ORMESSON The Glory of the Empire: A Novel, A History*

ARTHUR CONAN DOYLE The Exploits and Adventures of Brigadier Gerard

CHARLES DUFF A Handbook on Hanging

BRUCE DUFFY The World As I Found It*

DAPHNE DU MAURIER Don't Look Now: Stories

ELAINE DUNDY The Dud Avocado*

ELAINE DUNDY The Old Man and Me*

JOHN EHLE The Land Breakers*

MARCELLUS EMANTS A Posthumous Confession

EURIPIDES Grief Lessons: Four Plays; translated by Anne Carson

J.G. FARRELL Troubles*

J.G. FARRELL The Siege of Krishnapur*

J.G. FARRELL The Singapore Grip*

ELIZA FAY Original Letters from India

KENNETH FEARING Clark Gifford's Body

FÉLIX FÉNÉON Novels in Three Lines*

THOMAS FLANAGAN The Year of the French*

BENJAMIN FONDANE Existential Monday: Philosophical Essays*

SANFORD FRIEDMAN Conversations with Beethoven*

CARLO EMILIO GADDA That Awful Mess on the Via Merulana

BENITO PÉREZ GÁLDOS Tristana*

MAVIS GALLANT Paris Stories*

MAVIS GALLANT A Fairly Good Time *with* Green Water, Green Sky*